WEB OF JUSTICE

A Mara Brent Legal Thriller

ROBIN JAMES

Robin James Books

For the men and women of law enforcement who work tirelessly to protect our children and seek justice for those who have been harmed.

You are seen. You are enough.

Thank you for trying to save your corner of the world.

❧

For more information about how you can assist in the fight against child endangerment and exploitation, please visit and consider donating to the National Center for Missing and Exploited Children.

https://www.missingkids.org/home

1

There's a thing that happens in murder trials. It's not something they teach you or something you can prepare for. But I've seen it with my own eyes, every single time. As I stepped up to the lectern after Judge Ivey told me to call my first witness, I locked eyes with the twelve members of my jury. Seven women. Five men. Median age, fifty-two. They took a collective breath, as if they could somehow prepare for what was about to happen to them. The thing I called The Change.

Sure, they'd all grown up with a television in their house. Been desensitized, or so they thought, by the news or the ever more graphic violence in cop shows and thriller movies.

Then they came here.

Because of a random drawing based on their voter registration, they were called in to sit in those seats and hear about something most would never understand beyond what they had seen on a screen.

"The state calls Detective Brody Lance," I said in a clear, strong voice.

Lance was young, still. Two years younger than me. He'd cut his teeth in property crime before being called up to replace Sam Cruz when he made lieutenant. Now Sam was the sheriff.

Lance stood straight as the bailiff swore him in. He smoothed down his tie as he took his seat and met my eyes.

I quickly took him through his background. His ten years with the Maumee County Sheriff's Department. How he was plucked from field ops in his second year to serve as an undercover Vice-Narcotics detective before moving into property crimes. Young, yes. But experienced. Fully capable of handling the grisly reason for his testimony today.

"Detective Lance," I said. "Will you please tell me how you became involved in the Robert Forte matter?"

Lance shifted in his seat. He turned his gaze from me and looked directly at the jury box. He was getting better and better at this. Over my left shoulder, I could feel the eyes of two men boring into me. One of them, the defendant, Darryl Cox, had spent my entire opening statement smirking at me.

"I received a call from the first officer on scene, Stacy Kaminski. Deputy Kaminski had responded to a 9-1-1 call from a trash collector working his normal route along Mullins Drive in the south part of the county. That's an industrial drive. It was my understanding that this individual came upon what he believed to be human remains dumped in a drainage ditch. I responded to the call and arrived on scene at nine forty-one a.m. on Tuesday, December 7th of last year."

"What did you observe when you arrived?"

"Deputy Kaminski had blocked off the road leading to the drainage ditch on Mullins. He set up road flares and barricades.

I parked my vehicle at the barricade next to mile marker fourteen and approached the scene on foot. Deputy Kaminski and her partner, Deputy Boyle, were making sure no one else was coming in or out. There was a Maverick garbage truck parked along the side of the road. Deputy Kaminski had the driver and one other crewman, who I later learned was the individual who spotted the remains and called 9-1-1, seated in the back of her patrol car, waiting for me to question them."

"What did you do first?" I asked.

"I approached the drainage ditch. There was a body lying on its right side in what I'd call a loose fetal position in about two inches of water. Male. Caucasian. He looked to be about six feet tall, maybe two hundred pounds. I could see two wounds to the victim's body. What looked to be a gunshot wound to the left side of his head. Part of his face was gone. Then, there was another massive wound between his legs. As I said, the victim was lying on his side, his right leg drawn up, his left leg almost straight down."

"We'll come back to that," I said. I introduced the first of the crime scene photographs Lance had taken. The mild ones, showing the long stretch of road along Mullins Drive he described. There were shots of Deputies Kaminski and Boyle standing just as Detective Lance said they were. I stopped at one shot, looking lengthwise down the drainage ditch. You could see one white leg sticking up a bit on the wall of the ditch. But from this angle, the rest of the body nor the wounds Lance would later describe in more detail were visible.

"Detective," I said. "Were you able to make an identification of this individual?"

"I was," he said. "Fairly quickly, actually. The victim had a series of tattoos down both arms. Tribal symbols. A skull and crossbones. Also a date 9-18-2007 surrounded by angel's wings."

"Those had meaning to you?"

"They did," he said. "I recognized those tattoos as belonging to an individual by the name of Robert Forte, who goes by the street name of Big Robbie."

"Big Robbie," I repeated. "And how did you come to know him?"

"Years ago, when I worked undercover in Vice, Robbie was a well-known dealer. I arrested him twice on drug trafficking charges."

"I see," I said. "So, what did you do next?"

"I immediately called for more units to come out and assist Deputies Kaminski and Boyle with protecting the scene. I wanted that section of Mullins to be completely secured until I could get a crime scene unit out. I called Agent Kimberly Moss from the Bowling Green office of the Ohio Bureau of Criminal Investigation. She and her crew arrived at ten forty-two a.m. and began their work processing the scene. Taking more photographs, searching the area for more potential evidence, that sort of thing. I also called the county medical examiner. Dr. Pham arrived just before noon as BCI was finishing their work."

"And what did you do, Detective?"

"Well, as I said, I was familiar with Robert Forte and some of his associates. I had Deputies Kaminski and Boyle work on canvassing the area, talking to employees at the nearby tool and die plant to see if anyone had seen anyone dump the body or anything suspicious."

"Dump the body," I said. "You were operating under the assumption that the body was dumped there rather than being shot there? Why is that?"

"Well, it took a few hours for BCI to confirm it, but the body was covered in a white substance that to my eye and nose appeared to be lye."

"Understood. So what did you do next?"

"I reached out to an old informant of mine to find out who Mr. Forte might still be associated with. That's when the defendant Darryl Cox's name first came up. Also, Forte and Darryl Cox had been arrested together just six months ago for drug trafficking. I decided that's where I'd start. I found Mr. Cox's address and went to his residence hoping to speak with him."

"What happened next?"

"Mr. Cox wasn't at home, but his girlfriend answered the door. She identified herself as Tamara Harvey. I had immediate concerns about her well-being. Ms. Harvey had visible bruises on her arms, a black eye, and a cut lip. They looked to me like fresh injuries. I told Ms. Harvey that I was investigating the potential murder of Robert Forte and asked her if she would mind coming down to the Sheriff's Department and answering a few questions for me."

"Did she?"

"She became very upset. I would describe her behavior as bordering on hysteria. Uncontrollable crying. Hyperventilating. I took her outside and had her take a seat in the backseat of my cruiser. Ms. Harvey, when she was able to compose herself, told me she was in fear for her safety. I'll be honest. So was I based on her appearance and injuries. I asked her who hurt her. She repeatedly stated that Darryl was going to kill her too."

"Objection, hearsay."

I looked over my shoulder. Darryl Cox was using the services of a public defender. Nearing ninety, Earl Grandy might just have been one of the oldest still-practicing members of the Ohio bar. He'd worked in my office roughly fifty years ago. A good guy, prone to bluster, he liked to haunt the courthouse coffee shop regaling younger lawyers with stories of his glory days. He'd survived four different types of cancer and had new hips, ankles, and a pacemaker. For all of that, Earl had a mind sharp as an icepick, though he tried to disguise it with folksy charm.

"Your Honor, Ms. Harvey's statements were made during intense, physical duress as Detective Lance has stated. They fall under the category of an excited utterance and are also being offered to establish Detective Lance's motivation and course of action rather than for the truth of the matter asserted."

"I'll allow it," Judge Donald Ivey said. Grandy huffed, but sat back down.

"What did you do next, Detective?" I asked.

"At that point, I called for backup," Lance said. "Ms. Harvey indicated she didn't know where Darryl Cox was but that she was fearful of when he might return. She was concerned he was hiding, lying in wait, watching her. She indicated he had done this before. I assured her I wouldn't let anything happen to her but I did become concerned that perhaps her fears were well-founded, so I wanted to make sure Mr. Cox wasn't in the area. I told her that I could take her someplace safe if she were in fear for her life. I asked her to pack a few things and I would help get her into a safe house or a shelter. She asked me if I would come inside with her. At that point, Deputies Millburn and Harris arrived. I instructed them to do a search of the perimeter around the house and speak with some of the neighbors about whether they had seen Mr. Cox recently. I walked into the house with Ms. Harvey and followed her to the back bedroom while she packed an overnight bag with some clothes and toiletries. She then walked back through the house, exiting through the garage. She couldn't find her purse and wondered if she'd left it on a hook at the back door. I followed her at her insistence. As we stepped into the garage, I noticed three cans of lye stacked along the back wall."

"Lye," I repeated.

"Yes. In red and white cans. I asked Ms. Harvey if she knew what they were. She said no. But at that point, she started to cry again. She turned to me and asked me if Robert Forte was really dead. I said yes. She told me I needed to find Darryl. That she wouldn't ever be safe until I found Darryl."

"Detective, what were the next investigative steps you took?"

"I brought Ms. Harvey to the station for questioning. She calmed down considerably once she was away from the home she shared with Mr. Cox. I interviewed her for more than an hour. She was adamant that if Robert Forte was murdered, Darryl Cox was involved. She indicated that she and Mr. Forte had become romantically involved in the last few weeks before his murder. She told me she was afraid that Darryl had found out about it. She showed me a series of threatening texts Darryl had recently sent her. They were alarming."

"What kind of threats?" I asked.

"I would describe them as death threats."

"Against Ms. Harvey?"

"Against Ms. Harvey and against Mr. Forte."

Later, I would call Tamara to the stand and have her show the jury the same texts. "Detective, what did you do next?"

"I secured search warrants for Darryl Cox's home, car, computer, and cell phone. Those came through fairly quickly, by midafternoon on December 7th. By four o'clock that day, I met with Agent Moss from BCI. She had finished up at the Mullins Drive scene. She met me out at Ms. Harvey and Mr. Cox's residence, and we executed the search warrant. Mr. Cox's whereabouts were still unknown at that time."

"What did you find incident to your search warrant?"

"Well, it took a few weeks before all the phone and computer forensics came back. But that day, at the house, we found a mound of what looked like freshly dug earth on the side of the house."

I introduced the photographs. The mound was behind a blue garbage can. Lance had the presence of mind to take a video of Deputy Millburn digging through the earth. About a minute into the video, she yelled out, "Gun!" I stopped the playback.

"What did you find, Detective?"

"We found a 9-millimeter handgun. It was still loaded with a bullet in the chamber and four left in the magazine. Ballistics later matched it as the weapon that was used to kill Robert Forte. There were three fingerprints on the barrel of the gun matching Darryl Cox."

"What did you do next?"

"I secured an arrest warrant for Darryl Cox for the murder of Robert Forte based on the statement of Tamara Harvey. This was later corroborated by another associate of Mr. Forte's who had heard Mr. Cox threaten Mr. Forte's life. Based on the physical evidence on the murder weapon and later, evidence discovered incident to the forensic examination of Mr. Cox's home computer and phone."

"What did those examinations reveal?"

"Mr. Cox had made several internet searches about how to dispose of a body using lye and how long it would take for a human body to decompose after being covered in lye. He purchased the lye on the internet, and we found receipts for that transaction."

"I see," I said. "Detective, I'd like to direct your attention back to the crime scene on Mullins Drive as you discovered it. Was there anything unusual about the manner in which Robert Forte was killed?"

"Well," he said. "As I told you, I noticed two distinct gunshot wounds. One to the head, one to the uh ... groin area."

I took a breath. I'd seen these photographs hundreds of times. Knew them by heart. Had prosecuted more murders committed by gun violence than I could count. But still, I had to steel myself for what I was about to introduce to the jury.

The first photograph was a close-up of Robbie Forte's head. As Detective Lance described, there wasn't much there on the left side of it. But he'd been moved so there wasn't much blood. He almost didn't look human, so it was easier to let the mind disassociate from what this really was.

"And the second wound?" I said, putting my thumb over the clicker button that would advance the slide.

Brody Lance's lips disappeared as he grimaced. "It was tough to look at," he said. "Especially later after the coroner did his thing. The ... uh ... theory is ... that wound was made while Forte was very much alive."

"What happened, Detective?"

"The uh ... killer ... I don't quite know a delicate way to say it. Ah ... Robert Forte's manhood was shot clean off at very close range."

I had no choice. This was a capital murder case. The jury had to see. I clicked the button and advanced the slide showing what was left of Robert Forte's body, lying face up in that ditch.

A beat. A pause.

The Change.

Each member of the jury absorbed what they were seeing on that projector. Then two of the men on the far end of the box doubled over and threw up.

2

Earl Grandy took a moment to get situated at the lectern. I immediately knew it was for show. What I didn't immediately know was why. Was he hoping to garner sympathy on account of his age? Was he trying to make the jury think he was simply unimpressed with Detective Lance's testimony and thus in no hurry to get to his cross-examination? Maybe all the above. He stood there, chewing the inside of his cheek for a moment until Judge Ivey had finally had enough.

"Mr. Grandy?" he said. "We're waiting."

"Yes. Yes," Grandy said, finding a smile.

I let my eyes travel to my left. Darryl Cox wasn't looking at Detective Lance. He wasn't looking at the jury. He was staring at me. That same smirk lifting the corner of his mouth.

He'd been a good-looking kid. But somewhere along the way, he'd let his drug addiction take hold. It made his skin gray, his teeth brown and loose in his gums. I knew from his rap sheet he'd just turned twenty-nine. Graduated from Waynetown High eleven years ago with a lacrosse scholarship he never pursued. In fact, nothing about Darryl Cox's early life or upbringing could foretell he'd end up sitting at that table facing lethal injection for a murder, gruesome enough to send two jurors, grown men, running for the bathroom to lose their breakfasts.

Cox's father had been an engineer at Jeep. His mother, a homemaker and volunteer for Toddler Time at the Maumee County Library. They'd attended every game Darryl ever played in. Been there the day he walked across the stage to collect his diploma. He hadn't been abused. He'd never gotten so much as a speeding ticket before his nineteenth birthday. But something, somewhere, had gone very wrong for Darryl from that point on. His parents weren't around anymore to ask. They'd both died in a car accident by the time Darryl turned twenty-one. As an only child, their passing had left Darryl the sole heir to a six-figure life insurance policy that he burned through on fast cars and heroin by the time he was twenty-two.

The jury would hear about all of it if I got my way. Maybe Darryl's privileged life had been the thing that did the most damage. He felt the world owed him something. That the rules didn't apply to him.

"Detective Lance," Earl Grandy started. "I just want to go over a few things you said on direct. First up, you said you knew who Robbie Forte was right away when you saw him, didn't you?"

"I recognized him, yes," Lance answered.

"From your years in Vice. You knew he was a drug dealer."

"Yes."

"So, you assumed pretty quickly that his death was related to his long life of crime, isn't that right?"

"I never said that at all," Lance said. "What I said was, I wanted to question Robbie's known associates as quickly as I could. To be honest, once I saw the nature of Robbie's wounds, well ... I did not assume this was a drug-deal-gone-wrong scenario. Not one bit."

Good, I thought. Very good.

Grandy took a step back from the lectern, pushing himself off of it as if the thing had grown hot to the touch. He stood with one arm around his waist, the other folded over it, his chin resting on his fist.

"But you figured the odds were Robbie's dangerous lifestyle had finally caught up with him, didn't you?"

"I made no assumptions, Counselor. But I was interested in speaking to his known associates. As I testified earlier, an informant of mine told me Darryl Cox was Robbie's partner. That the two of them were dealing together as recently as the week prior to Robbie's murder. So I tracked down Cox's address and paid him a visit."

"He wasn't there though, was he?"

"No."

"Not at home. Nowhere to be found in the vicinity at all, isn't that right?"

"He wasn't home. No."

"And he wasn't at the neighbors. Wasn't watching you from a distance, isn't that right?"

"I don't know where Cox was when I first came to his residence the afternoon of December 7th."

"But Tamara Harvey was there?"

"Yes."

"You talked to her at length. She invited you inside. You had a look around."

"Your Honor," I said. "Is there a question in there somewhere?"

"Mr. Grandy?" Judge Ivey said, losing patience as quickly as I was.

"Sorry. Sorry. I just want it made clear. Tamara Harvey was the only person at the residence when you showed up that afternoon, uh ... December 7th. Right?"

"That's correct."

"Later on, you claim you found a gun buried next to the garbage can on the property, right?"

"I don't claim it. That's what happened. You've seen the recording of it yourself."

"Right," Grandy said. "While Tamara Harvey was the only one home. Detective, you were never able to establish when Darryl Cox was last at the house prior to your arrival, were you?"

"Ms. Harvey said he'd left sometime after ten the previous night."

"And you didn't get there until almost four o'clock the next day, right?"

"Correct."

"So, we're talking, what, eighteen hours or more that Tamara Harvey was alone in that house ... the house where you found what you're calling the murder weapon?"

"I'm sorry," Lance said. "That's a question?"

"Yeah. It is. You're saying Tamara Harvey was alone in that house for more than eighteen hours prior to your miraculous discovery of this so-called murder weapon?"

"Your Honor," I said.

Ivey already had a hand up. "Save the grandstanding for closing arguments, Mr. Grandy. I know you know better."

Grandy seemed genuinely irritated. He gripped the sides of the lectern with enough force to shake it.

"Tamara Harvey's the one who told you about these so-called threats against her life by the defendant, isn't that right?"

"She did, yes."

"And it was Tamara's word that Darryl Cox had some kind beef with Robbie Forte, right?"

"She described animosity between them over her relationship with Robbie."

"She was sleeping with him. She admitted that to you, didn't she?"

"She did."

"You ever ask her to take a poly?"

"Objection," I said.

"Mr. Grandy, again. You know better."

"Detective, you took a lot of what Tamara Harvey said at face value, didn't you?"

"I wouldn't say that, no. When I interviewed Ms. Harvey, my aim was to get her side of the story, then work on corroborating it. Her cell phone records, the evidence we found at Mr. Cox's home, there were a number of other pieces of evidence I considered during my investigation."

"Still ... let's say Tamara Harvey hadn't been at the house that day. Let's say she never said a word to you. You wouldn't have a case, would you? She's pretty much your star witness, isn't she?"

I felt the air shift behind me. I glanced over my shoulder. Sheriff Sam Cruz took a seat on the bench directly behind me. I gave him a quick smile and turned my attention back to the witness box.

"Mr. Grandy," Lance said. "Again, I'm not sure I understand your question."

"My question is, without Tamara Harvey's statement, you couldn't make probable cause to arrest Darryl Cox, could you?"

"I wouldn't say that, no. I believe I testified about the fruits of my search warrant. The internet searches on Mr. Cox's computer. His fingerprints on the weapon used to shoot Robbie Forte."

"But none of those things would have fallen into your lap without Tamara Harvey."

"Your Honor," I said, rising. "These questions have been asked and answered. Additionally, counsel is making speeches and arguing with the witness."

"Sustained," Ivey said. "Once again, save it for closing arguments, counsel."

"It's dangerous to be a drug dealer, isn't it, Detective?"

"I'm sorry?"

"What I mean to say is, in your, what is it, fifteen-year police career, you've seen a lot of people die after drug deals gone bad, haven't you?"

"Yes. I suppose so."

"So, somebody like Robbie Forte, he'd been dealing for a while, hadn't he?"

"I can't say how long he'd been in that life."

"But you haven't been in Vice for, what, eight years?"

"That's correct."

"So, he's been ... I'm sorry ... he had been at it for going on a decade at least, right?"

"At least."

"Guy like that would have racked up a whole lot of enemies, wouldn't you say?"

"Probably."

"But you can't name any of them for me today, can you?"

"Objection," I said. "Irrelevant."

"Oh, I think alternate theories of who killed this man are entirely relevant to the defense of my client, Your Honor. I'm permitted to explore them."

"You can answer the question, Detective."

"Mr. Forte would have perhaps had run-ins with rival dealers, yes. But that is not where my investigation took me."

"Where Tamara Harvey took you, you mean," Grandy said.

"That's not what I said."

"Sure. Of course. I have no further questions for this witness. I'm through."

I locked eyes with Brody Lance. He was angry. His color rose just above his collar, spreading up his neck and into his cheeks.

His testimony had been solid. He hadn't allowed Earl Grandy's tactics to rattle him. I had powerful ammunition coming in the form of the ME's report.

"I have no further questions at this time, but reserve the right to recall Detective Lance on rebuttal if necessary."

"Good enough," Ivey said. "Due to the lateness of the hour, let's adjourn to first thing in the morning. Be ready with your next witness, Ms. Brent."

I stayed standing while Ivey banged his gavel and left the bench.

As I gathered my things, Sam let himself through the wooden gate separating my table from the gallery. Two deputies stepped forward and led Darryl Cox out of the courtroom. Again, he glared at me. This time, Sam puffed out his chest and got in his line of sight.

"Sam," I whispered, touching his sleeve. "Don't let him get a rise out of you. He's not worth it."

The jury was gone. Lance approached my table.

"How'd he do?" Sam asked, half joking.

"Grandy's an idiot," Lance said. "You think Ivey's going to let him keep at that crap?"

"No," I said. "But that's obviously going to be his strategy. He wants the jury to think Tamara Harvey is the lynch pin of this whole case."

"Well," Sam said. "She kind of is, isn't she? Is she going to hold up?"

I wanted to say yes. Emphatically, yes. But Tamara Harvey had problems. Big ones.

Before I could answer, Howard Jordan, the other assistant prosecutor who worked out of my office, came rushing into the courtroom.

"Sorry," he said, breathless. "I couldn't get out of Judge Saul's courtroom."

"It's okay," I said. "I'll fill you in."

"I'm afraid you don't have time," he said. "Uh ... boss wants to see you. Immediately."

I didn't like Hojo's color. He looked worried.

"That bad, is it?" I asked.

Hojo shot a look at Sam. "I uh ... well ... just go. And maybe hurry."

I stuffed my notebook into my briefcase, said a quick goodbye to Sam and Brody Lance, then walked out of the courtroom, bracing myself for what I'd find back at the office.

3

One look at Caroline Flowers' face and I knew I'd rather face a firing squad. The longest-serving member of the Maumee County Prosecutor's Office, Caro, sat at the front desk keeping all of us on track. Currently, she had both hands resting flat on the desk, her eyes closed, her lips moving silently as she did a ten count. I waited. When she finished, she found a smile, took a breath, and turned her chair to face me.

"That bad?" I asked.

"It's been a day so far," she said. "How about yours?"

"It went. Jury is hard to read. Lance was a pro. Earl Grandy managed to tick Judge Ivey off half a dozen times."

"I don't know why that old badger doesn't just retire. No. I take that back. I know why. He's on his fifth wife and the other four are lined up to take his pension when he goes."

"Court appointments pay sixty-four bucks an hour last I checked. This thing isn't gonna make him rich."

"He's got a good heart," she said. "God knows he's had it worked on often enough."

"How's yours?" I asked. "Specifically, your blood pressure."

Caro's smile faded. "I honestly don't know how much more of this I can take. I was talking to my financial advisor about when I might be able to ret—"

"No," I said, cutting her off. "Don't say it. Don't even think about it. You're not going anywhere, lady."

Caro's desk phone lit up. She blew out her breath and answered it. "Yes? She is. I'm aware. I'll send her back. That's ... I haven't ... we don't ..."

She pulled the phone away from her face. She'd been hung up on.

"You better get back there," she said. "Boss is on a tear. I'm sorry."

"I can handle it," I said. "I've faced worse, Caro."

"Better you than me," she muttered. I tossed my briefcase into my office as I passed it. I smoothed a hair behind my ear as I walked to the office at the very end of the hall. The door swung open before I had a chance to even knock.

The boss, newly elected Maumee County Prosecutor Skip Fletcher, stood in the doorway glaring at me.

"Get in here," he said. "I've been waiting an hour."

"I've been in court, Skip. You knew that."

Skip Fletcher had narrowly beaten my ex-boss, Kenya Spaulding, in the last election. It was an upset on all accounts. Skip had fought dirty, tagging Kenya as part of the political establishment of Maumee County. She was anything but. But the voters were hungry for change and ousted incumbents up and down the ballot with little regard to their records.

"I need good news," Skip said. In the eight weeks since his swearing-in, Skip had removed every trace of Kenya from this office. Gone were the tasteful, muted tones of her decorating. Every square inch of the walls was now covered with Notre Dame Fighting Irish memorabilia. Skip himself had played as a cornerback during his freshman and sophomore years there until he blew his knee out during practice. A story he regaled us with enough times I could recite it by heart.

"Brody Lance was solid on the stand. Held up to Earl Grandy's cross pretty well. No worries."

"What's your read of the jury?"

"Too early to tell," I said. "And I don't have eyes in the back of my head. I could use Hojo at the table. Even a half-decent intern."

"Not happening," he said. "The county budget is bloated enough. If you can't handle your job on your own, I'm not going to throw more taxpayer money at you."

"We pay our interns minimum wage, Skip. If we pay them at all. And Hojo's salary is already baked into the budget."

"Do we have a problem?" he said, sliding around his desk, plopping into his chair. I didn't feel like sitting. I felt like getting out of here, going home, kicking my feet up, and having a glass of wine. It was quiet there now. My twelve-year-old son, Will, was on a class trip to Gettysburg and wouldn't be home for a couple of days.

"You keep asking me that," I said. "Seems to me I told you what the problem was the day after you were sworn in. We never should have certified this as a capital case. Robbie Forte is an unsympathetic victim. Darryl Cox is a menace to society, but Grandy will easily argue this was a crime of passion, not a premeditated murder. And Tamara Harvey is problematic. She hasn't been able to make it through a single interview without breaking down or changing tiny little details of her story. It's not too late to let me go to Grandy with second degree. He'll take it. I'm sure of it."

"Robbie Forte was found in a ditch with his private parts blown off. You've said you've got eight men on the jury. Trust me. They'll convict. They'll vote to put a needle in Cox's arm."

We'd had this argument at least a dozen times. I wanted Cox behind bars for life. I wanted justice for Robbie Forte, no matter how he chose to live his life. But this case? It wasn't capital murder.

"Skip, if Tamara Harvey cracks on the stand tomorrow, our window may be closed. You get that, right?"

"It's your job to make sure she doesn't crack. Are you telling me you're not up to your job?"

I couldn't look at the man. Instead, I focused on the glaring eyes of the three-foot leprechaun he had perched on the edge of his desk. Said leprechaun had his dukes up in his classic fighting Irish pose. Though I had nothing against him, the urge to knock him off burned through me.

"Skip," I said. "I told you from the very beginning. This was going to be a tough case to make capital murder. That hasn't changed. Yes. Robbie Forte's killing was grisly, but that's not enough. I'm begging you, let me test the waters with Grandy before Tamara takes the stand. A plea bargain isn't a loss. You're the one who mentioned taxpayer dollars. A protracted trial that ends short of your expectations won't be good for the county bottom line, either."

"You *make* sure it ends according to my expectations. I was put in this office because I swore I'd be tough on crime. I need my soldiers to be equally tough, Mara."

"Working out a plea deal that fits the elements of the crime is plenty tough, Skip. It's also good business."

"We're done here," he said. "You have your marching orders. If you can't hack it, I'll find someone else who can."

I bit my tongue. I didn't have the energy for this argument. He could bluster all he wanted, but I was the one in the middle of a murder trial. I had to save all my spoons for that.

I turned and put my hand on the doorknob.

"I didn't say you could leave," he said.

"You said we were done here, I thought ..."

"I know what you're thinking. I know what you're all thinking. I knew this was going to be a problem even before I got sworn in. You, Howard, even Caroline out there. You're all loyal to Kenya Spaulding."

"Skip, we all work for the county. That's true now and it was true before Kenya took office. It'll be true long after you're gone."

"You'd like that, wouldn't you?"

He was like a petulant child. Paranoid. Vindictive. Hojo had a theory he was doing it to make us all miserable enough to quit so he wouldn't have to fire us. He was doing a pretty good job.

"Anyway, I've said my piece," I said. "My recommendation is now and has always been that we offer second degree on the Darryl Cox case. You've overruled me. Fine. So I'm going to go in there tomorrow and every other day and put on the best case I can for capital murder. Despite what you want to believe, I'm good at this, Skip. The best you've got."

He let out a haughty laugh. "I'll make this as clear as I can. This case? It's your shot, Mara. Your only shot. You know I wanted to fire you the second I took office. Your baggage is a problem."

"My baggage?"

"You flew under the radar for years. You may have had Kenya snowed. You were friends. But I know it's only a matter of time before somebody digs up the skeletons in your particular family closet. You're a problem. One I get asked about daily. Your husband is serving federal time for corruption. Having you in this office is a bad look for me. But I'm willing to give you a chance. I'm not the monster you all want to make me out to be. If you don't deliver a guilty verdict on capital murder in this case, you're out."

"You're going to fire me?"

He didn't answer. He just stared straight at me, a smug smile on his face.

"You better hope your star witness delivers tomorrow. Now we're finished. You can go."

I swallowed the nasty retort that bubbled into my brain. He wasn't worth it. I had to focus. Robbie Forte's family was counting on me.

I turned my back on Skip Fletcher and walked out the door.

Caro and Hojo scrambled down the hallway, making a poor attempt to cover their tracks. Of course, they'd both been eavesdropping.

"It's no good," I said. "You might as well meet me in my office."

Heads hanging low, they followed me down the hall into my office. The walls were thin so I didn't want to gripe too much. I shut the door behind me.

"He can't fire you!" Caro whispered. "He'll take too much heat for that."

"I'm not worried," I said. "Not about that."

"Tamara Harvey?" Hojo said. "You're telling me your career hinges on what that girl says on the stand tomorrow?"

"Thanks, Hojo. I appreciate the added pressure."

"Sorry," he said. "It's just ... well ... bananas. Kenya never would have let this case go to trial."

"Maybe don't say that within Skip's earshot," I said.

"I hate this," Caro said, her eyes welling with tears. "I used to love coming to work. Now, I'm so stressed. I'm eating like a jerk. I've gained eleven pounds since that man was sworn in. My numbers are a mess. Blood pressure. Cholesterol. Triglycerides. Hojo, yours can't be any better. Look at you?"

Caro patted Hojo's beer belly. Leave it to her to make a near insult come out like an act of love. He knew it was.

"Everyone just needs to calm down," I said. "Skip's new. Green. Insecure. He can't stay on the warpath forever."

Caro and Hojo exchanged a look that didn't instill confidence in me.

"It'll be okay," Caro said, always the empath. "You're amazing in front of a jury, Mara. Skip would have to be insane to fire you. I mean ... he's not insane, right? Just mean."

"It'll be okay," I said. Caro came to me and flung her arms around me.

"If you go," she said, "I go. That's a promise."

"Great," I joked. "So, it's not just my career hanging in the balance. Thanks."

Caro laughed, then hiccupped into a sob. She really was wound tighter than I'd ever seen her. We all were. I took a breath and said a prayer. I needed a good day in court tomorrow. For all of us.

4

"What if I can't do this?" she said.

"You can. You are."

Tamara Harvey sat in a chair against the wall in the courthouse law library adjacent to Judge Ivey's courtroom. I had a few minutes before he took the bench to check in with her.

She was a small thing. Barely five feet tall and probably not even a hundred pounds. From a distance, you'd think she was twelve years old. But up close, the shadows under her eyes and lines around her mouth made her look at least twenty years older than her twenty-two years. She'd earned every one of those lines and shadows growing up in foster care, then attaching herself to a string of men who didn't value her. Little by little, I hoped she would learn to value herself. I'd gotten her into counseling with the help of the county's victim's advocacy group, the Silver Angels. One of their social workers was already sitting in the courtroom, ready to give Tamara a supporting face to look at while she took the stand.

"You don't know Darryl like I do," she said. "The way he looks at you. It can make you feel two inches tall."

"Listen to me," I said. "Darryl can't hurt you anymore. No matter what happens on the stand today. It doesn't matter what he thinks. Or even what anybody thinks. You just have to go up there and tell the truth, Tamara. You let me worry about the rest of it."

"If I do this ... if he gets out ..."

I wanted to tell her that he'd never get out. I couldn't. I wanted to tell her that no one would ever hurt her again. I couldn't. But I could help get her through this today. I could help her take back her own power. Something I'm not sure she ever believed she had.

"Mara?" Judge Ivey's bailiff, Tim Meegan, poked his head in. "Judge is ready to take the bench."

"Got it," I said. I turned to Tamara and smiled. "You ready?"

"I just want to get this over with," she said. It wasn't the most confident of answers. And when Tamara stood up, her hands trembled so badly, she had trouble picking up her purse. Tim shot me a look. He noticed too. Lord, I hoped I wouldn't lose Tamara on the stand. Her deposition had taken hours and she'd run from the room crying twice. Here, in front of the jury, that wouldn't read well. Jurors tend to lose patience quickly.

I took my place at the table. Tamara sat against the wall next to the Silver Angels' social worker. The deputies led Darryl Cox to his table where Earl Grandy already waited. It was the first time Tamara had been in a room with Cox since the day Robbie Forte had turned up dead.

"Ms. Brent?" Judge Ivey said from the bench.

"Your Honor," I said, rising. "The state calls Tamara Harvey to the stand."

Behind me, I heard Tamara's shuffle-footed gait as she walked up the rows. She had to pass right by Darryl's table as she made her way to the witness box. He smiled at her, turning on the charm. You could see why Tamara had been initially attracted to him. He had a sort of Kurt Cobain, lost-boy look about him, right down to the shaggy blond hair and pale blue eyes.

Tamara's hand was still trembling as the bailiff swore her in and she took her seat. I stepped up to the lectern.

"Ms. Harvey," I said. "Would you please tell the jury how you came to know Darryl Cox?"

"Um. We met through mutual friends. My ... my best friend, Alexis Dickey, her brother worked with Darryl at the refinery. That was, I think, four years ago. Almost four years ago. Jordan Dickey ... my friend's brother. He had a party at his house one night and I went to it. Darryl was there. He was with another girl. Actually, another friend of mine. Lacey. But they weren't getting along that night. Lacey got a little too drunk. She started flirting with another guy. I felt really bad for Darryl because he didn't know anybody else at the party. We got to talking. He was just really easy to talk to. After that, we started texting. Maybe a month or so later, he asked me out. We've been together ever since."

"You were romantically involved?" I asked.

"Yeah. I was Darryl's girl. That's how he'd introduce me to people. This is my girl, Tamara."

"How did that make you feel?"

Tamara's whole demeanor changed. She stopped shaking. Color came into her cheeks. I looked over at Darryl. He smiled at Tamara. I braced myself. She wasn't looking at her social worker for support. She was getting it from Darryl.

No. No. No.

"Ms. Harvey?"

"Sorry," she said, still blushing. "How did it make me feel? It made me feel important. Darryl was just one of those people other people like to be around. He can walk into a room and just own it, you know? He'd buy me flowers when it wasn't even my birthday or anything. He was just good to me in a way no guy ever had been before. He told me he would take care of me forever and I believed him. And he did. He made sure my car was running right. He'd put gas in it for me. That was one of the first things that floored me. He told me a lady shouldn't ever pump her own gas. I mean, I thought that was kinda silly when he said it. But then I liked it. He would wait on me. It just felt really good to have somebody looking out for me. I'd never had that before. I didn't have a dad or any brothers. Other guys I've dated didn't treat me all that well. Darryl was different."

"How did your relationship progress?" I asked. "Did it become more serious?"

"It sure did. And fast. I wanna say it was maybe three or four months in when he asked me to move in with him. At first, he was living in this little apartment on Chadwick Street. Just a one bedroom. But he promised me that was only temporary. As soon as some things he had going came through, he said he'd have enough money to get us a house."

"What things did he have going? Did you know?"

Tamara's shoulders tightened. She looked away from me.

"I didn't ask a lot of questions," she said. "I heard rumors. And I knew some of the people who would come to the apartment were involved in some shady stuff. Drugs. You know. But Darryl always promised me that he wasn't into that stuff. And I never saw him using. I rarely ever saw him drink. He hated it when I smoked pot. Not that I did a lot of that. But he'd tell me that stuff was poison, and you never really know what people put in it."

"Sure. Did that ever change? Did you ever see Darryl drink or use drugs?"

"Yeah," she said. "A couple of times, but that was way later. After we'd been living together for about six months, Darryl made good on his promise. He took me to the house on Raven Street where we ended up living. He was gonna buy it on a land contract. At that point, I was also making decent money bartending at Greenie's. So, I told him I'd move there with him, but I wanted to be on the paperwork too. I wanted us to own it together. He said yes. And then we moved in."

"I see," I said. "But when did you see Darryl Cox using drugs?"

"Oh. Sorry. Yeah. It was a housewarming party we had right after we moved into the Raven Street house. He invited a bunch of people to come over who I didn't know. Things got out of hand. I was furious. I'd spent a lot of time fixing up the house to look nice. And he invited all these people. They were all using. I came home from my shift at Greenie's and found them all there. I saw Darryl at the kitchen table, and he was snorting a couple of lines."

"What did you do?"

"I was so angry. I yelled at him and told him I wanted everyone out. I told him I was gonna call the cops."

"What happened next?"

"They all just laughed at me. When Darryl saw I wasn't kidding, he got so mad. He punched a hole in the wall."

"What did you do?"

"I was terrified. That's ... that's something my dad used to do when I was little. Punch things. I don't know. It just triggered something in me. I ran out of the house. Darryl ran after me. Our yard wasn't fenced at that time and I ran into the woods behind it. He caught up with me. Then ..."

"Then what?"

"Then ... he ... he got rough. He..."

"Objection," Earl Grandy said. "This is irrelevant, Your Honor. Ms. Harvey's testimony so far has nothing whatsoever to do with the crime in question."

"Your Honor, this is proper establishing testimony. Mr. Cox's propensity for violence, particularly as it relates to Tamara Harvey, is at the heart of this case."

"I'll allow it," Judge Ivey said.

"You can continue, Ms. Harvey," I said.

She looked down at the floor. I had to remind her to speak into the microphone. But then something came over Tamara. She squared her shoulders, looked up, and spoke in a clear voice.

"That was the first time Darryl hit me. He grabbed me by the shoulders, threw me to the ground, and smacked me, open-handed in the face. It was hard enough to make my teeth rattle. I bit my tongue and blood filled my mouth. He told me I'd better never talk to him like that again. Better never run away from him. He said I was his. He made me repeat it."

"Repeat what, exactly?" I asked.

"He made me say I belong to him. I belong to him. Over and over. It was the only way I could get him to calm down. So, I said it. Finally, he got off me. We walked back into the house. I locked myself in the bedroom. It got so loud. The partying. I was surprised the neighbors didn't call the cops. I finally fell asleep. Then, sometime after that, Darryl woke me up. He was on top of me. He was kissing me. Telling me how much he loved me. How sorry he was. And ... I don't know. I thought he was serious. He was serious, I think."

"Did he ever hit you again after that?" I asked.

She nodded.

"Ms. Harvey, I'm sorry. But you must answer verbally."

"Yes," she said. "He hit me a lot after that. Not right away. Things were good again for a long time after that. Months. Except at that point, Darryl stopped hiding certain things from me. He was more out in the open."

"In what way?"

"Well, he got pretty open about the fact that he was dealing. Crack. Heroin. Some pot. He and his friends would measure the stuff on the card table in our basement. He'd come home with stacks of cash. There would be people showing up to the house at all hours of the day and night."

"Did it ever occur to you to leave?" I asked.

She shook her head. "No," she said. "I was just ... I don't know. It's taken me a long time to really process everything that's happened. The choices I made. My counselor said I was going through a fawn response. Just kind of going very still, afraid to move. Afraid to run. I see that now. But back then, I was just not equipped to get myself out of a bad situation."

"How bad did it get, Ms. Harvey?" I asked.

She squeezed her eyes shut. "It got very bad. Darryl changed. Or more likely, I started seeing the real Darryl. It's taken me a long time to work through this too. But the Darryl I met. The guy I fell for. That was the act. The charmer. The real Darryl is different. Angry. Controlling. It went on for so long."

"Tamara, did you ever come to know Robbie Forte?"

"Yes," she said, a single tear falling down her cheek. "Robbie started coming around about a year and a half ago. I don't know how he and Darryl met. But they started dealing together. Darryl said Robbie had big connections. That their partnership was going to take him to the next level. And I think it did. Darryl started bringing in a lot of money. Thousands of dollars every week. Robbie was set up somehow to launder it, I think. He owned a car wash. At one point, they asked me to come work for Robbie there. Like as a cashier or something. I said no. That caused some problems between Darryl and me too. We got into a big fight. Darryl shoved me into the bathroom. He hit me again. Split my lip. Robbie pulled him off me. He knocked Darryl out. When he got up, Darryl took off. Robbie was there for me. He helped me get cleaned up. He apologized for Darryl. He was just so nice to me. I cried. I confided things I probably shouldn't have about how Darryl had been treating me. After that, we got close."

"You and Robbie?"

"Yes. I'm not proud of it, okay? But I just didn't know what to do. I knew I needed to figure out how to get myself out of the situation. Robbie said he helped his mom get away from his stepdad under similar circumstances. He offered to help me. But I was still too afraid. And I still loved Darryl. I know that maybe sounds crazy."

"No," I said. "It doesn't. Tamara, can you tell me what happened the night of December 7th of last year?"

"Yes. But you have to understand what happened a few nights before that. I'll admit it. I did something I shouldn't have. I let things with Robbie go too far. We started sleeping together. Robbie confided things to me about Darryl too. How he was worried that Darryl was sampling too much of their product. He was afraid it was going to come back to bite them in the ass, you know? Then one night, Darryl just lost it. I think at that point he started to suspect something was going on. He got into my phone. He saw some calls going back and forth between me and Robbie. We never texted. But we'd call each other. It was stupid of me. Darryl went nuts. Robbie came over and the two of them got into a fist fight. It didn't last long. Robbie was bigger and stronger. Darryl got his gun from the closet and waved it in Robbie's face. He said he was going to kill us both if he ever found out we were sleeping together."

"That must have been terrifying," I said. "What happened next?"

"Robbie left. I asked him to go. I knew I could get Darryl to calm down if he wasn't there. And I really thought Darryl was going to do it. You know. Shoot Robbie."

"What did you do?"

"After Robbie left, I told Darryl it wasn't true. That Robbie and I were just friends. That I'd never cheated on him."

"You lied," I said, saying the thing I knew Earl Grandy would try to make an issue of.

"I lied," she said. "Because if I didn't, I was afraid Darryl would kill me or kill Robbie. He did calm down after a while. He actually got really sweet. Kissing my feet. Literally. Telling me how sorry he was but that just the thought of me with anyone else made him crazy. I thought it was okay then. But later, like early the next morning. I woke up and Darryl was standing over the bed staring at me. He had the strangest look on his face. He leaned in and whispered in my ear. He said if he ever caught me with Robbie or any other guy, that he'd blow his um ... you know ... private parts off ... and then make me disappear."

"When was this?" I asked.

"It was on the morning of December 5th. I just froze. Darryl got dressed and left and I pretended I was asleep. I stayed there for so long, just frozen like that. Afraid to move. Afraid to even breathe. Then I got up and went to work. I tried to call Robbie. You know. To warn him that Darryl wasn't calm at all. I couldn't get a hold of him. That's when I got a bunch of texts from Darryl threatening me. Saying the same sort of stuff over and over. What he'd do to me. What he'd do to Robbie."

"Did you ever see Darryl again after that?" I asked.

"No," she said. "I stayed over at a friend's house that night. I went back to the house on the 6th. Darryl didn't come home. Robbie wasn't answering his phone either. I didn't hear from either one of them again. Then that detective showed up at the house on the afternoon of the 7th. That's when I knew. That's when I knew. Darryl killed Robbie. He did everything he said he would, only I didn't disappear. I didn't disappear. I'm still here."

Tamara Harvey dissolved into tears. But she was right. She did not disappear. She met my eyes. I was proud of her. She thought she was broken. But she had only bent.

"Thank you," I said. "I have no further questions."

Earl Grandy stepped up to the lectern. He tried to break her. He hammered home her lie, but I knew the jury wasn't buying it. I knew Tamara Harvey had just delivered the testimony that would ensure Darryl Cox would answer for the killing of Robbie Forte.

And Tamara stood up to it. She kept her back straight, her answers clear. She volleyed every attack Earl Grandy tried to make. I decided not to lodge a single objection. Tamara could take care of herself.

When it was over, Tamara left the stand. She flew into her social worker's arms and the two of them left the courtroom. Judge Ivey adjourned the trial for the weekend.

I gathered my things, feeling truly good about this case for the first time. And hating to admit that maybe Skip Fletcher wasn't completely off base, refusing to let me plead it out.

Earl Grandy walked past me. The deputies put cuffs back on Darryl Cox. He stepped around his table. His leg chains rattled as he launched himself straight at me.

He practically fell on top of me, forcing me backward against the half-wall separating the gallery. His breath was hot on my face. He clamped his jaw shut hard, threatening to bite me. His hands were shackled in front of him but he managed to grab one of mine and shove something into it.

"Cox!" one of the deputies shouted. They were on him, pulling him backward. My heart raced. The air went out of me. They wrestled him, easily overpowering him. Two more deputies came flying into the courtroom.

I took a step back, locking eyes with Cox. His swagger, his smirk, it all vanished and I saw the mask of rage that Tamara Harvey knew so well.

The deputies strong-armed him and pushed him forward away from me. My heart still thundered in my chest, but I wouldn't give the likes of Darryl Cox the satisfaction of seeing even an ounce of fear in my eyes.

"You okay?" one of the deputies shouted at me. I couldn't find the words yet. I simply nodded. They muscled Cox out of the courtroom as he laughed the entire way.

I clutched my hand to my chest. Slowly, I pulled it away and opened it. Cox had placed a tightly rolled piece of paper in it.

Maybe I should have tossed it in the garbage. Maybe I should have said something to the deputies. I don't know why I didn't. Instead, I unrolled the piece of paper, blinking hard as I read it.

5

"Mara!"

I stood with my back to him, still frozen in place at the table in Judge Ivey's courtroom. I closed my fist, concealing the piece of paper Darryl Cox had forced into my hand.

"Are you okay?" Sam said, rushing to my side. He put a gentle hand on my shoulder, his brown eyes filled with concern.

"I'm okay."

"What did he do to you? Did Cox hurt you? I'm gonna have some words with my deputies."

"It's okay. I'm fine," I said. "It happened so fast. They didn't do anything wrong."

"They didn't control their prisoner. It's their one job, Mara."

Sam ran his hands over my arms and looked me up and down.

"I'm fine! I promise. He just startled me, that's all. And he ..."

I sank into the nearest chair. Maybe Cox's behavior had startled me more than I wanted to initially admit. Sam sat beside me.

"Let's get you out of here. Can I get you a drink of water?"

"I'm really okay. I'm not that easily breakable. I appreciate the concern."

"Did the jury see any of that?" Sam asked.

"No. His lawyer didn't even see it. Where is Grandy, by the way? Did you pass him on the way in here?"

"No," Sam said. "Come on. Let's get you out of here. There are a couple of local reporters out there hoping for a story."

"Yeah. I don't want to talk to anyone."

"Let me get you back to your office," he said. I gathered my things, still clutching Cox's note in my hand. I didn't want to bring it up here. Not where there might be unguarded ears and loose lips. Gossip and rumors spread like wildfire in the courthouse.

Sam walked me the short block and a half back to my office. He scanned the street the entire time in threat assessment mode. He opened the door for me. By the time we walked by Caro's desk, word of Darryl Cox's courtroom outburst had already reached the office.

"You okay?" Caro said. She stood at her desk with her desk phone in her hand. "She's here now," she spoke into it, then quickly hung up.

"Good gravy," I said. "I'm fine. Hear that?" I shouted down the hallway. "I'm fine!"

Skip Fletcher's door stayed closed.

"Don't bother," Caro said. "He's not here. He left early for some meeting with the county commissioners. We probably won't see him until Monday morning, thank God."

This got a muffled laugh out of Sam. He followed me into my office. I set my briefcase down.

"Shut the door," I instructed him. He narrowed his eyes in confusion, but did what I asked.

"You sure you're okay?"

"Yes. I promise." I sat down at my desk. Finally, I uncurled my fist and pulled the crumpled piece of paper out of it.

"Cox gave me this," I said.

"He what?"

Sam crossed the room in two strides and stood over me. I flattened the half sheet of yellow notebook paper on the desk and let him read it over my shoulder.

"Need to talk. Have info you'll want. Can't trust Grandy. Deal."

"Cox gave you that?"

"I think it was his whole reason for that little outburst, Sam. He shoved it into my hand."

Sam went rigid. He curled his fists at his side. A tremor went through his jaw.

"He put his hands on you?"

"I told you. I'm fine."

"This is not fine. Are you sure you're okay? I have a few things I need to deal with."

"Sam," I said. "Don't lose your temper. Don't make a bigger deal out of this than you need to out of some sense of alpha male chivalry or whatever. I really am fine. The deputies were right there."

"You can't talk to him. Whatever that is. Cox is desperate."

"Of course I can't talk to him. I'm going to have to report this to the judge. And I need to get Earl Grandy on the phone."

"I want to be here for that," Sam said, tight-lipped.

"This isn't Grandy's fault either. At least I don't think so. Please. I can handle this from here. You don't need to babysit me. I'm just glad Tamara Harvey was already out of the courtroom. That girl was a rock star on the stand today. She stood up to Darryl in a way she's never had the chance to before. She was brilliant."

"Then that's what this is about," Sam said, stabbing a finger into Cox's crumpled note.

"Probably."

I picked up my desk phone and rifled through the other bits of loose paper I had on my desk. I zeroed in on a pink message from Earl Grandy made last week. It had his direct line on it. I dialed. It went straight to voicemail.

"Mr. Grandy," I said. "It's Mara Brent. There was an incident in the courtroom this afternoon after you left. Your client handed me a note. I need you to call me right away. I'll be in my office for about another hour."

I hung up. Sam had moved from my side and started to pace.

"You don't have to stay," I said.

"I don't like it. I don't want you talking to Cox. I don't even want you in the same room with him again."

"Well, that's gonna be pretty hard to pull off, seeing as how I'm prosecuting him for murder."

"I'm gonna talk to Ivey. I want that guy in chains at all times from now on."

"Grandy's gonna push back on that. It's a bad look in front of the jury."

"Don't care. Cox forfeited that consideration when he came at you."

Sam was too keyed up to reason with. I knew he was probably right. I just hated anyone making a fuss on my account.

Caro buzzed in. "Hey, Mara. I've got Earl Grandy on the line. He says you called?"

"Thanks," I said. "Sam. Seriously. Don't hover."

He let out a decidedly alpha male growl.

"Earl?" I answered the phone, hitting the speaker button. "Hey. We have an issue with your client."

"I'm listening," he said. His voice sounded tinny. I could hear traffic sounds.

"He kind of got into my personal space after you walked out. Darryl, uh ... well ... he passed me a note."

"Grandy?" Sam said, completely ignoring my request. "This is Sheriff Cruz. Your client assaulted Mara in court after you conveniently left. Here's what's happening from now on. He stays in irons every second he's not in a cell. That includes in court."

"You don't have that authority," Grandy said.

"Bet me," Sam answered.

"Stop!" I mouthed to Sam, but that freight train was already barreling down the mountain.

"Earl," I said. "I said Darryl passed me a note. I need to bring it to the judge's attention but I'm also fulfilling my ethical obligation by calling you. I'll text you a picture of it. But Cox says he wants to talk to me. Something about cutting a deal."

"You don't talk to my client, you got that? Mara, this is grounds for a mistrial."

"None of this happened in view of the jury," I said. "There's no mistrial, Earl. But you need to get a hold of and a handle on your client. Figure out what this is all about. Then call me. We clear?"

Earl Grandy let out a two-second heave of an exhale. "I'll call you back," he said.

"You do that," Sam said. It earned him an eye roll from me. I clicked off the call.

"That went well," I muttered.

"He's scared," Sam said. "Both Grandy and Cox. The sooner this trial is over, the happier I'll be."

"You always say that," I teased. "Come on. It's after five. Let's get out of here. I'll let you buy me dinner. Or better yet. How about I cook you dinner? Will's still on his class trip. It's quiet at the house."

Sam smiled. In the last four months, we'd been in a bit of a stalemate as far as our relationship went. Things had been too crazy for him since his swearing-in as the new sheriff. The upheaval in my own office had kept me off the board as well.

"I wish I could," he said. "That meeting with the county commissioners where Fletcher is? I'm supposed to be at it."

I let out a breath. "Then you better get going." I rose from my desk. Sam had time for a quick peck on my cheek. Then he was out the door.

I sank back into my chair, picking up Darryl Cox's note. Sam was right, I knew. This was just a desperate ploy from a desperate man who'd lost control of Tamara Harvey. She did real damage today. I liked my chances of a conviction a lot better than I did twenty-four hours ago.

I finished up a few pre-trial motions I had in other matters. I thought only an hour went by. My growling stomach finally got me to look back at the time.

"Oh geez," I said to no one. It was past seven o'clock. Caro hadn't even poked her head in when she left. I stuffed a couple of files into my briefcase. I had witness prep to do at home.

I clicked off the lights and made my way to the lobby. A text buzzed. I picked up my phone and looked at it. It was from Earl Grandy.

"Talked to Cox. We need to meet. It's urgent. I've made arrangements with the jail. Can you meet me there by eight tomorrow morning?"

I thought about that note and everything Sam said. Cox was a desperate man doing desperate things.

I typed in my response.

"I'll be there."

6

"They got here about an hour ago," Deputy Jon Liddy said as soon as I got to the jail the next morning. "Grandy's been yelling at everyone in sight."

"Please tell me you don't have cameras on them," I said.

"No, ma'am. We set them up in the lawyer's room. Doesn't mean we couldn't hear more yelling through the wall. I had Deputy Swift check in once. It got so loud we were worried they were literally at each other's throats."

"Thanks for the intel," I said. A pit of dread settled in my stomach. I could think of a thousand other places I'd rather be on a Saturday morning.

"You okay?" Liddy asked. "Heard you had a little excitement with Cox in court yesterday. Boss wasn't too happy."

"Boss is under a lot of stress. And thanks for asking. I'm fine."

The lawyer's room was two doors down from us. Earl Grandy poked his head out, red-faced. His color lightened a bit when he saw me.

"Oh good," he said. "You're late."

"You're early," I answered. "I'm right on time."

"You want me in there with you?" Liddy asked. "Cox is in cuffs and leg irons. Boss said that's non-negotiable."

I felt a little bad for Liddy and the other deputies. Sam generally had no anger management issues. But when he *did* get mad, it could be fearsome and pretty loud.

"We'll be fine," I said. "But thank you."

"I'll be right outside," Liddy said as much to Grandy as to me.

I followed Grandy in. As Liddy promised, Darryl Cox sat in cuffs looped through a bracket on the table. He kept his hands clasped and those pale blue eyes fixed on me as I walked in and took a seat at the far end of the table. Grandy sat beside Cox.

"What's this all about?" I asked.

"First of all," Grandy started. "My client would like to express deep remorse for his behavior yesterday. He's on trial for his life. You can imagine emotions ran high. He wasn't his best self."

"Your client would like to express that? Or you wish he would express that?"

"I'm sorry," Darryl interjected. "It won't happen again."

I wondered how many times he'd said something similar to Tamara Harvey. I bit my lip to keep myself from commenting exactly that.

I pulled the note he'd given me yesterday out of my briefcase. I slid it across the table to Grandy. Though he'd seen the picture of it I'd texted to him, I wanted to make sure he had the real thing.

"I'm sure your attorney has explained to you that it's entirely inappropriate to communicate with me this way, never mind your outburst. In the future, if at all, you need to communicate through Mr. Grandy. You both understand we're going to need to inform the judge about all of this."

"No need to blow things out of proportion," Grandy said. "My client has apologized. No harm done."

"Do you want to explain to me what you meant with that note?"

Darryl's gaze dropped. He pursed his lips as Grandy answered for him.

"My client is possessed of certain ... information he feels might be of interest to you. I need to make one thing very clear. I'm here at Mr. Cox's request. I have advised him against this course of action. He is proceeding in spite of my recommendation."

I looked at Cox. He shifted uncomfortably in his chair. I had the distinct impression that if it weren't for the cuffs and leg irons, he might actually wring Earl Grandy's neck.

"I'm listening," I said.

"First." Cox's word was an eruption. He leaned forward as much as he could, rattling the chains around his ankles. "You sign the paperwork. You drop the charges against me?"

I think I reared back as if his words took physical shape and smacked me.

"I'm sorry. What?"

"I want all charges dropped. I want to walk out of here. Today."

It took me a second to realize he was serious.

"You haven't said anything worthwhile, Mr. Cox. Perhaps you need to listen to Mr. Grandy. If—"

"I have information," Cox said. "The kind that'll make your career. Put you on the cover of *People* magazine or whatever. You drop the charges, and I'll give it to you."

My head started to pound. "You killed Robbie Forte. No. Sorry. You tortured and *then* killed Robbie Forte. I'm not offering a plea deal. If you've come here under the impression that I—"

"I can make you a hero," he said. "Wonder Woman. Whatever. Robbie Forte was a dirtbag. The world's better off without him. Nobody cares."

"I care. The people of the state of Ohio care."

"Whatever," he said. "Except you know they don't. They find it interesting because his junk was blown off. Which he deserved."

"Enough," Grandy shouted over him. "Ms. Brent, would you mind giving me a moment with my client?"

"No," Cox said. "I'm not admitting to any of it. That's not why I wanted you here. What I'm saying is Robbie was a loser. A piece of crap. Nobody cares. They care about pretty little blonde girls that go missing. Those are the ones that get in the news. What I'm offering is a chance for you to solve the case of the prettiest one of all."

He had that signature smirk on his face. The one that had charmed Tamara and countless others. The one that could turn to a sneer in an instant, just before he snapped.

I went a little numb. It almost felt like every ounce of water I had in my body suddenly dried up all at once. It got hard to breathe.

Little blonde girls.

My God. What had he done?

"My client believes he has information that could lead to the resolution of a cold case kidnapping," Grandy said.

"Your client would like you to leave," Cox said. There it was. The sneer.

"Not a chance," I said. "We will not be having this conversation or any others outside the presence of your lawyer. I don't really care what's going on between the two of you. But so far, this has been a monumental waste of my time. Whatever game you're playing ..."

"No games," Cox said. "This thing fell into my lap. I wanna be real clear. I had nothing to do with what happened to that kid. Twelve years ago, I was just a sixteen-year-old punk living in my parents' house. It had nothing to do with me. I don't even really want anything to do with it now except for how it can help me."

Twelve years ago?

"Mr. Cox. Darryl. No more riddles. What are you talking about? What little girl?"

"I want papers," he said. "That comes first."

"It doesn't work like that. If you have information that could lead to an arrest in an unsolved case ... even if I were inclined to entertain this ... which I'm not ... you show me yours first. You get me?"

Grandy simply threw his hands up in frustration. I got the impression he'd likely said the same thing to Cox in a variety of ways before I got here. Maybe that was the reason for all the shouting the deputies heard. Grandy gave me a "see what I've been dealing with" wide-eyed expression.

"Get me a pen and paper," Cox said. I reached into my bag and pulled out a notebook and ballpoint pen. I slid it across the table.

"What do you know about, Darryl?"

He grabbed the pen and clicked it open. He poised it above the paper, but kept his eyes on me.

"Violet Runyon," he said.

I let the name settle in my mind. Violet Runyon. It was familiar, but not something I immediately recalled.

Violet Runyon.

A memory surfaced. Twelve years ago. It wasn't my case. It happened maybe a year before Jason and I moved to Waynetown. A young girl. Was it a custody dispute?

Earl Grandy had his phone out. He tapped the screen then handed it to me. I kept my eyes on Darryl as I took the phone. Then I looked at the news article Grandy had pulled up.

Violet Runyon. Yes. The case had gotten national news. A five-year-old girl at the center of a bitter custody dispute. Her father had her overnight and failed to bring her back. She was never seen again.

I scrolled through the article. It was written on the tenth anniversary of Violet's disappearance two years ago. Violet's father, Bart Runyon, had maintained his innocence. He made unfounded claims of abuse on the part of Violet's mother. His story changed several times, but he told the police he'd given Violet to an organization that promised to protect her from abuse. Bart Runyon was now serving a fifteen-year stint for unrelated drug charges, plus interference with custody and child endangerment. But the police were never able to make a case for kidnapping.

My heart turned to stone. I handed the phone back to Grandy. "Violet Runyon is dead. Her father killed her. Disposed of her somewhere and she was never found."

"That was never proven," Grandy said.

"It's bullshit," Darryl said. "Listen. I can put you in touch with a guy who knows. He can tell you everything you need to know about the group Bart Runyon shipped his little girl off to."

"So, tell me what you know," I said.

"Are you offering me a deal?"

"I'm offering you an ear at this point. So far, I'm not impressed. You want to start by telling me how you came to be in possession of all this bombshell information?"

Darryl looked at Grandy. Grandy gave him a shrug. Whatever was going on between them, their body language didn't convey they were at all on the same page.

"I've been in jail for months on this crap. You hear things. People like to talk," Darryl started. "Well. Maybe three months ago, I got a new cellie. He was with me for a couple of weeks on a solicitation charge. Cops ended up dropping it, I think. Anyway, he was a talker. A bragger, really. Kept telling me over and over he wasn't worried about whatever they had him on. He said he had a card to play whenever he wanted. I couldn't stand the guy. He had the kind of attitude that can get you in real trouble, real quick. Only he didn't. He was protected. I never knew for sure by who or what he'd done to earn it. But he liked me."

"Naturally," I said, sarcasm dripping from my voice.

"A few weeks ago, he finally pissed off the wrong person in the yard. Somebody broke his nose for mouthing off. He came back crying. Then all talk again. Saying how he was gonna get his revenge. I knew he was scared though. When things got quiet again, he was in a talking mood. I told him I'd have his back the next time he went out in the yard. So, I did. I was the only one who'd even talk to him. Finally, maybe a week ago, he told me what this get-out-of-jail-free card was all about. He said he knew what really happened to Violet Runyon."

"He said that," I said. "Specifically mentioned Violet Runyon?"

"Yeah. And I didn't know who he was talking about. I looked her up later. After Marvin left. He had his charges dropped, just like he said they would be."

"Marvin," I said. "His name is Marvin?"

"Yeah. Hoyt Marvin. He said the cops had it all wrong. That Violet Runyon's dad didn't kill her. That her kidnapping was part of something way bigger that even the cops didn't fully grasp."

"Bigger how?"

"That part he never told me. But he said he knew how to get a hold of the woman who took her. Took Violet. He gave me a name."

"It's a lie," I said. "Bart Runyon never sent his daughter anywhere except to her grave."

"I'm telling you, this guy can prove he was telling the truth."

"Really?" I said, leaning forward. "Then what do I need you for, Darryl? Seems to me this *guy* is the one who's got the information that could get him out of trouble, not you."

"Ginger Ivan," he said.

I narrowed my eyes. He said the name as if it should mean something to me. Grandy looked just as puzzled as I was.

"Ginger Ivan," Darryl said again. Then he wrote it down on the pad of paper.

"You drop the charges, and I help you find Ginger Ivan."

"Am I supposed to know what that means?" I said.

"That's it for now," he said. "You go talk to your boss. I know you need authority from Skip Fletcher to cut me my deal. So, you take this to him. You get me my proffer, I'll tell you the rest."

He slid the pad over to me. I took it. I don't know why I took it. But I slipped it in my briefcase.

"There isn't going to be a proffer, Darryl. This dream you have of getting your charges dropped? Isn't going to happen. Even if you could draw me a map leading right to Violet Runyon's body. I've had enough. We're back in court on Tuesday. I'll be calling the M.E. next."

"You gotta listen to me," Darryl said. "I don't deserve the needle for this. I think you know it. I think you got steamrolled by your new boss into certifying this as a death penalty case. You're not feeling it. You just don't have the stones to stand up to him."

I glared at him. I felt heat rising up my neck.

"Yeah," Darryl said, satisfied with himself. "I'm nobody, Mara. Just something Fletcher can use to make himself look tough. Trust me. He'll salivate over finding Violet Runyon. So are you. Let me know what he says, sugar."

I wanted to smack the smirk right off his face. Cox licked his lips and raked his eyes over me in the most vulgar way he could.

"We're done here," I said, fuming. I stormed out of the room and slammed the door shut behind me, satisfied by the clanging, metallic echo it made. Let that be a sound Darryl Cox would have to listen to for the rest of his miserable life.

7

I came in early the next day, Sunday morning. I wanted to go over my notes on Dr. Pham's testimony. Juries usually loved David Pham. He had a way of presenting dry, medical terminology in a way lay people could easily understand. He had good looks and an affable nature that made his often grisly testimony slightly more palatable. Robbie Forte's postmortem would be rough to hear. I already had two pukers during Detective Lance's testimony.

I'd call Pham. I'd put the digital forensics detective on to go through Darryl's movements the day Forte was killed. His cell phone records alone would provide a literal road map of where he was that day. I could put him in the vicinity of the ditch on Mullins Road. That would be the clincher. I could probably rest after that.

A soft knock on the door drew my eye. Hojo poked his head into my office.

"Hey," I said. "What are you doing here?"

"I wanted to grab a couple of files when I knew Skippy wouldn't be around to make me wanna stab myself in the eye."

I laughed. "You better not let him hear you call him Skippy."

"Not my fault. The guy walks around with a dog's name. Sounds like a cocker spaniel."

"I'm glad you're here. I wanted to pick your brain on something."

Hojo opened the door wider and came in. "Pick away. If you can find anything in here." He thumped his fist against the side of his head. "Mostly hollow these days."

"You're hilarious."

Hojo took a seat at one of the chairs in front of my desk, then put his feet up on the edge. He was casual today, wearing a pair of blue track pants and a Buckeyes shirt.

"Darryl Cox wanted to meet with me yesterday. I haven't mentioned it to Skip yet and am trying to decide if I even should."

"Ah. Yeah. I heard some gossip about that. Is Cox ready to try to cut a deal?"

"Not exactly. Cox is trying to sell some snake oil. Thinks he's got information on a cold case worthy of me dropping his charges altogether."

Hojo's eyes went wide. "On a murder? You've got him dead to rights on this one. Tamara Harvey was your weak link and I heard she was a friggin' rock star on the stand."

"She was."

"You're not seriously entertaining this."

"I am not. What he gave me was secondhand information anyway."

"Lay it on me," Hojo said.

"Were you part of the Violet Runyon case? Little girl who went missing twelve years ago?"

Hojo dropped his feet to the floor. "Peripherally, yeah. Kenya prosecuted the dad. It was a rough one. A real heartbreaker. Cute kid. She was a pawn in a nasty custody dispute between her parents. Dad ended up killing her. It was big news at the time. That was right before you got hired."

"What do you remember?"

"Bart Runyon's a psychopath. That's what I remember. But it was a mess. Both parents were accusing the other of abusing that girl. Child Services got involved at one time, but I don't think they were ever able to prove anything. Dad had her on a weekend visitation and never brought her back. He had all kinds of stories about what happened. None of them checked out. He's in jail now, but not for kidnapping her. I wanna say it was some drug charges and interference with custody. Vivien Saul was the one who sentenced him. Tacked on everything she was legally allowed to. I think if you look online, there's a video of her ranting from the bench. A fiery speech about how he's the absolute scum of the earth. Pleading with him to do the right thing and tell the cops where to find that little girl's body."

"Yikes."

"Runyon's lawyer appealed over that. Trying to say Saul considered things that weren't part of the case. Bottom line is she did, and nobody shed any tears on that. But that old bat's not stupid. Her sentence was well within the guidelines. I wanna say Bart Runyon's serving something like fifteen years."

"But nobody ever found Violet?" I asked.

"Nope. Not a trace. I think the working theory is that he dumped her in a landfill somewhere."

I couldn't fathom it. How could a father do that to his own child?

"What does any of this have to do with Darryl Cox?" Hojo asked.

"Probably nothing. He says he was cellmates with a guy who claims he knows what really happened to Violet. That he can put me in touch with whoever kidnapped her."

"It wasn't a kidnapping, Mara. It was a stone cold murder by her own dad. Either Darryl's lying or his cellie was. There's no mystery there. Bart Runyon's in jail."

"But not for killing his daughter," I said.

"You believe this kid?"

"No. Not exactly. It's just ... odd. I kind of believe Darryl believes he has something worth trading."

"What's Grandy's take on all of it?"

"That's the thing. There was tension between them. I think Grandy's a realist. My guess is he's been trying to convince Cox to plead guilty to second degree."

"But that's not on the table. Thanks to Skippy the Wonder Dog."

I snorted. "Don't. Now I'm gonna have that in my head the next time he walks in here."

"What's Sam say about all of this?" Hojo asked.

"I haven't told him."

"Yeah. I think your guy is trying to convince you Bigfoot is real, Mara."

I reached into my briefcase and pulled out the notepad Darryl had written on. I ran a finger over his tight block lettering, then tossed the notepad on the desk. Hojo picked it up.

There wasn't much there. Just the outline of what Darryl had told me. I'd looked into Hoyt Marvin, his cellmate. He'd been arrested on a solicitation charge. Bottom line, he was a low-level pimp from what I could glean. He had a few priors, but wasn't what I'd describe as any sort of criminal mastermind. He was in county lock-up with Cox. That had been easy enough to verify.

"What's this word here?" Hojo said, handing the notepad back to me. "I can't make out his handwriting."

"Ah. Cox was pretty excited about that. He said his cellmate would know how to find this woman who'd be the key to finding out what really happened to Violet Runyon. I mean, this isn't even secondhand information. It's like thirdhand at best. I'm not even sure it's worth a conversation with this Hoyt Marvin's parole officer, let alone Marvin himself."

"But the name," Hojo said. There was something off about his expression. All traces of humor had left his face.

I tilted my head and translated Cox's notes. "Uh ... Ginger Ivan. He said that name over and over. Ginger Ivan. That Marvin could put me in touch with Ginger Ivan. Does that mean something to you?"

Hojo started tapping his foot furiously against the floor. "You're sure? That came from Cox?"

"Yes, Hojo. Why?"

"Yeah. See, Bart Runyon gave that name to the cops. I remember that. It's not a very common name. One of his stories was that he gave Violet to a woman named Ginger Ivan. That she was part of some underground group that was in the business of saving kids from abuse. It was all bullshit, Mara."

"Of course it was."

"Only ... what's some two-bit drug dealer or pimp doing with that information? Mara ... the only people who should know that name other than Bart Runyon are those who were directly involved with the investigation. Members of this office and the sheriffs."

I looked at Darryl Cox's note again. Ginger Ivan.

"You don't think ..." I started.

"I don't know. But you gotta go see Kenya. You gotta tell her about this. Before you say anything to Fletcher."

"I've tried," I said. "She's not answering my calls or texts. It's been weeks. Maybe months."

"You're scared of her?"

"Aren't you?"

Hojo smiled. "Oh, I'm terrified. But if there's anything you want to know about Violet Runyon's case, Kenya's the one to ask. She lived and breathed this one. It damn near ruined her."

I felt a pit forming in my stomach. The last thing I wanted to do was upset Kenya Spaulding any more than she already was. She'd taken the loss to Skip Fletcher very hard.

"Right," I said.

"It's the right thing to do."

"Uh huh. Yeah. I'll go. Tomorrow."

Hojo grimaced. "Good. Only ... do me a favor and wear a helmet."

8

"Does she know we're coming?"

I parallel parked at the curb in front of Kenya Spaulding's mid-century-modern three-thousand-square-foot brick ranch. She lived in an older neighborhood in the southwest corner of the county. She had a triple lot with nearly three acres of woods in her backyard abutting the Maumee River.

She called it her sanctuary. She'd inherited the place from a favorite aunt when she was just out of college. She'd spent the last twenty years making the place into exactly what she wanted.

"Not exactly," I said to Will. He'd gotten home late last night from his field trip to Gettysburg. He was puzzled when I woke him up early and told him we were going on a field trip of our own.

"Then maybe she's not even home," he said.

"She's home."

"She works out on Mondays. She likes the gym over on Roosevelt. She said there's a personal trainer she likes."

I looked at him. "How do you know all of that?"

"She told me."

"When?"

Will pulled out his smartphone. He gave me his now standard look of exasperation as he pulled up a text thread between him and Kenya. I scrolled up. They were texting a lot. A couple of times a week. She hadn't returned one of mine or anyone in the office all month.

I handed his phone back to him. Bringing him here was a last-minute whim. Now, I realized it might be a stroke of genius.

"Her car's in the driveway," I said, sliding out from behind the wheel. I walked around the front of my car. Will had already gotten out. I stepped onto the sidewalk next to him. My son had hit a growth spurt. He was my height. A strange thing, that. By next year, I'd probably have to look up at him. He was growing into his father's physique. That, too, was strange. From a distance, Will looked so much like Jason it often took my breath away.

"What if she doesn't want to see you?" he asked.

"Well, I suppose she'll at least want to see you."

He scowled at me. "So, you're using me?"

"Of course. Come on."

Will slipped his phone in his back pocket and begrudgingly met my stride as we went up the walk.

"You want me to knock?" he asked. "You want to hide in the bushes and jump out?"

"Funny. You're a funny guy."

I lifted the brass door knocker on Kenya's royal-blue oak door. She'd white-washed the brick and hung black flower boxes under the front windows. Cheery pink geraniums waved at me as I knocked on the door.

I stepped back. Will fidgeted with his sleeves beside me. I reached over and smoothed an errant hair away from his eyes. He jerked back, annoyed with me. He needed a haircut.

Will leaned forward, peering into the closest window.

"Don't," I whispered. "She'll think you're a stalker."

"Do you think she forgot what I look like?" Will said, his voice cracking. That was changing, too. Deepening. Everything about my sweet, lanky, gawky kid was. In just a few weeks, he would turn thirteen.

The front door flung open. Kenya stood there, tall, regal, wearing a green and teal kaftan and holding a champagne glass filled with something orange. A mimosa?

She eyed me, then took a sip from her cocktail. Will stepped to the center of the porch. Kenya smiled at him, then saved a scathing look for me.

"She didn't call," Will said. "I told her she should call first."

Kenya took another sip of her mimosa.

"We won't stay long," I said.

"By all means, come on in." She opened the door wide. Will walked in ahead of me.

"Dirty trick," she whispered.

"Hush," I said. "Time for you to rejoin the land of the living. We're all worried about you."

"Hey, Will," she called out. "I'm glad you're here. I've been working on this five-thousand-piece puzzle. It's a death mask. Tutankhamun. Half the damn thing is black. You wanna have a crack at it?"

Kenya closed the door with a flourish. Her kaftan billowed out. She was barefoot, perfectly pedicured. She wore her hair naturally, in wave after wave of luscious brown curls. I don't know if I'd ever seen her without her hair tightly pinned back or wearing a suit. The woman really was super-model gorgeous.

She walked ahead of me down her beautiful, terra-cotta flooring. She led Will to the back of the house where she'd turned a covered porch into a solarium. The puzzle in question was spread out over a large round table.

"You want some lunch?" she said to Will. "I made some chicken shawarma last night. There's leftovers in the fridge."

"We just had breakfast," he said, settling into one of the chairs. His eyes darted over the puzzle. Kenya had finished King Tut's chin, assembling his lapis lazuli headdress. Will started picking up random puzzle pieces. Within twenty seconds, he'd made several matches.

"It's vintage," she said. "My aunt bought that one during the seventies. She went to a touring Tut exhibit in Chicago."

"I can tell," he said. "The pieces are heavy. Not junk, like they do now. Probably made from a real jigsaw instead of laser cut."

"You got a few minutes?" I asked her.

I felt bad. Kenya clearly would rather sit and work the puzzle with Will. For his part, he was already fully immersed in the thing. Hours could go by and he wouldn't even realize it. I'd have my hands full trying to pry him away from it when Kenya and I had finished talking.

"Come on," she said, exasperated. "Let's get it over with."

She leaned in and kissed Will on the head. She smoothed down the same wild lock of hair I'd tried to fix. Will's mouth twitched with the hint of a smile, but he didn't bat her hand away.

"Show-off," I muttered. Kenya gave me a smug smile, then practically floated past me, drink in hand. I followed her to the kitchen.

She reached into the fridge and pulled out a glass pitcher filled with her mimosa. I waved her off. She put it back in the fridge and perched herself on a stool on her kitchen island. I went to join her.

"We miss you," I said. "Place isn't the same without you."

"I miss you too. But not the place. See. That's the thing." She lifted her glass and waved it in the air. "I thought I would. I lived for the work, Mara. I thought I'd be depressed or in some sort of funk. But I'm not. Two months away from that building and it's like I finally know what fresh air smells like."

"So now you're just flitting around barefoot and drinking champagne in the morning?"

"Don't knock it until you try it."

I had a retort, but swallowed it. It occurred to me that she might very well have a point.

"He's grown like a weed," she said.

"I know."

"He looks like Jason."

"I know that too."

"You talked to him?"

"Jason? Nope. Not since late last year. He sends letters to Will. So far, he hasn't opened any of them."

"Poor kid."

"Overall, I'd say he's handling it all pretty well. He knows Jason's the reason Jason is in prison. He's not quite ready to forgive him for it."

"I hope he does someday," she said. "For his sake, not Jason's. But ... you didn't come here to talk about Jason."

"No. I came here because ... Lord. Now that I've got to say it out loud, maybe I don't even know why I came here. Other than really wanting to see you. It sucks not having you around. The office, sure, but you. You're my friend, Kenya. What happened, the election? I hate it. We all hate it. Skip ..."

She put up a finger. "Don't wanna talk about it. Certainly not him. I'm fine. Really."

"You sure? How long are you planning on living your uh ... lost weekend?"

"A while. I've got a healthy savings account. My accountant says I can live off my investments for a couple of years if I'm frugal."

"Is that your plan?"

"I haven't decided yet. Right now, my plan is to finish that puzzle and start on another one."

"Uh huh," I said, unconvinced.

Kenya put her glass down. "So what's this really all about? This is a conversation we could have had over the phone."

"If you'd answer yours."

"I'm sorry. Sort of. I just haven't been in the mood for everybody's pity. I'm a politician, Mara. I lost an election. Don't cry for me Argentina and all that."

"Nobody feels sorry for you. If anything, we're feeling sorry for ourselves. Skip Fletcher is a menace. A brute and a blowhard. Hojo's convinced his endgame is to make us all so miserable we quit. I gotta be honest. The idea has appeal. I'm honestly not sure Caro's gonna last until summer. He treats her horribly."

"I'm sorry for that."

"It's not your fault. And no. It's not why I'm here. You can pretend you're off the grid here, but I know you've been following what's going on. You know Fletcher's got me trying Darryl Cox's case as a capital murder."

She took another sip of her drink. "Wouldn't have been my call."

"I know. And it would have been the right one. I told him that. Only ... I think I'm gonna get a conviction. First degree."

"You'd be the one to do it. I know what you're like in the courtroom."

"I appreciate the confidence. Darryl Cox wants me to cut him a deal. Thinks he's got intel good enough to have us drop the charges."

Kenya did an honest-to-goodness spit take. "He cut off that poor guy's—"

I held up my hand. Will was in the other room, but not completely out of earshot.

"Ginger Ivan," I said.

Kenya's eyes narrowed. "What?"

"Ginger Ivan. I met with Cox over the weekend. He says he was cellmates with a guy who knows who Ginger Ivan is and maybe where to find her. Cox believes he's got information that will lead to the real story of what happened to—"

"Violet Runyon," Kenya finished for me. "He said that? He's lying. He probably just did a google search of some of our higher profile cases. Not much more than drawing a name out of a hat. He's bluffing."

"Hojo's not so sure. See, Kenya. Cox told *me* the name Ginger Ivan. It's just me bringing it up to you. Hojo says nobody who wasn't involved in the case should know Bart Runyon told the cops a woman named Ginger Ivan took Violet. But Cox did. He swears he heard the name from this cellmate of his."

"He's lying. They're all lying."

"Probably. But then how did Cox hear that name?"

"She isn't real, Mara. Bart Runyon made it all up. He did something to his own daughter. Strangled her probably. Then dumped her body somewhere it couldn't be found. He's scum. Worse than scum. He might as well be the devil."

"You're still not answering the central question. How does Darryl Cox, or rather this cellmate, know Runyon told the cops about this Ginger Ivan? Whether she's real or not?"

"Who knows? Bart's been in prison for a decade too. He's probably the one shooting his mouth off. Word gets around. Thin walls. Runyon drops the name to someone, who drops it to someone else, then before you know it, your boy Darryl Cox thinks he's struck gold. Ignore him."

"You're sure though," I said. "Bart Runyon killed his own kid?"

"I'm sure," she said. "It was a terrible situation. An ugly custody battle. Runyon told his ex he'd make sure she never saw Violet again. Then he made good on his promise."

"Hojo said the case was rough for you."

"Of course it was rough. She was a five-year-old girl. Totally innocent. And she was murdered by her own father."

"I just thought maybe you'd like to sit in on my next conversation with Cox. If there is one, that is."

"Mara, he's feeding you a line. He's desperate. I would not under any circumstances talk to him again. What's Earl Grandy saying?"

"That's the thing. He's not. I don't think Grandy wanted Cox to even float the idea to me."

"Because Grandy's an idiot, but he's not stupid, you know? He's gotta know Cox is full of crap."

"You never had any doubt that there was something to Bart Runyon's story?"

"None. And neither did the cops. To be honest, I don't even know why you're talking to me about this one. If you want to know how tight the case was against Runyon, you should be talking to Sam. Violet's disappearance was his case. Did you not know that?"

I shook my head. "No. I suppose it stands to reason. I assumed it was maybe Ritter's. I hadn't gone that far down the rabbit hole. I just kind of wanted to get your gut on this one before I said anything to Fletcher."

"Don't. I wouldn't even take it to Fletcher. He'll laugh you out of his office. So would I."

"No, you wouldn't."

She smiled. "No. I suppose I wouldn't. But this one's a nothing burger. Trust me. Every word that's ever come out of Bart Runyon's mouth has been a lie. Let it go. You'll thank me for it."

Will walked back into the room. "I got most of the lower part done. Didn't want to do too much. It's your puzzle."

Kenya got up. I walked with her back to the solarium. Sure enough, Will had made quick work of the bottom third of the puzzle. Tut's lower jaw began to emerge.

"You should help me with this," Kenya said. "You have some time after school this week?"

"Yeah," Will said.

"Perfect. Have your mom drop you off. I'm making chicken parm Thursday night. I'll take you back home after dinner. Sound good?"

"With spaghetti noodles?" he asked.

"Of course."

Will had to tear his gaze away from the puzzle, but he finally walked with me back to the front door. He went on ahead, sliding into the passenger seat.

"I mean it," Kenya said. "Quit listening to Darryl Cox. It's a fool's errand."

"Bigfoot," I said.

"What?"

"Bigfoot. Hojo said it's like he was trying to convince me Bigfoot is real."

Kenya laughed. "Good analogy."

She wasn't expecting it, but I gave Kenya a hug. She stiffened at first, then she hugged me back with her whole body.

"I miss you," I said.

"I miss you too," she said, pulling away. "And tell Caro I'll call her this week. That's a promise."

I nodded. "She'll like that. See you Thursday when I drop off Will. Thank you for that, too."

She waved at Will. He had his headphones on, but raised a hand toward her.

Then I left her there, waving from her front porch. She was right, probably. At best, Darryl Cox was just repeating half-truths and outright lies. And yet ... I couldn't shake the feeling that I was missing something.

9

"This is one of those that's gonna go in the brain hall of fame," Dr. David Pham said. I had him seated in the law library ahead of today's testimony. He was doing double duty across the hall in a wrongful death civil trial.

"Brain hall of fame?" I asked.

He tapped his temple. "As in one of those cases that'll stick with me."

"Ah." I peered over his shoulder. He had a copy of his autopsy report spread out on the table. Some of the more gruesome photos of Robbie Forte were tabbed.

"They're going to want to know whether that happened when Robbie was still alive," I said, wrinkling my nose.

David pursed his lips. "No doubt in my mind. Don't worry. I know how to walk them through it. It's gonna be fine."

"I know. I trust you. Nobody is better at this, right?"

"You seem ... not like yourself," he said.

David was in a position to know. We'd briefly dated a couple of years ago. A fact I still felt bad about. Not that we dated, but that he had at one point taken it hard that we weren't anymore. He was a good friend and a phenomenal doctor and witness.

"I'm fine," I said. "It's just been a little ... interesting at the office lately."

"Yeah. I've been hearing things. Fletcher's a bridge burner."

"He's something all right," I muttered, though I didn't want to go into detail. I trusted David, but the courthouse walls were thin.

David checked his watch. "It's almost ten. What's holding them up?"

I poked my head out into the hallway. Earl Grandy was on his cell phone, pacing in front of Judge Ivey's courtroom.

"I think Grandy's trying to find out."

"Ivey's not gonna be too happy."

"I'm not too happy. This is keeping the jury waiting, too. I'm still presenting my case in chief. They'll blame me for the delay no matter who really caused it."

Tim Meegan, Judge Ivey's bailiff, came into the library through the adjoining door.

"Judge is done waiting," he said.

"The sheriffs haven't brought Cox down," I said.

"Like I said, he's done waiting. Grandy's here. That's all Ivey cares about at this point. Are you ready to go?"

"I'm more than ready," Pham said. He gathered his notes and slid them back into his accordion file folder. I picked up my coffee from the table. We followed Tim through the inner door straight into Judge Ivey's courtroom.

I settled myself at the table. Pham took a seat directly behind me in the gallery. I had a few minutes to gather my own notes before Judge Ivey took the bench and the jury filed in.

Each of them noted the empty defense table as they took their seats. Meegan walked out into the hallway. Earl Grandy came storming in after him. He plastered some semblance of a smile on his face as he took his place at the table, making Cox's empty seat that much more conspicuous.

"All rise," Meegan said.

Judge Ivey emerged from his chambers and climbed up to the bench. He scowled at the half-empty defense table, covered his microphone, and whispered something to the bailiff. Whatever Meegan said to him seemed to satisfy Ivey. He nodded. Readjusted the microphone and addressed me.

"Ms. Brent, is the state ready to call its next witness?"

"We are, Your Honor; we call Dr. David Pham."

Ivey waved Pham forward. He strode through the wooden gate separating the gallery and confidently climbed into the witness box.

After the formality of his swearing-in, I got right into the meat of his testimony.

"Dr. Pham, will you explain your involvement in this case?"

"Absolutely. I'm the chief medical examiner for Maumee County. I performed the postmortem examination on the victim, Robert Forte. I did his autopsy."

"Thank you. I'd like to get into the specifics of your examination, but first, were you able to determine Mr. Forte's cause of death?"

"Yes. Though Mr. Forte's examination revealed a number of major injuries, the fatal one was a single gunshot wound through the central glabella, the forehead, that penetrated his frontal lobe and exited the occipital lobe through the back of the head. He was shot at extremely close range. The gun barrel was actually touching his skin."

Pham made a gesture with his thumb and forefinger, pressing the latter to his own forehead just above his left eye.

I reached behind me and picked up the water bottle I had on the table. I took a small sip, then turned back to the lectern.

"Dr. Pham ..." I started. I didn't get the chance to finish. Two sheriff's deputies entered the courtroom from the back. Jon Liddy and Reggie Swift from the jail. Something was wrong. Liddy caught my eye. His skin was flushed. Even from here, I could see the pulse in his neck beating at a furious tempo.

"Sorry, Your Honor," Liddy said.

Judge Ivey put a hand up. "Let's take a ten-minute recess. Dr. Pham, stay where you are. Bailiff, can you take the jury back to the jury room?"

Grandy hauled himself to his feet. Liddy and Swift walked up to the side of Judge Ivey's bench. Grandy and I followed.

We waited a moment while Tim Meegan got the jury safely out of the room and earshot. Then Deputy Liddy faced the full wrath of Judge Donald Ivey.

"What the hell is going on? We're in open court, Deputy!"

"I'm sorry, Your Honor. This is an ... um ... emerging situation. I've just come from the jail. Darryl Cox is ... uh ... he's dead, Your Honor."

"What?" I think the three of us said it in unison. Me, Earl Grandy, and Judge Ivey.

"What the hell is going on? Where's my client?" Grandy yelled, as if he hadn't just heard the same thing I did.

The courtroom door opened again. Sam rushed in.

"Sheriff, you better get in on this," Ivey said, motioning him forward.

Sam came to my side.

"Where's Darryl?" Grandy asked again.

"He's dead," Deputy Liddy repeated. "He was found in his cell an hour ago. He appears to have hung himself."

"Appears?" Grandy boomed.

David Pham's cell phone started to ring. It didn't take a psychic to know what that was about. He checked the caller ID.

"You better get over there," Sam said to him. "The EMTs are still there."

"He's dead?" I asked. "For sure?"

Grandy rushed out of the room right on Dr. Pham's heels.

"What the hell happened?" Ivey asked Sam.

"We're still trying to figure all that out," Sam answered.

"Who the hell was in charge of him?" Ivey bellowed.

"Sir," Sam said. "This is an emerging situation. Believe me, I have the same questions you do."

"Well, you better get to the bottom of this, Sheriff. This happened on your watch. It's unacceptable."

"I will. But I'll remind you, you don't have oversight on this. I don't take orders from you."

Sam was fuming. He was generally an even-tempered guy. But when he blew, it could be epic. It shocked me a little that he had his guns blazing at Judge Ivey. Though his point was valid.

"Well, obviously, we're adjourned. Good Christ. What a mess. I wanna be kept informed on this, Cruz."

Sam bit the inside of his mouth. He didn't answer to Judge Ivey. On this one, Ivey had no more clout than an ordinary citizen. I put a light hand on Sam's arm, hoping to get him to holster his anger for now. Though Sam had been right on all points, it didn't do any good yanking Ivey's chain either.

"If you'll excuse me," Sam said. "I'm needed elsewhere as I'm sure you can understand."

Ivey waved a dismissive hand. "I suppose you are too, Ms. Brent?"

"I'd like to try to figure out what's going on too, Your Honor."

"Fine. Go. Both of you. All of you. I'll clean this mess up with the jury."

"Thank you," I said, though I wasn't sure why. There was a mess all right, but it had nothing to do with the jury. This case ended the instant Darryl Cox's heart stopped beating.

I quickly grabbed my briefcase and hustled out of the courtroom with Sam. He held the door for me, then practically slammed it behind us.

He took me by the arm and led me into the now empty library.

"Sam, what happened?"

He stood with his fists at his sides. "I don't know. I meant what I said to Ivey. I've got to get back over there."

"Of course. But ... what did he hang himself with? How in the world was he left alone long enough to do it?"

"I don't know. Ritter's already there. He'll probably beat Pham."

"There were no cameras in his cell? He should have been in holding this morning. He was due in court."

"Somebody screwed up, obviously," he said.

"I'm sorry. I don't mean to ask stupid questions. It's just ..."

"I'm sorry," he said, his shoulders dropping. He came to me. "I don't mean to be taking this out on you."

"It's not your fault. Whatever happened."

"You and I both know that's not how this will play."

My mind reeled. Darryl Cox was dead. Hung in his cell in the middle of his murder trial.

"What is it?" Sam asked. He held me away from him, his arms straight out, and leaned down so he could look me in the eye.

"It's nothing," I said.

"It's not nothing. Your wheels are turning. What are you thinking?"

"Sam, you know about that note Cox passed me."

"Yes. That's maybe going to be part of this. Gus is going to want to question you."

"Of course. I was going to tell you, but this weekend has been kind of crazy. And Kenya was certain it was nothing."

"Kenya? Mara, sit. Tell me what's happened."

I slid my briefcase off my shoulder and sat down. Sam stayed on his feet. I looked up at him.

"Sam, there's something you need to know. It might not be relevant. It's probably not relevant. But I met with Cox and Earl Grandy on Saturday at the jail. I assumed he just wanted to try to cut a deal. Plead to second degree. But that wasn't it. He thought he had intel valuable enough to get his charges dropped. He was talking about the kidnapping of Violet Runyon."

Sam's head reared back.

"He what?"

"I was going to come talk to you about it. I know you were lead on the Runyon case."

"Whatever he told you was a lie. Violet Runyon's dad killed her."

"I know. That's what Kenya said too. It's just ... Cox had a name. One that never made it into the press as far as everyone said. He said he spent time in the same cell as a guy who knew how to find Ginger Ivan."

A change went through Sam's face. Haunted shadows crossed his eyes. His jaw turned to granite. Of course he remembered the name.

"Mara ..."

He didn't get to finish his sentence. His cell phone rang. He pulled it out and checked the lock screen.

"It's Gus," he said. "Mara, I have to take this. We're going to have to finish this conversation later. I know I don't have to tell you, but don't talk to anyone about this. Not your conversation with Cox. Not any of it. I can't keep a lid on this for much longer. I've got to arrange a press conference within the hour."

"I'll be there," I said.

"You can't take any questions."

"Of course not."

My cell phone started to ring. I pulled it out. My lock screen showed Skip Fletcher. From where Sam stood, he could read it as well. He answered his call from Gus and walked out of the room.

When I hit the green button on my phone, Skip immediately started shouting at me from the other end.

"I'm coming back to the office now," I said, then hung up on him. It seemed Sam and I had our own firing squads to face.

10

I never made it back to the office. I only made it as far as the front steps. Skip Fletcher stood in front of half a dozen reporters, giving his own impromptu press conference.

"You can be certain. My office will work very closely with the attorney general to get to the bottom of what happened. It doesn't matter that this individual was incarcerated. He deserved basic human rights and protections ..."

"Are you saying he didn't receive them?" one reporter shouted out. "We are hearing that Darryl Cox may have reached out to your office with concerns about his safety inside the jail. Can you comment on that?"

My pulse raced. What? Hojo had come out of the building. He sidestepped the mob. I went immediately to him.

"What the hell is he doing?" I whispered to him.

"He took a call, stormed out of the office in a rage."

"Did he do this? Did he call this?"

"Yeah. I think so. What happened? Did Cox get murdered?"

"We don't know that," I said. "We don't know anything. David Pham was in the witness box when the deputies came in to tell us Cox was found dead. The body is literally still warm and hasn't been moved from his cell as far as I know."

"I have no information on that at this time," Fletcher called out. He noticed me talking to Hojo. His eyes flashed fire. "But I can assure you, as I said. My office will fully cooperate with any investigation. I am just as interested as you all in finding out where Mr. Cox was failed."

"Sam said they think he hung himself," I said. "He knows better than to comment on something like this. Especially now."

"I made a promise to the voters when they elected me," Fletcher continued. "I will pursue justice wherever it leads. If law enforcement is culpable in this matter, those responsible will be prosecuted to the fullest extent of the law. No special treatment. Not under my watch. That's a promise."

"Mr. Fletcher, is it true that a member of your office is involved in a romantic relationship with Sheriff Cruz? If so, how can your office possibly be impartial going forward?"

The question caused a flurry of murmurs within the press corps. Fletcher glared at me, then turned back to them, plastering on a fake smile.

"As I said, we will pursue justice in this matter for Darryl Cox wherever it leads."

"He was all gung-ho to see Cox fry," Hojo said. "Now he's martyring the guy."

"I can't listen," I said. "Sam's gonna kill him. I'm gonna kill him."

Hojo followed close behind me as I made my way into the office. Caro stood at her desk, watching the press conference outside from her computer screen.

"He didn't just say that," she said. "Mara, that man is going to throw you under the bus on this. You and Sam both."

"He's just grandstanding," I said. "Trying to keep his name in the news. Skip Fletcher has bigger ambitions than this office."

"He doesn't appear to care who he steps on to get there," Caro said. "Mara, I'm so sorry. You don't deserve this."

"Don't worry about me," I said. "I can take care of myself. And I'm not afraid of Skip Fletcher."

My timing couldn't have been worse. Fletcher stormed back into the office the second I said it.

"My office," he barked at me. "Now!"

Gritting my teeth, I made a dismissive gesture to Caro, telling her not to worry about me. Then I steeled myself and walked into Fletcher's office. He held the door, then slammed it behind me.

"That really necessary?" I asked.

"Sit," he said.

"I'm gonna stop you right there. I don't appreciate you yelling at me like that in front of the whole office. You had no business answering questions from the media while Darryl Cox's body isn't even cold."

"Did you meet with him behind my back? You wanna tell me that reporter was off base on that?"

"I met with him," I said. "Rather, I met with him and his defense attorney. I was in the middle of a trial. Cox reached out. It wasn't exactly a secret."

"I should have been your first phone call. I should have been in that meeting."

"You really want to micromanage that way? It was nothing. Cox had nothing to offer. And you made your opinion on the matter pretty clear. No plea deals. As I recall, the last time you lost your temper with me, that was the crux of it. So, which of your edicts would you like for me to have followed?"

"You're on very thin ice with me, Mara. You made me look like a fool out there by withholding critical information."

I bit the inside of my cheek to keep from reminding him that he made himself look like a fool without my help.

"Nobody withheld any information from you, much less anything critical. Cox threw a Hail Mary. He tried peddling second-hand information about a case that had nothing to do with him. If I'd have told you about it, you'd have had me in here, yelling at me that I was wasting your time. It was unvetted information."

"About what?"

"About the twelve-year-old disappearance of Violet Runyon. I was doing my due diligence trying to verify it, as I just told you. If there was something to it, I would have let you know."

"You damn well better figure out how to put a lid on this," he fumed.

"On what?"

"I'm out there twisting in the wind, covering your ass."

"Excuse me?"

"You heard me. You're out there playing house with the new sheriff. You don't think that's relevant to me?"

"Playing house? We are not ..." I took a breath. I realized arguing with him was a waste of my energy and mental space. Fletcher wanted to blame me for this no matter what.

"You didn't have to be out there at all," I said. "You shouldn't be the one answering questions about Darryl Cox in the first place. That's Cruz's job."

"Do we have a problem?" Fletcher said. He took two steps toward me and got very close to invading my personal space. His face had gone pure purple. Spit flew out of his mouth.

"Do. We. Have. A. Problem?"

"I'm going to need you to back up," I said. He froze and pointed a finger at my chest.

"Fletcher, I mean it. Get out of my face."

He flinched. He took a step back. "Get out," he said. "We'll talk about this later. Go home. You're suspended without pay until further notice."

"You can't do that," I said.

"We'll see about that."

"My union will see about that, Skip."

"You're done for the day," he said, backpedaling slightly. I wished that were true. I got an incoming text as he said it. I looked down. It was Sam.

"Need you to head over to the office. Gus needs to talk to you re: Cox."

I quickly texted back. "Be right there."

I slipped my phone back into my pocket and turned my back on Skip Fletcher.

"Where are you going?" he said. "We're not done here."

"You just told me to go home," I said. "I wish I had that luxury. I'm headed over to Gus Ritter's office."

"I haven't authorized you to do that."

"Really? Thought you just promised the press our office would fully cooperate with any investigation. This is me doing that, Skip. I don't recommend you interfering with that. It would look bad." I said the last part with as much sarcasm as I could muster.

He was still hollering as I opened the door and shut it in his face.

Caro and Hojo scrambled down the hall. Clearly, they'd been eavesdropping. Hojo stopped. "You okay? I don't like how aggressive he's being."

"I'm not afraid of him, Hojo. But I appreciate your concern."

"Mara, what if he fires you?" Caro said, turning back.

"He has no grounds."

She looked ready to cry. "Listen," I said. "Please don't worry about me. I'm going down to talk to Gus Ritter. He's going to want to know about my communications with Cox and his lawyer. That's all."

"You want me to go with you?" Hojo asked.

"What, as my lawyer?"

"No. More as your friend."

"I'm okay. Really. Skip is all bluster. He's shooting himself in the foot on this. He thinks he's scoring points with all these platitudes about going after law enforcement. I trust Sam. I trust that he'll get to the bottom of what happened." Caro and Hojo exchanged doubtful looks. I knew they were both just worried about me. I assured them one more time, then headed across the street to Gus's office.

11

"That's all he said?" Gus asked me. I sat at his desk. He'd listened to my whole story about my meeting with Grandy and Cox the other day.

"That's all he said. He mentioned he had a source, a former cellmate who could provide information about what really happened to Violet Runyon and mentioned the name Ginger Ivan. He identified this former cellmate as Hoyt Marvin. I haven't spoken with him. I haven't even been able to verify if he exists yet. I've been focused on prosecuting him for Robbie Forte's murder."

"It's crap, Gus," Sam said. "You know it is. Ginger Ivan doesn't exist. She never did. I went through this twelve years ago. Runyon changed his story at least five different times. First, he said he had no idea what happened to Violet and gave me a false alibi. His cell phone data didn't line up with where he said he was. Then he said he gave her to an organization that protected abused kids. Dropped her off at a truck stop. Then it was a park. Then he said he just woke up in his apartment and she was gone. He said he was called by someone named Ginger Ivan. Wrote her name down for me. But there was no record of that either. Then he changed his story again and said he made her up. It was all lies. He failed two polys. He killed his own little girl. Whoever this cellmate is, the story is bogus. Or Cox made the whole thing up himself."

Gus closed his notebook. "I'm gonna try talking to Earl Grandy. Anyone know where he went after he left the courthouse?"

"I assumed he went over to the jail," I said. "Didn't he?"

"He didn't show up while I was there," Gus said.

I looked at Sam. He wore his stress on his face. In the last year, he'd buried one of his closest friends, the former Sheriff Bill Clancy. He'd been thrust into Clancy's role. A job he hadn't originally had ambitions for but was beginning to grow into. Now, I knew Darryl Cox's death could spiral into a full-blown scandal if the media and my boss had anything to say about it.

"There was something going on between the two of them," I said. "They seemed pretty agitated with each other. I'm not sure if Grandy didn't want Cox to talk to me at all, or whether it was about the subject matter? Or maybe I was just reading the whole thing wrong."

"You don't usually do that," Gus said. "Read people wrong. I trust your instincts. I'll see where I can get with him."

"Do you really think this was anything other than a suicide?" I asked.

Gus shook his head. "Cox wasn't on any kind of suicide watch. Nothing about his behavior leading up to this morning would indicate he wanted to off himself. Nothing raised any suspicions. The security footage doesn't show anything out of the ordinary."

"Fletcher's already out there calling for my job," Sam said.

"He didn't exactly say that. But yeah ... he's trying to score points off this."

"I don't get that at all," Gus said. "This has nothing to do with him. We're all supposed to be on the same team."

"Skip Fletcher isn't exactly reasonable. He practically ripped my head off before I came over here. I think he just suspended me."

"For what?" Sam said, pushing himself off the wall. "He threatened you?"

I put my hand up. "Stand down, Sam. I can handle Skip. I know that look. You won't do yourself any favors by storming over there right now."

"She's right," Gus said. It was an odd role reversal. Sam was usually the one trying to talk Gus out of reacting from his temper.

"I've got all I need for now," Gus said. He closed his notebook and excused himself, sensing Sam might want to talk to me in private.

"You okay?" I asked.

"I was about to say the same thing to you."

"I'm fine, it's just ..."

"Just what?"

"I can't shake the feeling that all of this is connected somehow. Like what Gus said. Cox wasn't suicidal as far as any of us knew. And he turns up dead right after he tries to push information about Violet Runyon's case? I mean ... you don't think ..."

"No," he said. "I don't think. Mara, I am telling you. Bart Runyon is the one responsible for what happened to that poor kid. I have no doubt. Trust me ... if there was even a sliver of a chance there was more to the story, I'd be the first one trying to track it down. But there isn't. This isn't a cold case or an unsolved case. Bart's guilty. I don't know what happened with Cox. It's my job to find that out. I absolutely will. But this isn't about Violet Runyon. And I will not let it turn into some side show. Violet's mother has been through enough. Through hell."

"I can only imagine," I said. "I'm sorry. I'm not trying to make this harder on you. But I'm afraid we came up in Fletcher's ill-advised press conference. If you haven't heard about it, you will soon. He got asked a question. Is it true you're involved with someone from his office? And whether that means our office can be impartial in this. It's nothing. A cheap shot. But you should know."

His expression darkened, but he waved me off. "That's crap. Clickbait. I'm not worried."

"Neither am I. But it has occurred to me that maybe you and I should ..."

"Stop," he said. "I'm not letting Skip Fletcher dictate my life. I'm certainly not letting the media do it."

He came to me and put a soft kiss on my forehead. I could feel the tension rumbling through him though.

"Do what Fletcher said. Go home. Have a drink. Have one for me too. I'll probably be here all night sorting all of this out."

"You let me know if I can do anything," I said. "I mean it."

"I know."

I touched his hand and left the office. Sam's phone was already ringing with his next urgent matter.

I had a few hours to myself before Will came home from school. Unexpected private time. The whole rest of the week. Though I wouldn't accept a suspension, maybe I could take some accumulated personal time. I was supposed to be in a murder trial that was never going to happen now.

I drove home. By the time I got there, I had seven missed calls. One was from Tamara Harvey. Lord. I'd completely forgotten about her. I don't know how she'd take the news of Darryl's death after all of this. I tried to call her back, but it went straight to voicemail.

Two of my other missed calls were from Kenya. She left me a message. I hit play.

"Mara. I've been doing a lot of thinking. Then I made a phone call I probably shouldn't have. I heard about Cox. We need to talk. There's someone I think you should meet. I'll text you the address."

I tried to call her back but got no answer. Someone she thought I should meet?

I went to the fridge and pulled out a bottle of wine, not caring that it was only two in the afternoon.

12

I double checked the address Kenya gave me. It took me to the new subdivision off of Glenn Road in the south part of the county. I pulled up to the house. It was one of those modern farmhouse styles made popular on the home improvement cable channels. White with black shutters and a gable over the porch. A giant wooden welcome sign leaned against the black six-paneled front door. Kenya's red Mercedes was parked in the driveway. I slipped in right behind her.

Kenya walked out the front door to greet me. I stepped out of the car and slid my sunglasses up, perching them on the top of my head.

"Thanks for coming," she said. "We're just having iced tea on the back porch. Follow me."

"Who's we?" I asked. I followed her inside. She led me down a short hallway with cathedral ceilings. It opened into a great room. The modern farmhouse theme carried through the kitchen. The walls were covered with shiplap. A cheery red sign above the kitchen table read "Eat."

A portrait above the white-washed fireplace mantel stopped me. Above it, in white cursive lettering, was another wooden sign that read "Always in our hearts." Below it, a portrait of a beautiful blonde girl with shining blue eyes. I recognized her immediately from the news article I'd read as Violet Runyon.

"Kenya," I said.

The sliding door opened. A woman stepped through. She was pretty. Thin, but not toned. She wore a pink tee shirt and matching pink shorts. She had her bleach-blonde hair pulled back into a ponytail. She looked just enough like the portrait on the mantel.

"Mara," she said. "I'd like you to meet Carla Gribaldi. Carla, this is Mara Brent."

Carla smiled. She caught me looking at her daughter's picture on the mantel. Gribaldi. She had remarried. But I knew I was now in the same room with Violet Runyon's mother.

"Nice to meet you," she said in a sweet, somewhat breathy voice. "Kenya's always spoken so highly of you. It's nice to finally get to meet you."

She came forward, extending her hand to shake mine. Her bones felt so thin, like I could crush her hand if I wasn't too careful. In fact, everything about this woman seemed as if she could be crushed if I wasn't too careful. From her soft-spoken tone to the quiet way she walked, her footsteps not making a sound on the wood-plank flooring as she led us through the slider and onto the back porch.

Her hands shook as she poured me a glass of lemonade. Kenya took a seat beside her and gestured for me to take the empty one on her left.

"Uh ... thank you for having me over," I said, but glared at Kenya. I hoped to convey the nonverbal sentiment that I didn't appreciate the blindside. Kenya waved me off.

"I suppose this is a bit of a shock," she said, accurately reading my mind. "I told Kenya to let you know what you'd be walking into."

"I didn't think she'd come if I told her," Kenya said.

"Be nice," Carla scolded her. "You and I have been in this little club together a long time. Mara's brand new."

"I'm sorry. Forgive me if this sounds rude. But why am I here?"

"I told Carla what's been happening," Kenya said. "About your conversation with Darryl Cox and the baloney he tried to peddle you. She wanted to meet you. I didn't think it was such a great idea. She insisted. I've learned over the years to listen to her."

"Mrs. Runyon," I started, then corrected myself. "Mrs. Gribaldi. I'm truly sorry for your loss and for any additional pain my involvement, peripheral though it may be, has caused you."

"Oh, don't worry about me. I'm tougher than I look. Believe me, I know how I look. Poor, tragic Carla. How does she carry on? How does she even get through the day? Tony and I moved out here a year ago. It was a big step for me. I didn't want to leave the house where Violet lived. Kept thinking, how will she find me if she ever comes home? So yes. I guess I have been a bit of a tragic figure. But I like it here. Tony was right. He's been right about a lot of things. I'm sorry you can't meet him today. He's a sales rep for Mannix Windows. He's on the road a lot."

"Maybe some other time."

"Well," Kenya said. "You've had me drag her out here. Might as well ask your questions, Carla."

Carla smiled. She shot Kenya a withering look that told me she had about as much patience for Kenya's bluntness as I did.

"I wanted to hear it straight from you," Carla said. "What did Darryl Cox share with you about my daughter?"

I set my lemonade down. "Honestly, I'm not sure what I'm at liberty to talk about. You understand Darryl Cox was found dead in his cell yesterday? There's an ongoing investigation into that."

"You're not a cop," Carla said. "And you're no longer prosecuting him for murder. Right? I mean, his death is a pretty final disposition on that matter, right?"

"Right. That's all true, but ..."

"Mara," she said. "You mind if I use your first name?"

"Of course not. Please."

"Okay, Mara. I've heard it all before, okay? Don't think you have to spare my feelings or protect my mental state. If you truly aren't free to talk about this, that's fine."

"She is," Kenya said. "You're not under any kind of gag order. Spill it, Mara. She wouldn't just take my word for any of it."

I sat back. This was a strange dynamic between Kenya and Carla Gribaldi. But I ultimately trusted Kenya.

"Darryl Cox thought he had information that could lead to the whereabouts of a woman by the name of Ginger Ivan. He gave me the name of his former cellmate who claimed he knew her and had information about Violet. So far, I've been unable to vet that information."

"And Sheriff Cruz has probably told you it's crap, isn't that right?" Carla asked.

"It seemed pretty self-serving in light of the charges Darryl Cox was facing," I admitted.

"And yet, he knew a name he shouldn't have known," she said. "Ginger Ivan."

"That's right," I said. "That was the one point that caused us concern."

Carla got a faraway look in her eye. A full minute went by before she spoke again. I looked at Kenya, worried that maybe she was about to become very upset. Kenya nodded and scrunched her lips, giving me a sort of "just wait" expression.

"It wasn't always terrible between Bart and me," Carla started. "When I met him, he made me laugh. Deep, whole-body laughs, you know. Just quick-witted and self-effacing. Like he didn't have an ounce of ego. It was refreshing. I had a lot of trouble getting pregnant. Four miscarriages. We gave up on the idea of ever having kids. I took fertility drugs. It got demoralizing after a while. But Bart just hung in there, you know? Told me it didn't matter. That he was happy just being married to me. Finally, I got pregnant again. With twins. Then at eleven weeks, I lost one of them. Thought for sure I'd lose the whole pregnancy. But I didn't. We had our Violet."

"Carla," Kenya said. "You don't have to do this. Not again."

Carla waved her off. "She was so perfect. Like a little doll. Barely ever cried. Even when I brought her home from the hospital.

Right away she slept for four-hour stretches at night. I thought it would make us okay, you know? See, there was already some trouble in our marriage before Violet came. Bart was controlling. It was little things at first. He didn't like a certain dress on me. He didn't care for the friends I brought home from work. I should have seen it. I thought having his child would fix it. It was really like being boiled alive little by little. By the time things got really bad, I found myself wondering how I'd let it go so long."

"You've beaten yourself up enough," Kenya said. "You found a good man in Tony."

"Bart became convinced I was sleeping with this guy I worked with at the bank. Our assistant manager, Fred Damon. Poor Fred. He was married. He had a family of his own. There was absolutely nothing going on between us. He drove me home from work once because my car wouldn't start. Well, Bart became incensed. You know, after Violet ... the police questioned Fred. For six hours. Bart accused him of hurting Violet. He was one of the many false stories Bart told the cops."

"He also told them Carla had been abusing Violet," Kenya said.

"They sent CSB out to investigate," Carla said. "It was awful. They had a social worker out here three different times. Bart said I sold pictures of Violet to some pedophile. It got so ugly after I filed for divorce. Violet was only two years old then. She didn't even have a memory of her parents living together in the same house. She only knew being shuttled between us."

"That must have been awful for you."

"You know something about that, don't you?" Carla asked me.

"I know about custody battles, yes."

"Your child's father is in jail too, right?"

"He is," I said. Carla reached across the table and took my hand.

"I'm not saying what your husband did is the same. But ... you know. You know what it's like to think you know someone. That you love someone and they're one thing. Then you realize they're something else. And you had a child with them. And your child loves them anyway because how can they not? Right?"

I swallowed past a lump in my throat. This was a conversation to have over something stronger than lemonade. And yet, here we were.

"Violet loved him," she whispered. "That's the thing. She loved her daddy. All those CSB investigations came to nothing. I just wanted peace. For Violet. You understand. If I thought Bart would do something. If I thought he would harm so much as a hair on her head ..."

"Of course," I said. "You can't blame yourself."

"Sure, I can. I was her mother. It was my job to protect her. Just like it's your job to protect your son. But she begged me to let her go with him that weekend. She was just five years old and had already learned ... or that it was her job ... to regulate *our* emotions. I let her go with him. And then he never brought her back. See, the thing about Bart ... the side of him nobody but me ever got to see. He was sadistic. He took pleasure in causing me pain. After Violet was born, he was angry with me for gaining weight. I bought new clothes in a bigger size and one day when I was at work, he chopped them all to pieces. He told me if I couldn't fit into my size fours, I didn't deserve new clothes."

"I'm so sorry," I said.

"It's his way, you see? The stories he told the cops. Just these tantalizing little clues. Things to give me hope. Then he'd change it. Pull the rug out just when I thought we had a viable lead. He was never trying to save himself. That's not what his lies were about. He kept changing his story because it was a new way to torture me."

"She's done everything," Kenya said. "Tell Mara how much money you spent on that private investigator who turned out to be just another huckster."

"Twenty-five grand," she said. "My life savings at the time."

"She's gone," Carla said. "I know that now. It's taken me a lot of years and a lot of therapy to accept that hurting Violet was Bart's ultimate way of hurting me. But I have."

Kenya got up from the table. She cleared the glasses and lemonade pitcher. When she shot me a look, I rose and helped her carry everything back to the kitchen, leaving Carla Gribaldi sitting alone under the pink umbrella on her porch.

"What's this about?" I said to Kenya.

"I needed you to meet her. I need you to hear her story in her own words."

"Why?"

"Because I know you. I know it's going to nag at you. A loose thread you aren't going to be able to help yourself from pulling. Darryl Cox was just another liar and opportunist in a long line of them who have touched and soiled Carla's life."

"I get it, okay? Sam's on the same page you are."

Kenya smiled as she loaded Carla's dishwasher. "Only you're still thinking about it. I know you. You're turning this thing over in your head. Wondering whether Darryl Cox's sudden suicide was about something else. Maybe it was. But it wasn't about this. It can't be."

As she spoke, the eyes of Violet's mantel portrait followed us. It was unsettling, to say the least.

I went back to the sliding door and opened it. "Mrs. Gribaldi. Thank you again for talking with me. The last thing I want to do is dredge up old wounds for you. I'll leave you alone now."

Carla kept that far-off expression on her face. Then she smiled at me.

I closed the door. "I'm leaving," I said. I couldn't help it. I was a little mad at Kenya for bringing me out here.

"She wanted to meet you," Kenya said, following me out the front door and down the driveway. I backed out. Kenya pulled out and drove away. I was about to put my car in drive and go. A dashboard alert came on. My phone wasn't syncing to the Bluetooth. I realized I didn't have it with me. I left it on Carla Gribaldi's patio table.

"Dammit," I muttered. I put the car in park and dashed back up the driveway. Carla must have found it. She opened the front door and met me, holding my phone in her hand.

"Sorry," I said. "I really am sorry for bothering you. Kenya shouldn't have ..."

"She worries about me," Carla said. "She's always had this kind of protective, alpha dog way about her when it comes to me. I may bend a lot, Mara. But I assure you, nothing can break me anymore."

She handed me my phone. I thanked her.

"Do you understand what I'm telling you?" she said.

"I ... think so?"

She smiled. "Nothing can break me again, Mara. The worst that can ever happen to a person has already happened to me. My daughter is gone. She's never coming back. Kenya is worried about me, but she's worried about the wrong things."

"What do you mean?"

"Darryl Cox," she said. "He really shouldn't have known that name he gave you, should he?"

I clamped my mouth shut and then said, "No. No, he shouldn't have."

"Find out," she said. "Sam Cruz. Kenya. They don't want me to have to go through anymore."

"I think they're right though."

She cocked her head to the side, studying me. "Do you? Do you really? Because I think you think there might be something worth pursuing. Do you think Darryl Cox's death was more than just a suicide?"

"I don't ..." Lord. The last thing I wanted to do was give this woman false hope. Again, she seemed to know what I was thinking.

"I told you," she whispered in that haunted voice of hers. "The worst thing that can happen to me? It's already happened. Since Bart, I've gotten much better at judging people. Ironic, really. All I'm asking ... Mara ... follow your gut. Okay? Wherever it leads. You can't hurt me."

She did something strange then. She reached out and touched my cheek. It brought a smile to her face.

"Find out," she said. "That's all I'm asking. No matter what Kenya or Sam say. Find out. For me."

Then she quietly closed the door.

13

"I'm sorry," Hojo said. "It's complete crap. It's not going to hold up, but for now, Fletcher's within his rights suspending you with pay. But barely."

I sank into one of my kitchen chairs, holding the phone against my ear. "For how long?" I asked.

"A couple of weeks tops. Maybe a month," Hojo said. "Look, just think of it as a paid vacation, Mara. Lord knows you deserve one of those anyway."

"Has he put out a statement yet?" I asked. "I don't care about the suspension. I mean, I care. But I care more about what lies he's telling the media about what happened."

"It's going to come out right in the wash," Hojo said. "Ritter's lead on Darryl Cox's death investigation. Nothing's going to come of it. We all know you didn't do anything wrong."

"Only Fletcher's taking the position that I withheld information from him."

My back door opened. Will walked in carrying an armload of grocery bags. Right behind him, my mother came in. She looked impeccable as always. With her latest facelift, at seventy-three, her skin was smoother than mine was. She wore a cream-colored silk pants suit, her black hair in a flattering bob that didn't move. She carried a single green grocery bag and sat on the counter in front of me. I peered into it. Natalie Montleroy had picked up three bottles of her favorite brand of Pinot Grigio.

I held up a finger, letting her know I just needed another minute on the phone. I scooted out of the kitchen chair and walked into my study off the dining room hoping for a little privacy. Only the double French doors weren't exactly soundproof.

"Mara, nobody believes anything he says. He's just trying to throw his weight around."

"He's trying to make me look bad," I said. "Erode any clout I had after the Clancy murder trial. And he's got it out for Sam, too."

"We aren't going to stand for it, okay? Caro and I have been talking. We'll walk out in protest. Then Fletcher won't have any litigators in the office with you and I both gone. And he certainly can't run things without Caro."

"Don't," I said. "Don't do that. Especially Caro. She can't afford to lose her job over this nonsense."

"She doesn't care. She's miserable, Mara."

"Just ... don't do anything rash. I didn't do anything wrong."

"It's gonna be okay," he said. "It has to be."

"I appreciate your support. Caro's too. I'll give her a call tomorrow. Tell her not to worry about me, okay?"

Hojo assured me he'd convey my message. Then we clicked off. My mother hovered near the dining room entrance. She stood with one hand on her hip, the other holding her bottle of wine.

"Where's your opener?" she asked me, though I knew she was well aware of how to find everything in my kitchen.

"It's not even noon," I said, coming out to join her. I picked up my electric wine bottle opener from under the cabinet and handed it to her.

She took two glasses from the same cabinet.

"I'm good, thanks," I said. She ignored me and proceeded to pour each of us a glass.

She took a seat at the kitchen table and motioned for me to join her. Will busied himself with emptying the grocery bags and putting everything away.

"Looks like I got here just in time," my mother said, lowering her voice even though Will was close enough to hear her whisper.

"In time for what?" I played dumb.

"Mara, don't stonewall me. You're in trouble. It's obvious."

"Why?" Will said. He held a box of Ritz crackers in his hand.

"I'm not in trouble," I assured both of them. "It's just office politics. Completely boring."

"It's not just office politics," my mother persisted. "It was in the papers this morning. This new prosecutor is trying to scapegoat you for what happened to your client, isn't he?"

"I don't have clients," I said. "I work for the county, remember?"

"For how long?" she asked. "Mara, read the writing on the wall. You've been on shaky ground here since Jason went to prison." She whispered prison as if a.) Will couldn't hear her and b.) He didn't already know exactly where his father was.

"Are they going to fire you because of Dad?" Will asked. He didn't seem concerned, not yet. But I knew where this would lead if he let his head start spinning. My almost thirteen-year-old son knew far too much about my finances. Down to the penny of every bill I paid each month. It was something his dad had started teaching him, not realizing how Will might start to obsess about it.

"They are not going to fire me," I said. I glared at my mother. She was oblivious to my concerns about Will.

"We can't afford the mortgage payment without your salary," Will said, immediately spinning to the place I didn't want him to.

"I'm not getting fired!" I repeated. "You can both just relax."

"I liked it better when Kenya was your boss," Will said.

"Me too, buddy."

"This is ridiculous," my mother said. "I cannot believe we are even discussing how you're going to save a job you shouldn't even be working at in the first place. You make what, sixty thousand dollars a year? That's barely enough to pay for the groceries."

"She makes seventy-eight thousand a year," Will said. "She'll get a one point five percent cost-of-living raise next January."

"How do you know that?" I said.

"You're a public employee, Mom," he said. "Anyone can look it up on the internet."

"You don't need to be looking up my salary on the internet."

"The mortgage costs one thousand eight hundred and twenty-three dollars a month with the taxes and insurance rolled in," he added. "With Mom's savings ..."

"Stop!" I said.

"It's poverty," my mother said. "Mara, when are you going to stop being so stubborn? I've been telling you for years, there's a job waiting for you in New Hampshire. Sawyer-Carlson. Avery Sawyer owes me so many favors, Mara. You'd make ten times what you're making here in this dead-end town."

"That means her net pay would be over fifty thousand a month," Will said.

"I don't want to work for Sawyer-Carlson," I said. "I like the job I have. And we've been over this a thousand times. Waynetown is home. It's Will's home. We like it here."

Will finished putting the groceries away. He seemed nonplussed by my mother's machinations and the dollar signs attached to them. He left the kitchen and headed up to his bedroom.

"You can't keep doing that," I said to my mother. "He may not seem like it now, but Will is going to ruminate over all of this. He's gonna wake me up at like three in the morning with my entire debt-to-income ratio figured out."

"Well, someone's got to. I never had a head for numbers. That was always your father's department. And my father before him."

She was full of crap. My mother was as financially shrewd as they came.

"I'm fine," I said. "We're fine. If I ever need help, you'll be the first to know."

"Liar," she said. "You'd sooner beg in the streets than ask for help from me."

"I don't want to talk about this anymore. How was your outing with Will? Did he like the movie?"

"I sure didn't. Too loud. Too fast. It gave me a headache."

"Well, thanks for taking him. He was looking forward to it all week."

My mother rose. She dusted off her suit. I would have paid money to see her sitting in the middle of the Waynetown multiplex watching the latest Marvel movie with her grandson. Her country club friends would be shocked. Avery Sawyer would be shocked. But for all her bluster and vanity, my mother had turned out to be a fantastic grandmother.

"I've got to head out," she said. "I'm meeting an old friend for dinner in Ann Arbor."

"Oh? Is this a male friend?"

She blushed. "None of your business."

"Are you coming back tonight?"

"No, darling. I'm catching a flight this evening."

"Do you need a ride to the airport?"

She shook her head. "All taken care of. My friend will drop me off."

"Interesting," I said, teasing her. "So this is a ride-to-the-airport type of friend? Sounds serious."

She playfully batted me away.

"Have fun," I said. I meant it. I hoped her mysterious Ann Arbor, airport friend was worthy of her.

"You want to say goodbye to Will?" I asked.

"We already did that," she said. "You don't have to drag him back down here again."

I gave her a hug. "Thanks for coming. I'll see you next month?"

She grabbed her Prada bag off the counter. Reaching into it, she pulled out a pair of designer sunglasses and slid them up her nose. Then my mother flitted out the front door, leaving a whiff of perfume in her wake.

My untouched glass of Pinot Grigio sat on the table.

"The hell with it," I said, taking the first sip. It wasn't like I had to get to the office anytime soon.

Hojo was right. I couldn't remember the last time I'd taken any personal time off, mandated or otherwise. Maybe the thing to do was plan something fun for Will and me. He'd been asking for months for me to take him to COSI in Columbus. There was an exhibit on bioluminescence he'd been bugging me to see.

I was just about to head up to ask him about it when my phone buzzed. A text came through. I picked it up. It was from Kevin Barnum. He was Hoyt Marvin's parole officer. I'd left a message for him the other day after Darryl Cox gave me his cellmate's name.

"Hey, Mara," it read. "Sorry it took me so long to get back to you. I've got an address for Hoyt Marvin if you still need it. As far as I know, it's current. He's overdue for an appointment with me as it happens. Here you go."

A moment later, Barnum shared a map link. It was an address in Stonehouse in the southern part of the county. It was showing as a twenty-minute drive from my house.

I stared at my phone screen for a few more seconds. Carla Gribaldi's words haunted me.

Find out. For me.

It was nothing more than a conversation, I told myself. A dead end, no doubt. My fingers hovered over the phone screen. Then I sent Kevin Barnum a thumbs up emoji and finished my wine.

14

"I'm not getting out."

Kenya sat with her arms folded, her lips drawn into a thin line. She clutched her purse to her chest and stared out the windshield.

"Fine," I said. "You don't have to." I rechecked the address in my GPS. This was it. We were here. The most current address of Hoyt Marvin, Darryl Cox's cellmate, as reported to his parole officer.

It was actually a pretty decent part of town. Wildwood Avenue was just behind the newly constructed Wildwood Villa assisted living facility. A large number of the 1940s-era brick bungalows were purchased by the developers to make way for the assisted living complex. The holdouts were well-maintained, brightly painted ranch houses on the north side of the street.

We parked in front of 8218 Wildwood Drive. A silver Honda Civic was parked in the driveway. The license plate matched Marvin's. He allegedly worked nights at the spark plug factory off I-280. It was two o'clock in the afternoon. Marvin was home.

"This is a terrible idea," Kenya said. "I never should have let you drag me out here."

I turned to her and unlatched my seatbelt. "Who are you kidding? You came because you're just as curious as I am. Besides, you're the one who introduced me to Carla Gribaldi. She asked me ... no ... she begged me to track Marvin down. So that's on you."

Kenya shook her head. "How was I supposed to know she'd do that? That woman has been through enough. I wanted you to understand that."

"I do. But your plan backfired. Besides, you lost your election and I got suspended. What else do either of us have to do today?"

"A root canal," she said. "A colonoscopy. I can think of a dozen other things."

"You're too young for that," I said. "And you could have told me no." I got out of the car. Kenya kept her arms folded, indignant.

"Fine," I said. "So, wait here."

I slammed the door shut and went up the walk. The front door to 8218 Wildwood opened. I had a picture of Hoyt Marvin on my phone. His last mugshot. That was him all right, standing in the doorway, looking me up and down.

I knew he was my age. He had thinning hair and skin covered in freckles. A cigarette dangled from his lips. He put it out against the door frame as I approached.

"Hello," I said. "Thanks for meeting with me. I'm Mara Brent. Kevin Barnum told you about me?"

"He said talking to you wasn't a condition of my parole or anything."

"That's true," I said. "But I've come all this way. I just have a few questions to ask you. You're not in any kind of trouble or anything."

"I know that," he said. Marvin opened the door. "You can come on in. I'll give you ten minutes, then I've got somewhere I need to be." He looked over my shoulder, spotting Kenya still in the car.

"She coming in?"

I looked back. Kenya caught my eye, then immediately turned her focus elsewhere.

"Doesn't look like it," I said. Marvin ushered me in.

He took me through the living room and into the kitchen. There, he invited me to sit at a small round table with red leather kitchen chairs. I did. There was an ashtray on the table with six cigarette butts in it. It was his house. I wouldn't have minded, but Hoyt Marvin didn't light another one the entire time we spoke.

"I'll get straight to it," I said. "If you've looked me up online, you know I was prosecuting a murder case against Darryl Cox."

"You think I had something to do with that?"

"Not at all. But Darryl mentioned your name to me. He was trying to broker the information he claims you gave him regarding the disappearance of Violet Runyon. I'm here to ask you if there's any truth to what Darryl Cox said."

Marvin regarded me. I don't know what I expected. He could have told me to pound sand. He could have told me Cox was mistaken. He did neither.

"He told you what I said about Ginger Ivan," Marvin said. "Darryl Cox was a worthless, weak weasel. And he had a big mouth."

"He said you knew where to find this Ginger Ivan. Is that true?"

I heard movement off the kitchen. There was a short set of stairs leading down to the basement. A young woman, early twenties at best, came halfway up the stairs. As soon as she saw me, she backed down and disappeared.

"That's just Leesha," he said.

"Your girlfriend?"

"Yeah."

She was pretty. Thin. Blonde. With Hoyt Marvin's criminal proclivities, I had an instant suspicion that Leesha may be more than his girlfriend. Odds were, she was working for him. Turning tricks, most likely. From the moment our eyes met, I recognized a certain submissive fear I'd seen all too often in women like her.

"What did Cox tell you?" Marvin asked.

"He said you claimed you could tell us how to find Ginger Ivan. That she was a real person and could lead us to what really happened to Violet Runyon twelve years ago. He implied that her father, Bart Runyon, had been telling the cops the truth. That he didn't kill her. Do you know anything about that? Have you spent time with Bart Runyon?"

Marvin slammed a fist on the table.

"He said all that? Cox told you I talked to Bart Runyon?"

"No. I'm asking you if you did. See, the thing is, none of this would mean much to me. Cox was desperate. He was facing the death penalty. He thought he could use this information to bargain for his life and his freedom. To be honest, I wouldn't have held much stock in anything he had to say. Only ... that name. Ginger Ivan. Cox swore he heard it from you. So, I'm trying to figure out where *you* heard it."

"What good does that do me?"

"I'm sorry?"

"Me telling you where I heard it. What good does that do me? I'm straight now. I did my time. I don't have any charges on me."

I folded my hands in front of me. "You know about Violet Runyon?"

Marvin's hand started to shake. "This is your house, Mr. Marvin. If you need to smoke ... smoke."

He pulled a fresh cigarette out of a pack in his front pocket. He put it to his lips but didn't light it. He just let it dangle there.

"She was five years old when she disappeared," I said. "Violet. Her body was never found. I met with her mother the other day. To be honest, that's the only reason I'm even here. She asked me to come back and talk to you. She's been chasing down leads ... ghosts ... for twelve years. Even though we all know Violet's dead. But if you know something. Even the sliver of something that might lead to what happened to that girl. To her remains. Her mother deserves closure."

He lit the cigarette. "You're sitting there telling me I should tell you what I know because it's the right thing to do?"

I heard a screen door open in the basement. Footsteps. I couldn't see much down the darkened stairs, but Leesha was back.

"Go outside!" Marvin barked at her. She ran. The screen door slammed shut behind her.

"Yes," I said. "Telling me what you know is the right thing to do."

Hoyt Marvin laughed. "I told you. Darryl Cox was a weasel. What I told him wasn't for him to sell. You got me? That little piece of information was for me. In case I ever needed it."

"But you're straight now," I said. "Right? So why would you need to hold on to what you know?"

"You never know what can happen. And yeah ... I looked you up online. I'd say you're the last person in a position to do me any good. They're about to fire you."

"Nobody's firing me."

"Sure. Only it's Tuesday in the middle of the day. You're not a cop. You're not a private investigator. And you're not even a lawyer right now. You're just some nosy bitch who showed up on my doorstep thinking I owe you a favor."

"I never said that."

"I think we're done talking. I've got nothing to say to you."

"Darryl Cox is dead. You know that, right? I mean ... if you took the time to look me up. The last conversation I had with Darryl before he died was about you, Hoyt. You're right. I'm not a cop. Or an investigator. But there may come a time really soon when you might need a favor from someone like me. The cops think you were lying to Cox. I think you were telling the truth. I think someone like you shouldn't know the name Ginger Ivan. But you do. From what I've been able to figure out, you've never even met Bart Runyon. Never been in the same jail. Never traveled in circles that would put you in each other's path. So, my gut is telling me he's not the source of your information. You know things you shouldn't know, Hoyt. Why?"

"You need to leave," he said. His fingers shook as he tapped his ashes on the tray.

"I hope you are clean now, Hoyt. I really do. For your sake and for that girl you just threw out of here."

"Look, I never should have said anything. Not to you. Not to Darryl. You don't get it. These people? The ones protecting Ginger Ivan, they aren't playing. You don't believe me? Ask Darryl!"

With that, he pushed his chair back and got up. "I'm done talking. Nothing left to say."

There was a knock on the screen door. "Mara?" Kenya was on the porch, peering in.

"Coming," I said.

Hoyt Marvin didn't say goodbye. He turned his back on me and disappeared downstairs. I went out the front door.

"How'd that go?" Kenya asked.

"Terribly. But he's scared of something. And he didn't deny telling Cox he knew about Ginger Ivan. In fact, during our entire conversation, he was behaving like Ginger Ivan was a real person. One who's being protected by someone he doesn't want to cross."

"It's crap," Kenya said. "Marvin's a nobody. He's just trying to make himself sound important."

"What he sounded," I said as we walked back to my car, "was scared."

That's when I saw her. A young woman was walking briskly away from us, almost a block down the street.

"Kenya, hang on," I said.

"Mara!" she called after me, but I was already on the run.

"Leesha?" I called out. "Wait. Just wait."

Leesha made it to the next stop sign before I caught up with her. When I did, she turned toward me. She had tears in her eyes.

"Leesha," I said. "It's okay. You know who I am?"

"I have to go," she said. "I'll be late."

"Are you working for Hoyt? He's still turning you out, isn't he?"

Kenya caught up with us. She stood beside me.

"It's none of your business," Leesha said. "Hoyt's good to me. It's not what you think. He got me away from them."

"From whom? Leesha, who is Hoyt mixed up with?"

"I can't talk to you. I can't even be seen talking to you."

Kenya and I exchanged a look. She reached into her purse and pulled out a business card we both kept. I took it from her.

"Listen to me," I said. "If you need help, you can call this number."

I handed Leesha the card. There was no logo on it. No business name. Just a number written in raised red letters.

"A shelter?" Leesha said. She tried to give the card back to me.

"A safe house," I said. "Any time. Day or night. I can help you get away, Leesha." I wrote my own cell phone number on it.

A bus pulled up.

The girl was terrified. Her eyes had a haunted look. Pale and blue. There was something so familiar about her. There were faded track marks on her arms. At most, I guessed she was twenty years old.

As the bus doors opened, Leesha crumpled the business card in her palm and climbed onto the bus. She didn't look back as the doors closed and she took her seat.

"That went well," Kenya said. "Got any other lost causes you'd like to try to chase down or save today?"

We turned and started back toward my car. As we climbed inside it, Hoyt Marvin stood on his front porch, glaring at me.

15

"She said her name is Leesha. What do you know about her?"

Kevin Barnum, Hoyt Marvin's parole officer, met me in the courthouse coffee shop between hearings. We were tucked in the far corner, but I suffered no delusions that we couldn't be overheard.

"He's never mentioned her," Kevin said. I'd worked on hundreds of cases with Kevin over the years. I found him to be a straightforward, decent guy. But like the rest of us, he was trying to juggle a caseload more suited to at least three people.

"She's young," I said. "She may be a minor. And she had that look about her. You know? He's turning her out. I'd bet my next paycheck on it."

Kevin smiled as he tapped his sweetener packet into his coffee. "Don't know that I'd take that bet right now, Mara. You sure you're gonna survive Skip Fletcher's wrath?"

Prior to my coffee with Barnum, I'd just come from a meeting with my union rep. The news wasn't what I wanted to hear. My suspension with pay would stand until a formal hearing could be held in a couple of weeks. I was effectively benched.

"I'm not going down without a fight," I said. "He can't prove I've done something fireable."

"We all know that. And I'm sorry. I probably shouldn't have made a dumb joke."

"It's okay. This whole thing is ridiculous. Might as well laugh about it."

Kevin blew over his coffee before taking a sip. "Well, back to Hoyt Marvin. If this girl's a minor, that alone is a violation of his parole. Is that your sense?"

"Like I said, she looked very young. She could be eighteen, but just barely."

"Maybe I need to pay Hoyt a visit unannounced."

"I think I might have spooked her," I said. "Kenya and I tried to talk to her outside after I was done with Hoyt. She wasn't interested in anything we had to say. Couldn't get away from us fast enough."

Kevin raised a brow. "You and Kenya went out there? How'd you get her out of the house?"

"Dragged her kicking and screaming."

"You two have the makings of a buddy cop comedy," Kevin laughed.

"I'm worried about this girl." I couldn't say the rest of what I was thinking. It was preposterous. Far-fetched. Only I couldn't shake the idea that Leesha had a lot of the same facial features and coloring as that portrait I'd seen of Violet Runyon. I hadn't mentioned it to Kenya yet. But I'd gone so far as to call my contact at NCMEC, the National Center for Missing and Exploited Children. There'd been no age progression photographs done for Violet Runyon in years. On what currently amounted to little more than a whim, I asked for one. They were backlogged and it might take a few weeks, but I could see no harm in the request.

"I'll look into it," Kevin said. "I promise."

"What do you think about this story he told? This woman Bart Runyon claims he gave his daughter to?"

Kevin shrugged. "Hoyt has never mentioned it to me. As far as I know, he's never tried to bargain himself out of trouble with it."

"But now I know Darryl Cox wasn't lying. Hoyt admitted he told him he knew how to find Ginger Ivan. He just wouldn't tell me."

"Because he's probably lying about the whole thing. Sure, he told Cox, but maybe it was a lie to begin with. Maybe he looked it up in the paper or something. Made up a story."

"But Ginger Ivan's name was never in the paper. That's the part that keeps me picking at this. What do you know about Hoyt's background? His affiliations?"

"Hoyt's a two-bit criminal. Talks a big game. Always operated on the periphery from what I've seen. None of the big players, whether it's drugs or prostitution, want much to do with him. I think he tried to get somewhere with a couple of the local biker gangs. A hanger-on. They'd never have a guy like that. He got thrown out of one of their bars a couple of years ago, beaten to a bloody pulp. He's the kind of guy the real bad guys like to make an example of, not confide in."

"If he's hurting this girl Leesha, like I think he is, he's bad enough."

"I'm sorry you wasted your time with him."

"Well, I do appreciate your insight. If you wouldn't mind following up with him. This girl, my instinct is that she's not safe around him. If he's as powerless as you're saying, she's the one who stands to get hurt. Eventually, he's going to get her mixed up with someone Hoyt can't protect her from. I told you. She's young. Fresh-looking. Pretty. If she's being trafficked, she'll get eaten alive."

"Yeah," Kevin said. "I get it. Just give me a couple of days. If you and Kenya spooked her, she might be lying low. They both might. But I'll find out what I can."

"Thank you," I said.

Kevin's attention went elsewhere. He frowned and stared at something over my shoulder.

"You know him?" Kevin asked.

I turned and followed his gaze. A man, someone I'd seen before but couldn't immediately place, scowled at me through the glass. He had papers in his hand. Ellen Cline, one of the court clerks, walked up to him. She put a hand on his shoulder and pointed him toward the elevators.

He left with his paperwork. Ellen gave me a pained look, then walked into the coffee shop toward me.

"Thanks again, Kevin," I said.

"Something wrong?" he asked.

"Probably," I answered. I tried to put a twenty on the table, but Kevin waved it off.

"This one's on me. You catch the next one. And there will be a next one, Mara. You've got a lot of people rooting for you, including me."

I thanked him and met Ellen. She gestured to me to follow her out into the hallway.

"Who was that guy?" I asked. "I've seen him before."

"Yeah," she said. "He's not exactly your biggest fan. I wouldn't even say anything, only he's already filed so it's public record now. That's Anthony Gribaldi."

Anthony Gribaldi. Tony Gribaldi. Violet's mother, Carla's second husband.

"Why'd he look at me like that?"

"He's filed for a temporary restraining order," Ellen answered.

My mind raced through the multitude of possibilities. Before I could ask, Ellen put a hand on my shoulder.

"Against you, Mara," she said. "He wants a TRO against you."

"He what?"

"Listen, don't get upset ..."

"Where's he going?" I asked. "You pointed him to the elevators."

"He's heading up to Judge Saul's courtroom. She's on call for TROs today. She's not going to sign it without a hearing. But ..."

The elevator doors opened. Tony Gribaldi stepped out, but he wasn't alone. Skip Fletcher had a hand on his back. The two of them looked pretty friendly with one another.

"I don't believe it," I said. Kevin Barnum came out of the coffee shop.

Gribaldi saw me. His face turned red. He charged toward me, raised a finger, and jabbed it near my face.

"Hey!" Kevin shouted. I put my hand up, not wanting Kevin to make things any worse than they already were.

"I know what you're doing," Tony shouted. The half dozen or so coffee shop patrons stopped eating and stared in our direction. Great. Every lawyer and public servant in the county would know about this within the hour.

"Mr. Gribaldi," Skip said. "I assure you, this will be handled. I understand your concerns."

"She's a menace," Gribaldi said. "You stay away from my family. You hear me? You have no idea what you've done. Carla doesn't need to have all of this stirred up again. If I have to sue you for emotional distress, I'll do it. I've already talked to a lawyer. And your office too!" He turned to Skip.

"What is this about?" I asked. "I'm sorry. I'm at a complete loss here."

"It took Carla years ... years to learn to live with her grief. To rebuild a life with me. And it's taken you one afternoon and your reckless behavior to spiral her again."

"What's wrong with Carla?" I asked. "What's happened?"

"You," Tony said, spittle flying from his mouth. "You happened. Well, I'm not going to let it. Any of you."

He jerked away from Skip's grasp and stormed down the hallway.

"Why are you here?" Skip said through gritted teeth. "What are you even doing in the building right now, Mara? You're on suspension."

"She was having coffee with me," Kevin said. Ellen Cline looked physically ill. She mouthed "I'm sorry" to me, then headed back to her office down the hall.

"You couldn't leave well enough alone, could you?" Skip said.

"Whatever this is?" I said. "Let's not do it here."

We'd already drawn a crowd.

For once, Skip didn't argue with me. He turned and punched the up button on the elevator. I wanted nothing less than to get into it with him, but it looked like I had no choice. I said a quick goodbye and a thank you to Kevin Barnum, then climbed into the elevator with Skip.

He didn't say a word on the two-floor ride up to our offices. He just fumed beside me. Caro and Hojo looked stunned when the two of us stepped off together.

I expected Skip to charge back to his office down the hall. He didn't. Instead, he whirled on me right there in the middle of the bullpen in front of Caro's desk.

"You might as well all hear this together," Skip yelled. "Mara, you've made a complete mess of this. You heard Tony Gribaldi. He's threatening to sue this office because of your actions."

"For what?" I said. Hojo said it at the same time.

"For harassment. For prosecutorial misconduct. Negligence. Abuse of process. You name it. He claims you went over there and gave his wife false hope that their daughter might still be alive."

"I did no such thing," I said. "You know exactly what I've done. I didn't start any of this. Darryl Cox did."

"Right. And you withheld that information from me, didn't you? That's why you're on suspension. Well, now I've got a full-blown PR nightmare on my hands because of your carelessness. Did you or did you not go over to Carla Gribaldi's house and put ideas ... fantasies into her head?"

"I was invited there," I said. "And it was on my own time, Skip."

"Invited there by whom? Not Carla. Certainly not Tony."

"Carla is still friends with Kenya Spaulding. I ..."

"Christ," Skip shouted. "You went behind my back. You have been determined to undermine my authority at every turn. You don't work for Kenya Spaulding. You work for me."

"No," I said. "I work for the county."

"We'll see about that! Tony Gribaldi demanded I fire you today. If it were completely up to me, I would have done it."

"Then you'd have to fire me too," Hojo said.

"Don't," I said to him.

Skip's eyes darted between Hojo and me. His color turned purple.

"I think you need to get out of here," Skip said to me. "Go home. Stay there. And stay away from the Gribaldis or anything to do with the Violet Runyon case. You've done enough damage as it is."

Skip turned on his heel, marched down the hallway to his office, then slammed the door behind him.

"What in the fresh hell was all that about?" Hojo asked.

I shook my head. "I'm not even sure I know. I need to talk to Kenya. I need to talk to Carla Gribaldi."

"Are you sure that's a good idea?" Caro said. "Look, I'm not saying I agree with anything Skip just said. He's out of line. Tony Gribaldi is out of line. But maybe ... I don't know ... maybe you should just let this one go. Huh?"

I felt terrible. Not about anything I'd done regarding Darryl Cox or Carla Gribaldi. But Caro hated conflict. The stress of the situation was taking its toll on her. I hated putting her in this position.

"It's going to be all right," I assured her. I hoped it would.

Before I could say anything else, my phone started to blow up. There were texts from Kenya. Carla. Sam. And finally, David Reese, a reporter for Channel 8 News. The story of Tony Gribaldi's restraining order had already hit the internet.

16

"You should comment," David Reese said. He had his phone in my face, ready to record anything I said.

"For the third time," I said. "I'm not going to."

"Mara, you're on suspension for allegations of misconduct surrounding a murder defendant who just happened to turn up dead within a day of you talking to him. Exactly why was he talking to you in the middle of his trial?"

"You should ask his lawyer," I said. I kept walking. Reese caught me just outside the Sheriff's Department. Gus Ritter had called me and asked me to come down.

"Earl Grandy," Reese said. "I've been trying. He isn't taking any calls. As far as I know, he hasn't been back to his law office since news of his client's death broke. You don't think that alone is strange?"

"I don't keep Earl Grandy's schedule."

"Does Darryl Cox's death have something to do with the disappearance of Violet Runyon? Because that's the rumor I'm hearing. This is all going public, Mara. Tony Gribaldi's petition for a restraining order against you is a matter of public interest. You could do yourself a favor and get your side of it out before people start jumping to conclusions."

"I have no comment," I said just as I reached the front doors of the police station. "These are matters that will either be resolved by the courts or are part of an ongoing investigation. Both of which I will fully cooperate in."

I realized I'd just made a rather lengthy comment after swearing I wouldn't. A stupid mistake. I knew better. Waving Reese off, I opened the door and walked into the station. Luckily, Reese wasn't bold enough to walk in after me. He wasn't exactly the most popular guy with law enforcement.

I waved to the desk sergeant as I headed upstairs to Gus's office. I found him standing in the hallway with Sam. Neither of them looked happy to see me.

Terrific, I thought. I had the distinct feeling my day was about to go from bad to worse.

"Come on in," Gus said.

"I should warn you," I said. "David Reese from Channel 8 tailed me coming in. Asking all sorts of questions about the Darryl Cox investigation."

"He's a nuisance," Gus said. He took a seat behind his desk and gestured for me to take one in front of it. Sam loomed over the both of us, standing against the wall. He had yet to say a word.

"Thanks for coming down," Gus said. "I'm sorry about Reese. I should have seen that one coming. It might not be the worst idea if you steered clear of downtown for a little while."

"Just tell me what's going on. I can handle myself."

Gus shot Sam a look. I turned. Sam seemed to have adopted a permanent scowl.

"Will you cut that out?" I said. "You're hovering like a gargoyle. I get that you're mad at me, but get in line. Between Skip Fletcher, Tony Gribaldi, and who knows who else, I'm just tired of it."

Sam's face fell. He had the decency to at least look like he felt bad. He came over and took the chair beside me.

"Listen," Gus chimed in, before Sam could say anything. "I wanted you to hear this directly from me. I probably should have just headed over to your place this evening, but there's going to be a press conference we can't put off."

"Darryl Cox," I said.

"Yeah," Gus answered. "His death will officially be ruled a suicide. As of now, there's no reason to suspect foul play. There's no reason to conclude anybody other than Darryl himself is responsible for what happened to him. There was no indication he was suicidal ahead of this. He hung himself with a piece of cloth he made from part of his shirt and the bed sheets. Dr. Pham just forwarded his final findings. The injuries to his neck were consistent with self-strangulation. There was nothing about the body that indicated signs of a struggle. He just flat out offed himself. We don't know why. We probably never will."

I let out a breath. Gus's words reverberated in my mind. No signs of a struggle. No suicidal ideations. He just offed himself.

"What are you thinking?" Sam asked.

"I don't know. I'm just ... I'm trying to process all of this. I can't fathom it. I've never been able to. The man I saw two days before wasn't acting like someone about to take his life. He was making plans. Trying to work a deal."

"You think our guys did something wrong?" Gus asked with a bit of an edge to his tone.

"No, no. I'm not saying that. I'm sorry. It's just ... thank you. I appreciate you letting me know firsthand. Have you talked to Earl Grandy? His lawyer?"

"Not yet," Gus said.

"Reese," I said. "He mentioned he's been trying to reach him for an interview. He said Grandy's been missing from his office since the day we found out Cox was dead. Do you think that's strange?"

"Do you?" Gus asked.

"I don't know the man well."

"Maybe he's just trying to avoid talking to the media," Sam offered. "If I had the luxury of disappearing for a few weeks during all of this, I'd surely take it."

"I'm sorry," I said. "I know this has been a tremendous strain on you. Even with Pham's autopsy findings, you're still going to take more heat on this. Reese is like a bloodhound. He thinks he's on a scent."

"Like you said, I can handle myself too," Sam said. There was a certain amount of tension in his voice. Gus picked up on it. Gus and Sam had been partners for a lot of years before Sam was promoted. They had their own shorthand communication. Gus rose from behind his desk.

"I'm gonna go get more coffee. You two want anything?"

Gus had a perfectly good coffee maker right in his office. As if he could track my thoughts, he said. "Stuff in the break room tastes better to me today."

"Thanks," I said. "None for me."

Sam waved Gus off. He excused himself and left the two of us alone.

"Were you gonna tell me about Tony Gribaldi?" Sam asked, getting right to the heart of what was bothering him.

"Tell you what? Tony's got nothing to do with me."

"You sure about that? Because what I heard is, he's going around saying you've been harassing Carla, dredging things up about Violet's disappearance."

I met his eyes. "And what do you think?"

"What do you mean?"

"I mean, you know me. You really think I've been harassing that poor girl's mother? Does that sound like something I'd do?"

He tightened his lips. "No. But ever since you had that meeting with Darryl Cox ... a meeting I wish you'd clued me in on beforehand ... you're the one who's been acting like a bloodhound on the scent of something. You're not that different from David Reese on this one."

"This thing fell into my lap. Cox reached out to me. And since when have I needed to clear meetings with criminal defendants with you? His lawyer was present the whole time."

"It was my case," Sam said. "Violet Runyon was my case. You weren't here when that all went down. For two years, I ate, slept, and breathed what happened to that little girl."

"Sam," I said. "When Darryl Cox asked to meet with me, I had no idea he had anything to say about Violet Runyon."

"You knew after. I wish you'd come to me straight away."

"Like you said. I wasn't here when that girl disappeared. I wasn't part of Bart Runyon's prosecution. When Cox threw out Ginger Ivan's name, it didn't even mean anything to me. You can't be mad at me for not including you in that meeting. It had nothing to do with you. It still doesn't."

"Except Cox decided to off himself within a few hours after it. In my custody."

"We can't keep having this same argument. Cox's death isn't your fault. But it isn't my fault either. As far as Tony Gribaldi? I don't know what to tell you about that. His behavior has caught me completely by surprise."

"You went out there," Sam said. "To talk to Carla. You didn't tell me about that either."

"Kenya invited me. It wasn't my idea. And she brought me out there to make sure I wasn't going to be one more person to give Carla false hope about finding her daughter."

"But you did anyway, didn't you?"

"Not on purpose. Carla was the one who approached me and told me to keep digging. She begged me, Sam."

"She does that," he said. "Kenya should have known better than to take you there."

"Tony's reaction seems overblown for what actually happened," I said. "It feels ... I don't know ... suspicious. Don't you think?"

Sam's scowl came back.

"It's like the Streisand effect," I said.

"The what?"

"He wants everyone to just leave Violet's case alone for his wife's sake. Only filing for that TRO against me is having the opposite effect. It makes this whole thing public. Now I've got reporters like David Reese asking questions about it all over again. Tony's put it back in the news, not me."

"He's just trying to protect his wife, no matter how misguided it is."

"I don't know. Maybe. He was in the picture when Violet disappeared, wasn't he? They were dating."

"Don't," Sam said, sighing. "Just don't. I know how your wheels turn. Tony was cleared. He wasn't even in town when Violet went missing. Do you think I didn't know how to do my job back then? Christ, Mara. Part of me wants to put you in a room with Bart Runyon. So you can see for yourself. He did this. Nobody else. He's a liar. A psychopath. A killer. He changed his story time after time. We've got him tracked by his cell phone. Violet's blood was in his damn car. He killed that girl to punish her poor mother. Do me a favor, don't help him."

"I'm not trying to," I said.

"Really?"

"Sam, stop. Right now, it feels like the whole town is against me. I'm not sure I can handle it if you are, too."

Sam's expression changed. He reached for me.

"I'm sorry. I'm not against you. God. I'm sorry if it's coming out that way. It's just this case. Mara, I still have nightmares about it, okay? It still haunts me. But I got it right. I know I got it right. And Bart Runyon sits rotting in his prison cell with all the power. Still."

"What do you mean?"

"Because he knows. He knows exactly what happened to Violet because he's the one who did it. And every few years, he finds a way to twist the knife in Carla just a little bit more. It's things like this. Whatever he told Hoyt Marvin or Darryl Cox if that's how they got their information. Giving her false hope. Dragging someone new into this. When he could end it. He could just confess. Or he could tell me where he dumped Violet's body so Carla could give her a proper resting place. So she could finally say goodbye. I would just really appreciate it if you'd stop poking this bear. I don't want you to be another one of Bart Runyon's victims. You could lose your job over it."

"I won't lose my job."

He stared at me. I still had the sense he was holding something back.

"What?" I asked.

"Were you going to tell me you met with Kevin Barnum? Hoyt Marvin's parole officer?"

"It wasn't a secret," I said. "We had coffee in the courthouse. Half the county judiciary saw us."

"You went to see Marvin, didn't you? And you asked NCMEC to do another age progression. One of their agents called me about an hour ago. Said it would be ready in a couple of weeks. Mara, what are you doing?"

Maybe I should have told him about that girl with Hoyt Marvin, Leesha. No. I know I should have. And yet, something stopped me. I could tell myself it was his anger. Or the fact I didn't want to torture him. As much as he said he was pleading for Carla Gribaldi, I knew that wasn't all of it. This case had been torture for him too all these years. It wasn't just Carla who needed closure.

I said nothing. A moment went by. Sam reached across Gus's desk and grabbed a pen and a sticky note. He wrote a name and a number down on it.

"Here," he said. "You want to talk to somebody who knows as much about this case as anyone? Who understands what kind of master manipulator Bart Runyon was? You talk to Christine Schuler. I'll tell her to expect a call."

Christine Schuler. The name was familiar. Where had I seen it before?

"She's the social worker who investigated Runyon's bogus abuse allegations for Children's Services. She interviewed everyone involved in Violet's life. Including Tony Gribaldi. You talk to her. You hear what she has to say about Bart Runyon. Then you come back and tell me if you have any doubts about what I did."

"Sam ..."

He got up. He walked toward the door. He turned back at the last as if he were going to say something else. In the end, Sam quietly let himself out.

I stared at the hot-pink sticky note. I probably should have just left it right there on Gus's desk and walked out myself.

For the rest of my life, I'll wonder what would have happened if I had.

17

"I appreciate you taking the time to talk with me."

Christine Schuler didn't work for Maumee County anymore. She'd left her position with Children's Services nine years ago. Three years after Violet went missing. She now worked for New Hope, a private agency that helped troubled teens find alternative housing and other services. Her offices were in the newly renovated Glasgow Building right on the river. It had previously been a factory that shut down over forty years ago. A local historical society had lobbied to keep it from being torn down. The two smokestacks towered over the river and could be seen for miles. A local landmark that made it on almost every Waynetown postcard.

I caught Christine as she was coming back from lunch. She juggled a banker's box on her hip and hit the lock on her key fob.

"Do you need some help?" I asked.

Smiling, Christine pushed her mirrored sunglasses to the top of her head. She was pretty. Pale green eyes. A slight dusting of freckles across her cheeks and the bridge of her nose. She had a talent for applying make-up that I lacked. Bottle-blonde hair that she wore loose around her face.

"Just some plants from home," she said. "Trying to personalize my space now that we're fully moved in."

She extended a hand to mine. "Good to meet you, Mara."

"You too. Is it Christine? Chris?"

"Christine. Always hated nicknames. Christie in particular. Come on. I'll take you in through the side door."

We made our way up the walk. Christine flashed her ID badge across the metal panel at the door and it opened automatically. I followed her in.

"Wow," I said as we entered the building. They'd left the brick walls bare. High arched ceilings with silver wrapped pipes. My heels clacked along the slate floors.

Christine had a first-floor office. It was still in disarray with unpacked boxes stacked along one wall. She had her desk and computer set up. Her single guest chair wobbled a little when I took a seat.

"Sorry about that," she said. "This is temporary furniture. Mine won't come in for about a week. Though they said the same thing last week. We make do."

"It's no problem. Really."

Christine set her box of plants on the floor and took her own seat. "So, Sam clued me in a bit on what you're dealing with. You've met Carla already?"

"I have."

"I love her. That woman is a rock. Even with everything that's happened, she just keeps on going. I should call her. We used to have lunch every other month or so. We got to be friends after everything that happened. I don't know. In a weird way, I think it helped her feel connected to Violet. She wanted people in her life who knew her too."

"It makes sense," I said. "You met with Violet a lot?"

"We had a rapport," she said. Christine got up and walked over to one of her stacks of boxes. She ran her fingers along the side.

"Figures," she said. "It's second from the bottom. You mind giving me a hand?"

I went to Christine's side. She lifted the top box and set it aside. I moved to the next one, stacking it on top of the one she'd set down. She moved one more, then picked up the box near the bottom. She heaved it on top of her desk and took off the lid. It contained standing files. She thumbed through them then pulled one out. It was stuffed at least an inch thick with paper.

"This isn't the official file," she said. "That's still in the bowels of the CSB office somewhere. Plus, Sam has a digital copy. These are mostly my handwritten notes. Pictures I took. My work product. If you tell me what you're looking for, I'll see if I can help."

"Thank you. The thing is, I don't entirely know what I'm looking for. If it were up to Sam, I wouldn't even be pursuing this."

"She got to you," Christine said, smiling.

"Carla?"

"No. Violet. She does that."

I cocked my head to the side.

"Sorry," Christine said. "That sounded a little crazy, maybe. She's gone. We all know that. But Violet had a bit of an aura about her. She was a special child. Believe me, I've worked with hundreds. Maybe a thousand. They're all special in their own ways. But Violet? She was just ... this is going to sound strange, but it's like she was already an angel when she was born. She was smart. But it was more than that. They say things like old soul. Maybe that's the best way to describe it. She was only five years old when I met her, but she was just so aware of what was going on around her. She felt things. Deeply."

"I can see why Carla wanted to keep in touch with you. I'm sure it's been a comfort knowing how you felt about Violet."

"An empath," Christine said. "I think that's the word. Violet would kind of tune in on the emotions of the people around her. I see that a lot with kids. Especially the ones who come from volatile homes. They're keyed into the emotional states of the adults around them. They become very good at managing them. Which is kind of terrible."

"It's a lot to put on a little kid," I said. "Can I ask ... how did you initially become involved in Violet's case?"

"It was Bart," she said. "He filed a report with the state. He accused Violet's mother of abusing her. He had concerns about the company she was keeping. Carla and Bart were separated by the time I got involved. And had been for, gosh, I want to say two years. Their divorce was pending the custody arrangement."

"I understand the court mediator recommended Carla have primary custody. So, they weren't suspicious of any issues in Carla's home?"

"No," Christine said. "But I can't say I always put a lot of faith in the court-appointed mediators. Don't get me wrong. They're good people who care about kids. There just aren't enough of them to go around and they don't always get to do an in-depth investigation like I could."

"Sure. So, you had a chance to get to know all the people in Violet's life?"

"Most of them, yes. I interviewed both Bart and Carla, of course. Violet was in pre-school at the time. She was old enough for kindergarten, but Carla decided to hold her back a year. With the divorce, there was a lot of turmoil in her life. She felt it was better for Violet. I thought it was a good decision."

"I did have a chance to read your final report. Like you said, it was part of Sam's investigation file. You ended up not finding any evidence of abuse or neglect within the home?"

"That's right. Bart's allegations were completely unfounded. Violet was a healthy, well-cared-for little girl. She was sensitive. I'm not saying she hadn't suffered some psychological trauma incident due to the parental dynamic. But it wasn't anything that would have required intervention. There's no such thing as a perfect parent. Now ... I had some concerns about the psychological abuse Carla was experiencing. He was controlling. Manipulative. Jealous. He was angry with Carla for moving on with her life. That's what his report was about. Unfortunately, I've seen that kind of thing often. One parent claiming abuse as a way to get back at the other parent."

"But you're certain that's all this was?"

"At the time, yes."

"But you ended up being wrong," I said. "I'm sorry to put it so bluntly."

Christine blinked rapidly. She placed a flat hand on the top of Violet's file. "Yes. To be honest, it shocked me when Carla reached out to me after Bart's trial. I've carried a lot of guilt over what happened. It's why I'm no longer working for the county. I needed a change. This case haunts me."

"You're not the first person who's said so," I said. "Sam and Kenya feel the same."

"Kenya." Christine smiled. "How is she? I've been meaning to send her a text. I felt terrible about the last election. She was robbed."

"She's doing," I said. "She's enjoying her forced vacation, let's say."

"How's the new guy?"

"The new guy is indirectly why I'm here."

Christine nodded. "Yeah. I kinda figured. Saw that piece on the news about your suspension. It's ridiculous. He's trying to force you to resign?"

"Probably." I didn't want to say too much. Christine was friendly with both Sam and Kenya, but I'd never met her before. I had no idea who she might gossip to after I left here. On the other hand, my even being here, if it got back to Skip, wouldn't do me any favors.

"So," she said. "You wanna ask or should I just tell you?"

"I'm sorry?"

"Tony Gribaldi. You know he was in the picture when Violet went missing. Now I understand he's causing trouble for you. A restraining order?"

"Something like that. Yes."

"I never liked him. I interviewed him too. Extensively. I know Sam did after Violet went missing. He was the new man in both Carla and Violet's life. He was a natural target of suspicion. Then, there's what Bart told me."

She thumbed through her notes.

"Which was?"

"The thing you need to understand. Bart Runyon was a lot of things. Quick-tempered. Insecure. That man has one of the worst inferiority complexes I've ever seen. He overcompensates with all these big stories he tells. It started with his report to me. The day I issued my findings, he marched into my office, ranting and raving. Saying how if anything happened to his little girl, it would be on my head. Two sheriff's deputies threw him out of the building. But ... there was one point on which I agreed with him. Tony Gribaldi isn't much better. I've always felt like Carla traded one jerk for another. Like she's drawn to men who boss her around."

"Tony's story is that he's just trying to protect Carla from having all of this stuff dredged up again," I said.

"Let me guess; that's not how Carla feels. I'm betting she told you to go for it if you thought you could turn over some rock the rest of us might have missed."

It was my turn to smile. "I guess you do know her."

"She's unafraid. That's what I know. And she's a hell of a lot stronger mentally than Tony gives her credit for."

"So, there was nothing. Not in any of your interviews. Your home visits. Nothing that raised your suspicions that Violet was in danger from Tony?"

"No. Tony barely had any interaction with her at that point. Carla was pretty adamant about that. He didn't sleep over. She didn't have him there during the holidays she had Violet. She wanted to take her time. Make sure Tony was a keeper before she introduced him into their lives. Carla was getting family counseling. She was doing all the right things. I spoke to Violet's preschool teacher. Her babysitters. Parents of some of her little friends. That child was being raised in a loving home. And as much as we now know about Bart, on the surface, at least when I was involved, he was a good dad. Until the very end. The final two weeks."

"In what way?"

"Whatever issues he and Carla were having, Bart didn't seem to be airing it in front of Violet. He had her every other weekend and alternating holidays. They were working out summer visitation. Bart all of a sudden changed his mind and tried to get full custody. He was denied. When the court issued that ruling, that's when things went south. That's when he filed his report with me. And when I issued my findings, that's when it took a turn. That's when he started getting verbally abusive to Carla in front of Violet."

"You were called back in?"

"Yes. Carla filed a petition with the court. Violet started coming back from her visits with Bart with behavior problems. She started wetting the bed. She'd show up wearing the same clothes

Carla dropped her off in three days before. She became withdrawn. A new case was opened. I never got a chance to complete my investigation. Carla's petition to change custody was supposed to be heard the Wednesday after Violet went missing. Until then, as you know, Carla was still under a court order to turn Violet over to Bart for his normal weekends. I was working with her. If she couldn't get his visitation revoked outright, she was going for supervised visitation. I would have likely been involved in that. Like I said, I had a rapport with Violet. She felt comfortable with me. I would have been the one supervising."

"But you said Bart got verbally abusive with you, too? You said you had deputies remove him from your office? How would that have worked?"

"These were all things that would have been ironed out. We just never got the chance. I'll tell you. The moment I got the call that Bart hadn't returned Violet after their scheduled weekend, I knew. I just knew. He did something to her."

"You didn't suspect Tony at all?"

"Not initially. I, of course, told Sam my impressions. But as I recall, Tony was cleared pretty quickly. He was out of town, I think?"

"He was. Yes."

"But you still have a bad vibe about him?"

"I'm trying not to let his actions cloud my judgment. Trying not to take it personally."

Christine nodded. "Good luck with that. But I need to know. Why now? I can see it on your face. You're not completely convinced Sam had it right, are you?"

"I'm sure he did. It's just ... I don't know what he told you ..."

"He told me you had a murder defendant sell you some story about knowing the woman who Bart said kidnapped Violet."

"That's about the size of it, yes."

"He was lying. Your informant."

"But he knew the name Bart gave the police. That was never in the papers, but my informant knew it."

Christine raised a brow. "He gave you a name?"

"Yes."

"Well ... shit."

"It bothers you too?"

"Well if you're sure nobody else was supposed to know that name," she said.

"That's the thing."

Christine shrugged. "Who knows? From what I've heard, Bart's gone silent over the years. Stopped talking to the cops altogether. But maybe he told someone who told someone. I think your boy just threw a dart at the wall."

"Maybe. Probably. Only ... he's dead now. My, uh, boy."

"Right. Sam told me that too. I'm sorry about that. And I'm sorry you got drawn into all of this."

She reached back into her file and pulled out a square yellow envelope. She fingered it, then handed it to me. It was a DVD sleeve. There was a disk inside labeled with a sharpie.

"Violet Runyon. Third Interview."

"You should watch it," she said. "Of all the things that still haunt me. That does. I'm surprised you haven't already seen it. There's a copy in Sam's file."

I saw my own reflection in the disk. My eyes were too wide. My skin too pale. She'd caught me off guard with this.

"I skimmed Sam's file. That's all."

"Well, that right there is Violet Runyon speaking from the grave. Take it. It's just a copy. I told you, Sam's got one. The original is in the county file. I'm fine if I never watch it again."

"No," I said. "I can't take this. I've wasted enough of everyone's time as it is."

"You'll watch it," she said. "I know the look. I told you. Violet's got a hold of you now. Maybe you owe it to her to watch it. So you can put this thing to bed for yourself once and for all. Believe me, I've been trying to do that for twelve years."

I thanked her. I slipped the disk into my purse.

"Christine?" The receptionist poked her head in. "I'm sorry. But your two o'clock is here."

"I won't take up any more of your time," I said. I could feel the circular outline of the disk in my purse as I walked out. Christine's words echoed in my mind.

She said it was Violet Runyon, speaking from the grave. As I left the Glasgow Building, I could almost feel her ghost following me.

18

I had one DVD player in the house. It was hooked up to the television in Jason's old study. I'd converted it into Will's playroom, though the only toys he had were Lego sets and puzzles. I set up shelving on every wall for all of his creations. He started by getting thousand-piece kits when he was two years old. He built replicas of the Millennium Falcon and every Star Wars spacecraft made. By the time he was seven, he'd begun to design his own models just from his head. I sidestepped his largest work, a complete replica of the *Titanic* before she sank.

I pulled the chair away from his worktable and set it in front of the flat screen I had mounted to the wall in the one space not used up by shelving. I pulled out Christine's DVD and popped it in the drive.

My hands shook. My palms felt clammy. I realized I didn't really want to see what was on this disk, but the overwhelming urge to bear witness kept me staring at that screen.

The video began to play. The camera was placed in the corner of a small room. It looked like a classroom set up with toy stations. Stuffed animals. Barbie dolls. A train set. There were colorful beanbag chairs in the center of the room.

Christine walked in. Her body obscured the camera for a moment as she adjusted it. Though this footage was over twelve years old, she looked much the same as when I met her yesterday. The same flattering haircut. Light layers framing her face. She dressed casually in a pair of jeans and a pink sweater. She had a lanyard around her neck with her county ID badge.

A moment later, the door in the far corner opened and a little girl walked in.

I held my breath.

Violet Runyon appeared on the screen. She was timid at first, surveying the room. Then she saw Christine and her pretty round face lit up.

"Good morning!" Christine said. She took a seat in a chair to the right of the camera. You could only see part of her left shoulder for the remainder of the video. I checked the counter. It was only twenty-two minutes long.

Violet wore a red jumper over a white shirt with puffy sleeves. She had her hair pulled back in front and tied with a red bow. It was a strange thing to see her face lit up and animated. I'd only seen the photographs law enforcement had plastered over the internet before plus Carla's mantel portrait. In those, she looked ethereal, angelic. She was that. But here she was also a five-year-old little girl making goofy faces and fidgeting in her seat when Christine asked her to sit in one of the beanbags.

Christine encouraged Violet to select a toy to play with if she wanted. She was timid at first. Then she picked up a floppy-eared stuffed dog. She delighted in making barking noises and taking it for a "walk" by dragging it along the floor with a leash tied to its neck. She found a plastic water dish and felt dog bone. She proceeded to feed the dog.

For several minutes, Violet seemed to be in her own world, playing with the dog. Christine began to ask her questions, blending them in as she asked Violet what kinds of animals she liked. Whether she wanted a dog of her own.

Violet was compliant. Pleasant. She spoke with a slight lateral lisp I found endearing. She had certain mannerisms I found familiar. The way she never really made eye contact with Christine. She flapped her right hand when she got excited as her imagination took over with the dog. These were all things my own son did. Things that would result in phone calls from teachers and school psychologists, just making sure I was aware.

Finally, Christine managed to get Violet to focus.

"How's school going?" Christine asked. "Do you like your new teacher? Mrs. Simms?"

Violet nodded. "She smells good. Like the shampoo my mom uses sometimes. She says it's 'spensive."

"Mrs. Simms says it's expensive? Or your mom?"

"Mom says it. She won't use it on my hair."

"Gotcha."

"What do you use when you go over to your dad's?"

Violet had been making the stuffed dog "eat" from the bowl in front of her by bobbing his head up and down. She pulled its head back and let out a fake burp, then laughed at her own joke.

"He uses this stinky stuff in a green bottle. I don't like it."

"Did you tell him that?"

Violet nodded.

"What did he say?"

"Said I'm not gonna let you be spoiled." She spoke in a fake, stern voice, mimicking her father.

Something happened then. Violet frowned. She stopped making the dog eat. "You hear that?" she said to it. "That food is 'spensive. This collar is 'spensive. You better 'preciate it all."

She stayed in the deeper fake voice she'd used to mimic her father. All the joy left the child's face and she threw the dog to the ground. Violet climbed back into the beanbag and crossed her arms in front of herself.

"What kinds of things do you do when you visit your dad, Violet?" Christine asked.

Violet wouldn't answer.

"What kinds of things do you do when you visit your mom?"

"She takes me to school. She makes me dinner and my lunches. We play."

"What's your favorite thing to play lately?"

"Barbies."

"We have some here, I think. Do you want to play?"

Violet shook her head.

"Why not?"

"I might break them."

"Why would you break them?"

"Because I'm not 'sponsible."

"Responsible?"

Violet nodded.

"Did someone tell you that?"

She nodded again.

"Who?" Christine asked.

Tears burst from Violet's eyes. She kept her arms tightly wrapped around herself and twisted at the waist so Christine couldn't see her face.

"Violet, it's okay. You can play with anything you like here. I'm not worried about you breaking anything."

"I'm not 'sponsible," she whispered. "Things cost too much money."

Christine let her sit for a moment. Then Christine got up, went to a yellow bin in the corner and brought back a Barbie and a Ken doll. She put them on the table in front of Violet. Violet stayed rigid and twisted away from Christine.

"Honey," Christine said. "It's okay. I promise. Here you don't have to worry. I don't care what gets broken."

Violet turned. She had her eyes tightly shut. She was murmuring something, but I couldn't make it out. I turned up the volume.

"Violet, what is it? Honey, you know you can tell me anything. We've talked about this. Is something wrong?"

"I hate it," Violet said.

"What do you hate?"

"He yells all the time."

"Who, honey?"

"He says I'm not 'sponsible. But I am. The lamp just broke. It fell over. I tripped. I didn't try to break it."

"Where was this lamp?"

Violet shook her head back and forth.

"Violet?"

"It was ugly. It had stupid fish on it. But I didn't break it on purpose. I tripped."

Violet stuck her leg out. She pulled up her pant leg and showed Christine a Band-Aid she had on her shin.

"Did you cut yourself?"

Violet nodded. "The pieces got all over. I tried to pick them up. I was 'sponsible. I was going to clean it all up. But he yelled and yelled and yelled and yelled."

"Who yelled at you?"

"Dad," she said. "It's so much yelling. It makes my head hurt. I don't want to go there. You said I could tell you. I don't want to go there. He's mean. Mean, mean, mean, mean, mean!"

Violet started to cry in earnest. She drew her legs up in the beanbag chair and rocked back and forth.

Christine tried to gently question her. She was careful not to put any words in Violet's mouth. It took a few minutes, but Violet finally calmed down.

"Can I stay with Mama?" she finally said, hiccuping through the last gasp of her tears. "Can you tell them? I just wanna stay with Mama. I told him. He took the lamp. He threw it so hard."

"Your dad broke the lamp?"

Violet nodded. "He said not to say it. Not those words. That Mama's just gonna spoil me and I need to 'preciate."

"How did the lamp get broken? How did you cut yourself, honey?"

Violet put both hands together. She raised them high over her head and rose up out of the beanbag. She scrunched up her face, baring her bottom teeth. Then she made a sharp, downward gesture with her hands as if she were throwing something on the ground with great force.

"Like that," she said. "It broke all over."

"Where were you?"

"On the floor. It fell on the floor. Right next ta me."

"What happened after that?"

"My leg got all stingy. Then there was blood."

"The lamp cut you when it broke?"

Violet nodded. "He didn't mean it. Dad didn't mean it. It just jumped up. A big ugly piece of fish. It just jumped up and bit my leg."

"I see."

"I wanna stay with Mama."

Violet got up then. She walked over to the bin where Christine had gotten the dolls. She selected a different one and began to play with it in the far corner away from the camera. Christine turned and switched off the camcorder. The screen went blank. I picked up the remote and rewound the video until a point where Violet looked straight at the camera. I hit pause.

I knew from the date stamp on the DVD it was one of the last sessions Christine had with Violet. The incident with the lamp hadn't made it into Sam's report.

"She's like me."

The voice behind me made me jump. I'd been so engrossed in watching the video, I hadn't heard Will walk in.

"Honey. My gosh. You startled me."

"Sorry. Who was that?"

"Oh. It's just a case I'm sort of working on. It's nothing."

"She's like me," he said. "She stims."

"Oh. Yes. The hand flapping when she gets excited. Yes. I've seen you do that a million times when you work out a puzzle piece or something."

Will nodded. "Is she okay?" He picked up the paper sleeve the DVD came from. Violet Runyon's name was printed on it.

My heart stuck in my throat. He would Google the name. I knew it.

"No, babe. She's not okay. She didn't make it. But it was a long time ago."

Will cocked his head to the side. He stared at the screen. Violet, frozen in time with a goofy smile on her face.

She looked so familiar in a way that haunted me. Yes. She was like Will. Though I'd never spoken to Carla about it, Violet might have been on the spectrum, or perhaps had ADHD.

"You okay, Mom?"

Violet's clear blue eyes transfixed me. I couldn't shake the feeling that she looked so much like the mysterious Leesha. I should have gotten on that bus with her, perhaps. Pressed her.

"I hope you win whatever it is you're doing for her," Will said. "Or her parents."

"Thanks, honey."

He walked out of the room. I looked back at the screen. Just then, my phone rang. The caller ID made me take a breath. It was Kevin Barnum, Hoyt Marvin's parole officer.

"Hi, Kevin," I said.

"Hi. Hey. I just wanted to follow up with you. Hoyt Marvin's in the wind. I'm going to have to violate his parole. He missed an appointment and when I went out to his address, he was gone. Neighbors said he packed up a few nights ago. Hasn't been back since. He hasn't shown up for work. Two days now."

"I'm not surprised."

"Me either. Listen, I also talked to the neighbor about that girl you told me about."

"Leesha," I said. I pressed a hand to the television screen.

"Right. Listen. I think your instincts were right. The neighbor said she saw her getting dropped off multiple times by different men. A couple of times, she seemed upset. Crying. Once, the neighbor approached her. Leesha had a black eye and was wearing a pair of fishnet stockings that were all torn up, she said. She had bruises on her arm. The kind you get when somebody grabs you. Anyway, this neighbor tried to help. Offered to let her stay at her place. Leesha said she couldn't. That Hoyt would never allow it. Then Hoyt came out and chased the neighbor off. I guess it got heated. He was rough with Leesha. Grabbing her by the hair."

"Did she call the cops? This neighbor?"

"No," Kevin said. "She was afraid to get involved. She'd heard rumors that Hoyt might be connected to some bad people. Obviously, she couldn't prove it. But she said she one hundred percent got the impression Hoyt was turning this girl out."

I took my hand off the screen. "That poor kid."

"I'll do what I can," Kevin said. "I've got a few other addresses where Hoyt Marvin used to stay. Some associates of his I can run down. I'll find him. Can't promise you how long it'll take. But he'll turn up."

"What about the girl? I really need to talk to her again. When you put feelers out, can you see what you can find out about her?"

"I'll try. But I think it's obvious she's not safe, Mara. When I find Hoyt again, he's going back in. I'm not messing around. I don't care what he's telling you he knows about that cold case."

"No. I know."

"You tell Skip I told you that. He can't cut any deals with this guy."

"I'm not sure I have a lot of sway with Skip Fletcher these days, Kevin. I'm still on suspension."

"Jesus," he said. "I'm sorry about that. It's crap. What do we have to do to get rid of this guy?"

"Wait four years, I think."

Only we both knew girls like Leesha didn't have that kind of time.

"Well, hang in there," Kevin said. "You've got a lot of people in your corner. People who'll be happy to stick their necks out for you if there's some kind of review board."

"I appreciate it. Truly." And I did.

I just wasn't sure if any of it would help.

I said goodbye to Kevin after thanking him again for what he could do about Hoyt Marvin. A text came through from Hojo.

"Judge Saul ready to rule on Tony Gribaldi's bullshit TRO motion. The judge wants you there. Nine a.m. I'll be right there with you. Don't let the bastards get you down."

I sent him a thumbs up, then sank back into the plastic chair. Violet smiled down at me. Letting out a sigh, I clicked the remote and watched the television screen go dark.

19

"This woman has no idea the kind of stress her actions have caused for me and for my wife." Tony Gribaldi stood at the lectern. Judge Vivian Saul stared down her readers at him. I sat in the gallery. An odd place to be while I was the subject of the hearing.

"My wife has worked hard to bury the past. Every year on the anniversary of Violet's disappearance, we have to deal with reporters or keyboard detectives reaching out and harassing us. We've had every crackpot and psychic in the country claiming to have seen Violet. Each time, it devastates my wife. She doesn't eat. She doesn't sleep. She cries all the time. Now, because of the callous, careless, reckless actions of Ms. Brent, the whole thing has been stirred up all over again. I mean, look at this?"

He gestured to the benches behind me. David Reese and two other reporters had shown up to cover the hearing. I recognized a few faces from the local online forums as well. Helpful "tipsters" who covered true crime. They'd made themselves known to my office over the years.

"Mr. Gribaldi, I'm sensitive to your wife's mental state. She's had to endure a nightmare I cannot even fathom. But you filed this petition on your behalf, not for her. You understand you must prove to me why the actions of the respondent, Ms. Brent, have caused you irreparable harm. Can you do that?"

"Isn't it obvious?" Tony said.

Judge Saul scratched her forehead. She looked at me. "Ms. Brent, I'd like to hear from you. Mr. Gribaldi, take a seat."

"I'm not finished, Your Honor."

"If I have any questions for you, I'll let you know."

I rose and waited for Tony to clear the lectern before making my way through the gate.

"Ms. Brent, would you like to respond to Mr. Gribaldi's allegations?"

"Yes, Your Honor," I said. "First, I want to make it abundantly clear. My deepest sympathies are with Mrs. Gribaldi. But as it relates to her, I've acted first within the scope of my duties as a prosecutor. And second, any additional inquiries I've made into her daughter's case were at her direct behest."

"What do you mean?" the judge asked.

"She's a liar!" Tony shouted.

Judge Saul banged her gavel. "Mr. Gribaldi, please. You've had your turn to speak. I've reviewed your pleadings. Ms. Brent as the respondent has a right to speak as well."

"Your Honor, there are certain aspects to this matter that I am not willing to discuss in open court or in public. Violet Runyon's case may be cold, but it isn't closed. I don't feel comfortable, therefore, getting into the particulars. To be honest, as far as the additional media attention this hearing has drawn, it's of Mr. Gribaldi's making, not mine. And to reiterate, any action I've taken as it relates to this matter was done on Mrs. Gribaldi's request. Mr. Gribaldi, as the court has pointed out, has offered no evidence to back up his claim that he personally has suffered irreparable injury, loss, or damage. I think it's telling that Mrs. Gribaldi has refused to participate in these proceedings."

"How dare you!" Tony shouted. "She's my wife. She's been through hell! And you want me to drag her back into this courthouse? The same courthouse where she had to listen to her ex-husband, the murderer of her little girl, spew lies about what happened?"

"Mr. Gribaldi!" Judge Saul banged her gavel. She looked physically pained. As frustrated as I was with Tony Gribaldi, I had sympathy for the position he'd put Vivian Saul in. Behind me, I could hear the constant tapping of fingers on laptop keyboards as the media and amateur sleuths in the courtroom took down the events. None of this would do Carla any good. I knew Skip Fletcher would also use it as further ammunition against me.

"All right," Judge Saul said. "I've heard enough. Mr. Gribaldi, please believe me when I say I have the deepest sympathy for what's happened to your wife and to your family. But as a matter of law, you simply haven't met your burden of proof such that I can grant you a restraining order against Ms. Brent. Perhaps if your wife was willing to testify or at least offer an affidavit in support. But she hasn't. I'm sorry. Your motion is denied, and this matter is dismissed with prejudice."

"Your Honor," Tony said. He rose and came through the gate. He brushed me aside and stood at the lectern. "I don't want this woman near my wife. I don't want her near my home. She's a menace. She's abused her position and added legitimacy to all those conspiracy theorists you see in the back of the courtroom typing away. She should be censured. She should be disbarred."

"None of those remedies are within my power to grant, even if I agreed with you. My ruling stands."

"I'm not done," Tony said, turning on me. There was fire in his eyes. He took a step toward me and raised a finger, ready to jab it into my chest.

"That's enough!" Judge Saul pounded her gavel. "We're finished here, Mr. Gribaldi. Go home to your wife!"

"Are you threatening me?" I said, unable to control my own bubbling rage.

"You heard what I said," he hissed. He saved a menacing glare for the judge, then stormed out of the courtroom. David Reese jumped up and began to follow him. Terrific. More fodder for Skip Fletcher.

I took a steadying breath and prepared to leave the courtroom.

"Mara?" Judge Saul called out. "Can I see you in chambers for a moment?"

I was glad Reese was already out of the courtroom by the time she said it. No doubt he would have printed his own version of what happened next.

"Of course, Your Honor," I said. She stepped off the bench and disappeared through the door behind her. Her bailiff gestured for me to come in that way rather than through the hall. I was grateful for the added privacy that would give me, but not looking forward to whatever Vivian Saul had to say.

She unzipped her robe and tossed it over her wing-backed leather chair. Instead of sitting in it, she went to the futon she kept in the corner.

"What's going on?" she said.

"I wish I knew," I said. "Thank you for that out there, by the way."

"Don't thank me. He had no legal footing to stand on. If he had, if the wife had backed him up, I would have ruled against you."

"You actually think I'm in the business of harassing family members of murder victims?"

Vivian pressed her thumb and forefinger to the bridge of her nose and let out a deep sigh. "No. But I'm not going to lie. I'm worried about you. More than that, I'm worried you're not worried enough. Skip Fletcher is looking to clean house. Why are you giving him a mop?"

"I can't control what Fletcher does. And I haven't done anything wrong here. More to the point, I haven't done anything Carla Gribaldi hasn't approved of."

"What do you have? Because those vultures out there are going to have their clickbait stories online before we even finish this conversation. Is there new evidence in the Runyon girl's case?"

"If there was, I'm not sure it would be appropriate for me to discuss it with you. You're still the presiding judge over Bart Runyon's case, aren't you? He's doing fifteen years, thanks to everything you tacked on. He's still winding his way through the appellate courts."

She waved me off. "I'm not worried. Runyon's not going anywhere, and I had legal cause for every second I sentenced him. I'm just asking you ... you've sent up a hell of a lot of smoke on this one. Is there fire?"

I looked her squarely in the eye. "I'm not sure. That's the truth. I'm just not sure."

"But you're not acting in any kind of official capacity. You're suspended. To be honest, I didn't call you in here to even rehash all this stuff about Runyon. I called you in here because you're in trouble and I don't even think you realize how deep. Fletcher's going to get his way. You know that, right? He's going to fire you. And that makes me sad. We need you in that office. I need you in my courtroom doing what you do. You're good at it."

I smiled. "I appreciate your support."

"Don't look at me. Nothing I can do to save your ass this time, Mara. I'm just giving you a heads-up. I don't know what you did to ruffle Skip Fletcher's feathers ..."

"I drew breath," I said.

"Be that as it may, try to undo it. Make him happy so I don't have to go through breaking in another prosecutor. One that won't be half as good as you are."

"You're a good egg, Vivian," I said. "And I do appreciate it. But ..."

"But ..." she said. "You're not about to give up on whatever it is you're doing. Chasing ghosts. Or red herrings. Because the other thing I've heard ... is you have doubts that Bart Runyon is the one who killed that little girl. I'm telling you. He did it. He's as evil and black-hearted as they come. Tony Gribaldi is a blowhard, but he's harmless."

"You really think that? You think it makes sense for him to be coming at me as hard as he did out there? Because to me, he's starting to act like a man who has something to hide."

She leaned back and closed her eyes. "I need a drink."

"It's only one thirty," I said.

"You and your facts."

That got a laugh out of me. Before I could say anything else, there was a soft knock on her door. Judge Saul's clerk poked her head in. "Sorry to interrupt. Mara, I've got someone in the judge's office looking for you."

"Go," Judge Saul said. She'd stretched out on her futon, resting her feet on the armrest. "Get out there and ruin your career. See if I care."

She was teasing. I gave her a half-hearted salute and stepped out of her chambers and into her outer office. The person looking for me was Hojo. His face was flushed. He held a pink message sheet in his hand.

"Good," he said. "I ran over here to catch you before you left the courthouse."

"You caught me," I said. Judge Saul's clerk excused herself and went back in to speak with Saul. It left Hojo and me alone in the office for a moment.

"Caro managed to intercept this before Skip got a hold of it," Hojo said, waving the pink piece of paper in front of me.

"Well, that's cryptic. What's up?"

"He wants to see you. Today, if you can get up there."

"He?"

"I should have ripped it up. But his lawyer was going to keep calling. And if he ran into Skip, God help you."

"What are you talking about? Whose lawyer? Who wants to see me?"

Hojo handed me the piece of paper.

"You can't go," he said. "There will be a record of it. It'll be a disaster. Seriously, Mara. The final nail in your career coffin."

I read the message. I checked my smartwatch.

"Christ," Hojo said. "You're gonna go. Aren't you?"

I crumpled the piece of paper and tossed it in the nearby trash can. I thought of Violet Runyon's sweet face in the video interview I'd played yesterday.

"He's mean," she had said.

The message had been from Bart Runyon's current lawyer. Bart had something he wanted to tell me. He wanted me to pay him a visit. Today.

20

Four hours later, I found myself sitting across the table from the man Violet Runyon called Daddy. The man she trusted to protect her. The man who people I trusted were one hundred percent certain had killed that little girl and dumped her body somewhere.

I've sat across from killers before. Hundreds, maybe. You want them to look the part. You try to see things in their eyes that make sense of the evil you know they harbor. You can, sometimes. The coldness. The lack of remorse. The sadistic glee they have when talking about their victims. The lack of empathy. But most of the time, they seem just like someone you'd meet in line at the grocery store. Polite. Humble. Even personable.

Bart Runyon was none of those things. Instead, he presented as manic, desperate, and terrified. He bit the nails on his left hand to the quick as he sat across from me. Beads of sweat made his forehead glisten. His blue prison jumpsuit hung from his shoulders. His skinny arms poked out from the gaping sleeves, showing sores all up and down his arms. He scratched at some of those, making them bleed after he'd finished with his fingernails.

"Why did you want to see me, Mr. Runyon?" I asked.

"I saw you on the news," he said. "You've talked to Carla. You want to know about Violet."

"Yes," I said, deciding I had no time for anything but directness. I didn't want to be here. And yet, I couldn't stop myself from coming.

"What have you heard?" he said, going back to chewing what was left of his pinky nail. "Tony says you've been harassing Carla. Is that true?"

"No. It's not true."

Bart shook a finger at me. He rubbed the top of his head with the other hand. He'd changed a lot from the pictures I'd seen of him during his trial a decade ago. His wavy brown hair had thinned and turned stringy. He had large puffy pockets under his eyes. His lower teeth were yellowed and crooked. One was missing in the front. If I had to guess, he was on something. He had that look about him. The demeanor. The skin picking.

"You see. You met him. You know. You can't trust Tony. I knew from the very beginning. He was no good for Carla. He was no good for Violet. She didn't like him."

"She never met him," I said. "Violet. Carla was careful about that."

"That's what she told everyone. I knew. I know. He's trouble. He's a liar. You ask him. You spend some time with him, and you'll see what I see. What Violet knew."

"Are you trying to tell me Tony Gribaldi did something bad to her?"

He shook his finger again. "See? I know you. I know what you're doing. You want me to say something. Trip me up. Tell me I'm lying."

"I'm just trying to figure out why you asked me to meet with you today, Mr. Runyon. Why don't you do us both a favor and tell me?"

"You think I killed her? I told you. I know you. You and Detective Cruz. Sorry. Sheriff Cruz. You think he's some hero. Some great man. He never cared about the truth. Took one look at me. Believed everything Carla told him. She lies. She turned my baby against me. I know what she did. I see her. She goes on the news with her new face. Her new hair. Her new husband. Gets people to fall all over her. Like she's some saint. She's no saint. Violet was scared of her."

"That's not what Violet told the social workers, Mr. Runyon."

"She coached her. Taught her what to say."

"Look, I'm not here to listen to you relitigate the breakup of your marriage or your custody issues. I shouldn't have come at all. There are a lot of people in my life that won't be happy when they find out I gave you the time of day. But here I am. So, say what you want to say."

He pushed his bottom lip over his top lip and furiously shook his head. Then he slammed a flat palm against the table. "You're one of them. Dammit. I knew it. I thought you had an open mind."

"I do have an open mind. I wasn't in the prosecutor's office when Violet went missing or you went on trial. Most of what I've learned about Violet's case ... your case ... is new to me."

"She's your friend though, Kenya Spaulding."

"Yes. She is."

"I'm sure she's given you an earful. She's another one. Prejudiced against me. She hates men."

"I've never known that to be true. But I'm not here for Kenya either."

"She deserved to lose her election. I got a real laugh out of that. Nice to see her taken down a peg or two."

I gathered my purse. "I think we're done here. I knew I shouldn't have come."

"I heard a rumor," he said. "I saw the news. You had an informant tell you something about what happened to my Violet. I deserve to know what he said."

I folded my hands on the table. Everything Sam, Kenya, Carla, and even Judge Saul said ran through my mind on a loop. This man was a liar. A chameleon when he needed to be.

"Ginger Ivan," I said, and waited. Bart Runyon instantly stopped fidgeting. He stared at me, his pupils narrowing to pinpoints.

"Ginger Ivan," I repeated. "That's what my informant said. That he knew someone who knew how to find her."

The only movement from Bart Runyon was the slow trickle of sweat down his right temple. Then finally, "No," he said. "No way."

"I'm thinking you told someone. A cellmate, perhaps. It made its way to my informant, and he tried to trade it for his freedom."

"No. I never said anything about that. That's not what happened. Your informant was lying. There is no Ginger Ivan. I made it up."

Of all the things Bart could have said, that was the one I didn't expect.

"Excuse me?"

"I never said there was a woman. I never said I gave Violet to a woman. That's a lie. I never knew her name. I never told anyone her name because I didn't know it!"

"Bart, you're lying to me right now. You're on record. All of your interviews were taped. You told Detective Cruz that woman's name. You said you were contacted by her. And you're right. No one believes you that she was real. You know what they believe. That you killed your own daughter. That you dumped her body in a landfill somewhere most likely."

"No. No. No! I never hurt my baby. Not a hair on her head."

"Her blood was in your car."

"You have a kid, don't you? You want to sit there and tell me if somebody searched your car. Right now. Right this very minute. That there wouldn't be blood in it. Your son's blood. They scrape their knees. They get cuts and bruises. She was a little kid. She fell off a swing set and busted open her knee. I took her home. But she was bleeding. I told them. I told Detective Cruz."

"You lied about where you were. Even when you were caught by your cell phone records. Why do you expect me ... why do you expect anyone to believe a word you say?"

"Because I'm telling you the truth. If you talked to someone who says they know who Ginger Ivan is, they're lying. I told you. I made it all up. I was scared. They pushed me for a name. I was out of my mind. My baby was missing. I knew she was dead. Everybody knew she was dead. They always say, if you don't find them in the first forty-eight hours, you're never going to."

Everything Sam warned me about had been spot on. Bart was changing his story mid-sentence. Nothing tracked. Nothing stayed the same.

"So, you expect me to believe you just made up a name out of thin air? Bart, that makes no sense. Not if you were truly worried about finding your daughter. Why would you purposely misdirect the police?"

"Because of her!" he yelled. "Fucking Carla. I knew what she was saying about me. She was telling them I was some kind of monster. The second I sat down, I knew they'd already decided I was guilty. She'd railroaded me, set me up for months. It was all Carla. She's the one who was putting Violet in danger. The whole time. The whole time! Everything I did, I did to protect Violet."

My head started to pound. Everything single thing Sam had said was true. Talking to Bart Runyon was like trying to pin a wet noodle to the wall.

"So, you want me to believe that you never mentioned Ginger Ivan's name to anyone after the police interviewed you?"

"That's the only time I ever said that name," he said. "And I told you. It was made up. I panicked. I was out of my mind with grief and then I knew what Carla was trying to do. Her grand plan to frame me. There's no Ginger Ivan. Just forget you ever heard that name."

"Do you think maybe Darryl Cox wishes he'd never heard that name? Or Hoyt Marvin?"

Bart Runyon went very still. "I don't know what you're talking about. I never met either one of them. Who are they?"

He seemed genuinely confused, but who could really tell with him?

"Bart, you could do yourself a favor. You could make sure Violet can truly rest in peace. Just tell everyone what they want to know. Where's Violet? What did you do with her?"

He squeezed his eyes shut. "I only tried to protect her. To get her away from the people who were really going to hurt her. I swear it. On Violet's soul, I swear on it. She's with people who know how to keep her safe. At least, that's what they promised. I trusted them. But then when the police started asking all those questions, they were gone. Invisible. They hung me out to dry."

"The invisible people."

His eyes snapped open.

"I think even you can hear how you sound, Bart. Crazy. You sound crazy. You might as well be speaking in tongues."

Now, tears began to mix with the sweat rolling down his cheeks. "No. I never hurt her. I swear to you. I never hurt her. I never told anyone to hurt her. I would never have done anything to put her in danger willingly. I swear to God. My only crime is trusting the wrong people. That's it."

"Where is she?"

He dropped his chin to his chest. "I don't know. I really don't know."

"But you admit that you gave her to someone. That you're the one who took her away from her mother."

"Yes!" he hissed. "Yes. And I'd do it again. But I was protecting her. If I have to rot in here forever, I'll never regret doing what I did. She's safe now. She's in a better place because of me."

It was my turn to drop my head. I knew it was the closest thing to an admission I or anyone else would ever get from Bart Runyon. I'd heard enough. I slowly rose from my chair and went to the door. I pressed the button beside it, alerting the guard we were finished.

"You can't leave. Not until you promise you're going to finish what you started. You have to tell them the truth. I know you. I can see it in your eyes. You want to find Violet as much as I do."

I turned to him as the guard opened the door. "You're the only person who can do that, Bart."

He yelled at me as I left the room. The clang of metal as the door shut pierced through me like gunfire. It felt so final. Almost like the closing of a coffin lid. Violet's coffin. As long as Bart Runyon clung to his lies, Violet would never find a peaceful rest.

I kept seeing her face floating in front of me as I left the prison and made my way back to my car. As I climbed behind the wheel, two texts came through. One was from Hojo. The other from Sam.

Hojo's message read, "They set your just cause hearing in front of the review board. Three days. Your rep will be there with you. Anything you need from me, you got it."

I sent him a quick, "Thank you," then read Sam's text.

I hadn't told him I was coming here today. I knew he'd try to stop me. His simple text told me he likely already knew.

"We need to talk."

21

The look on Gus Ritter's face as he walked out of Sam's office spoke volumes. He put his head down as he saw me. He looked over his shoulder, then carefully steered me away from the door and down the hallway.

"Just give him a few minutes before you go in there," he said.

"How bad is it?"

Gus waited while two deputies walked by us and we had at least a minimal level of privacy.

"He's just under a lot of pressure. There's a law enforcement watchdog group putting pressure on the attorney general's office to open an independent investigation into Darryl Cox's death."

"They'll try to scapegoat Sam."

"Probably. But there's nothing there, Mara. They won't find anything. This one's as clean as they come. They'll blow their smoke. Make sure we've got every safeguard in place so it doesn't happen again. And that's okay. Oversight doesn't have to be a bad thing. That's what I told Sam."

This got a smile out of me. "Well, Gus Ritter, you're a changed man. Your leave at the beginning of the year made you mellow."

He gave me a sly smile. "Don't get used to it. I'm just certain I'm right about Darryl Cox."

Sam's door opened. His civilian assistant, Debra, slipped out, walking with purpose, carrying a notepad in her hand.

Sam and Gus exchanged a look. "Hey, Mara," Sam said. "Thanks for coming down so quick. Come on in. I've only got a few minutes before I've got to head across town."

Gus winked at me, then gave me a subtle thumbs up. Somehow, it did nothing to make me feel any better about what Sam might say.

He closed the door behind me and took a seat behind his desk.

"Ah," I said. "So, it's that kind of meeting."

Sam's shoulders dropped. "Don't start. You knew I was gonna get a call from the penitentiary?"

"Was it before or after I got there?"

"What?"

"Come on. I'd wager you got a call the minute Bart Runyon put the word out he wanted to see me."

"Why didn't you call me?"

"Because I knew what you were going to say. You were going to tell me not to go."

He sat back. His leather chair rocked, then creaked as he rested one ankle over the opposite knee.

"Figured you could use plausible deniability. I went on my own. It had nothing to do with you."

A flash of anger colored his face, but a moment later, he seemed to find some inner calm. He took a breath. Let it out.

"What did you think?"

I crossed my legs. "I think Bart Runyon probably hasn't told the same story twice in twelve years."

"But what do you *think*?"

I considered the question. I knew what he was asking.

"I think Bart Runyon probably killed his own daughter."

A wave went across Sam's face. Relief maybe. "But I got answers I didn't expect," I said.

"Such as?"

"It would have made sense for him to repeat the story he told you about this Ginger Ivan woman. He could have played the angle that Cox and Marvin, two new people completely unrelated to Violet's case, were corroborating his initial story after the fact."

"But he didn't?"

"He did not. He very adamantly denied ever even mentioning the name Ginger Ivan."

"He's on record. On tape."

"I reminded him of that. Then he changed his story again and said it was all a mistake. That he made her up."

"He contradicted himself within the same conversation. That sounds about right."

"I know. But like I said. I didn't expect that. I expected him to tell me he told you so. That this woman is out there somewhere just like he told you twelve years ago. Instead, he seemed terrified, Sam."

"Of you?"

"As far as we know, Runyon has had no contact in prison with either Darryl Cox or Hoyt Marvin. But he knew about Cox's death. It felt like ... I don't know ... like Runyon was worried something similar might happen to him."

"Did he say that?"

"No. But he came off as extremely paranoid. I don't know. I just think ... I guess I'd like to know who Runyon's been talking to. Has he had any run-ins lately? Is there any scuttlebutt surrounding him? Should we maybe talk to the COs?"

"Runyon's been a marked man since he went inside. Prison justice has a way of dealing with men who hurt little kids. That's nothing new."

"Maybe. I don't know. It just seemed so odd to me based on his history, that he wouldn't pick up the thread Darryl Cox and Hoyt Marvin left."

Sam stared at me but didn't say anything for almost a full minute. Finally, I leaned forward.

"Sam, I'm sorry, but I'm not sorry. I don't know if that makes sense. I've been chasing something down based on little more than gut instinct and Carla Gribaldi's request. The last thing I wanted to do was cause you grief."

He sat up. He came around the desk and sat on the edge of it, right in front of me.

"I'm not mad at you. I'm not."

"Violet was scared of Bart. I know that. You were right. Talking to Christine Schuler was a good idea. It helped me put a few things into perspective. Your perspective, for one."

"He's going to get out," Sam said. "That's the thing I can't shake. Bart Runyon is in year eleven of a fifteen-year sentence. He's up for parole next year. I don't think the board will grant him early release. But in about four and a half years, he's going to be a free man. He'll be under a court order not to go anywhere near Carla. He'll be a town pariah. But he'll be free. And he's never going to tell anybody what he did with that girl."

"Sam," I said. "I just can't keep myself from coming back to this one thing. Hoyt Marvin shouldn't have known the name Ginger Ivan, but he did. Darryl Cox is dead and now Marvin is missing. Bart Runyon has backtracked off the main story he told you all those years ago when it's in his self-interest to stick to it now. Someone knows something. I feel it. You feel it too."

"I don't know what I feel. But I'm worried. Not about Bart, but about you."

"I'm fine."

"You're not fine. You've let this thing sink its hooks into you. You're in imminent danger of losing your job. I'm doing everything I can to try to save it. But the fact that you and I have a relationship is going to be the thing Skip Fletcher ultimately uses to get rid of you. I don't care what they say about me. I don't care about the fallout from Darryl Cox. I can handle everything they throw at me, but it's killing me what they're doing to you because of me."

I smiled. The concern in his eyes melted me. I just didn't share it.

"I'm not afraid of Skip Fletcher."

"What are you going to do if he gets his way? Mara, you'll lose your health insurance. You have Will."

"Sam," I said, reaching up to touch his face. "I don't need to be rescued. I'm touched. Really. But I can take care of myself."

"Your hearing is in two days. Have you even prepared for it? What if Skip wins?"

"I haven't done anything wrong. If I've done anything at all, it's with a mind toward getting answers about a little girl who was murdered. I'm not sorry about that. I'm also not going down without a fight. Skip can't fire me without a just cause hearing. I still like my chances."

"He'll stack it against you. There are enough people who want to get rid of you just because of your association with your ex-husband."

"They can't do that. I'll sue the county if I have to."

"What about Will?"

"Will is fine."

"He isn't. Mara, he called me. He's worried about you, too."

"Will called you?" I didn't expect that.

"He says he's worried you're going to take the job in New Hampshire that his grandmother said she could get for you. The one that'll give you ten times more take-home pay a month or something."

Sam smiled at the same time I did. We laughed together.

"I'll talk to him," I said.

"Would you take it?"

"What?"

"The job. It's a lot of money. A lot less stress."

"Are you worried I'm going to leave?"

Sam inhaled. I got the impression he was going to give me one answer, then changed his mind mid-breath. "Yes," he said. "I'm worried."

He took my hands in his. "I know when it comes down to it, you'll do whatever you have to to protect your son. I just hate the idea that means I might lose you."

I rose. He held his arms open and I stepped into them. Things were so new between us. We each hesitated with putting a label on it.

"Thank you," I said. "The boom hasn't been lowered on me just yet. I still have a few tricks up my sleeve to deal with Skip. And I trust my union to do their job and back me."

"You do? Because I don't. I've been hearing things."

"They haven't even scheduled a formal hearing yet."

"Just watch your back," he said. "Don't assume people won't stab you there. If I hear anything concrete, I'll let you know. But ..."

"But doing that might be seen as a conflict of interest. I don't want that. I don't want you sticking your neck out for me."

My phone rang. I glanced down. The caller ID read Kevin Barnum. Sam saw it too.

"Do you need to take that?"

"One second," I said. I picked up the phone and walked to the corner of Sam's office.

"Hi, Kevin," I said.

"Hey, Mara. Listen. There's no word on Hoyt Marvin yet. There's a bench warrant out for him now though. I expect he'll get popped for something soon enough. He can't help himself from getting into trouble. But you asked me to keep my ears open about the girl you saw him with. This Leesha? I got a little bit of information on her. A friend of Hoyt's told me she goes by Leesha Stevens. I did some digging. I've got an address. Hoyt's associate told me Leesha's there now. He saw her two days ago and she looked pretty bad. Like someone had roughed her up."

"What's the address?" I asked. I made a writing gesture to Sam. He grabbed a pad of paper and a pen off his desk and handed it to me. I wrote down the address Kevin relayed.

"The friend said she works nights. Some bar downtown. He didn't know the name of it. But he said she usually gets in really early. Like seven o'clock in the morning. The last five mornings in a row. If you want to talk to her, that's your best bet on catching her."

"Thanks, Kevin, I really appreciate it."

"You're welcome. Mara, don't go out there by yourself. It's a rough part of town."

I didn't have Kevin on speaker, but his voice was loud enough. I was pretty sure Sam heard every word. He scowled.

"Thanks," I said. "I'm not planning on doing anything stupid. I'll let you know if I hear anything else about Marvin on my end. You'll do the same?"

"You bet," Kevin said. "Talk soon."

Then he hung up.

"Mara ..." Sam stood beside me. He read the address I'd written down.

"It's this girl," I said. "The one Hoyt Marvin was turning out. Sam, I know this is crazy. But I want to talk to her. She looked ... scared. But she also looked familiar."

"Familiar?"

"Well, she looked like Violet."

Sam reared back. "You think this girl is Violet Runyon?"

"No. Not really. Not literally. But she's about the same age Violet would be now. She's in trouble. I know it."

"You think you can save her?"

"I think I need to try."

Sam let out an exasperated sigh, but I knew what he'd say. Because in the end, Sam Cruz would always do the right thing.

"I'm going with you," he said. "We'll try talking to her together. What time am I picking you up?"

Warmth flooded me. I went to him and kissed his cheek. "Pick me up at seven tomorrow morning. This will be quick. I promise."

"Until something goes wrong," he muttered.

"Nothing's going to go wrong. Promise."

He was grumbling something behind my back as I picked up my purse and left his office.

22

"You're sure this is the right address?" Sam asked. His face had fixed into a permanent scowl. He parked four houses down from the address on Redwood Street at the east end of town. Half the homes on this street were boarded up. They were century-old houses built for factory workers coming back from the Great War. Then the factory closed in the sixties. Now, several of the blocks in this neighborhood had become notorious crack dens. There had been seven shootings on this very street over the last five years.

"This is a bad idea," Sam fumed.

"We'll knock on the door. See if she's there. See if she'll talk to us. Then we'll leave. I'm not looking for a whole drama."

"I'm afraid a whole drama is going to come looking for you," he said. "But it's early. It's later in the day things are gonna start getting really dodgy. Still, I'd feel better if I had a marked cruiser out here."

Sam had driven in his unmarked Crown Victoria. It was gray, nondescript, but absolutely had the look of exactly what it was. A cop car trying not to look like a cop car.

I checked my phone one more time to make sure I had the street number right. 413 Redwood. It was a gray, craftsman-style home in the center of the block. The cement walk was crumbled. From here, it looked like one of the front porch steps was missing. There had once been a screened-in porch, but one wall was torn away. From here, I could make out an olive-green refrigerator shoved into one corner of the porch.

"Let's get this over with," Sam grumbled. He got out of his vehicle and scanned the street. He kept his right hand resting on his service weapon. He wore plain clothes, a blue suit, but had his badge clipped to his belt.

He gestured for me to follow him. He went first, keeping his head on a swivel as we approached the house.

"Do me a favor," he said. "Don't just walk up to the door and stand in front of it. Let me knock. And stay behind me. Okay?"

"You're the sheriff," I said. It got me another grumble in response. But I did what he asked. I let Sam approach the door. He hit the doorbell, then gave it three knocks. He gently pushed me to the side, away from the front window and the door itself.

No answer. But we could easily hear movement from inside. People were talking. I could make out a male voice, then a female.

Sam knocked on the door again. "Come on," he said. "I know someone's in there. Just have a question."

I distinctly heard someone "shushing" someone else inside. I wanted to peer into the window but knew Sam would flip. He had a point. If Leesha were in there against her will, my plan to just come knocking suddenly seemed very unwise.

Finally, a man pushed the curtain away from the window and looked out at us. Frowning, he turned and called out to someone else inside. Then he unlocked the deadbolt on the door and swung it wide. Sam kept his hand on his gun.

"You're a cop?" the man said. His age was hard to guess. Maybe mid-thirties, but his front teeth were missing. His neck and half of his face were covered in tattoos.

"I'm looking for Leesha Stevens," I said. "My name is Mara Brent. She knows me."

"You got the wrong house," the man said. One of his neck tattoos read "Ace."

"Listen, Ace," Sam said. "We don't have the wrong house. I'm not here to arrest anybody, okay? Don't give me a reason to. We're just asking if the girl is here."

Behind Ace, I saw two girls sitting on a couch in the living room. They looked young. Sixteen at most. Sam saw them at the same time I did.

"Ace," he said. "Why don't you step outside?"

"You got a warrant? Because those are my sisters."

"Right," Sam said.

"Leesha!" I shouted. "It's Mara Brent. If you're in there, can you just come out? You're not in any trouble."

"Get off my porch," Ace said.

"This isn't your house," Sam said. "It belongs to Florence Parsons. She's eighty-seven years old. Is she in there too?"

Ace sneered at Sam, then slammed the door in our faces.

"Nice," Sam said. "This is a waste of time."

"Something's wrong," I said.

"Yeah. I don't like it."

We heard another door slam. Then a shout.

"I didn't tell them!" a woman's voice yelled. She sounded terrified. "I swear. This has nothing to do with me."

"Leesha," Sam and I said it together. He pounded on the door again.

Something crashed on the floor and broke.

"You gotta be kidding me. Ace! Open the damn door." Then to me, "I'm calling this in."

"Good idea," I said. No sooner had I gotten the words out before we heard yet another door slam, this one coming from the side of the house. I stepped off the porch.

"Mara!" Sam called out. "Don't ..."

Three girls ran out the back, followed by an older man who jumped the neighbor's fence and kept on going.

"Ace!" Sam called.

"She's there!" I yelled. A third girl ran out the side door, her blonde hair trailing behind her.

"Leesha!" I called out. "Don't run. You're not in trouble. I just want to talk!"

I wanted to run after her, but knew it wasn't safe.

"Come on," Sam said. "That alley backs up to the gas station on Brentwood Avenue. She won't get very far on foot."

We left the porch and ran back to Sam's car. I barely got the door shut before he peeled out and maneuvered the car through the alley. Sure enough, we saw the three girls, including Leesha, heading down it. Ahead of them, two men ran. They darted in two different directions. Then two of the girls, including Leesha, got into a nearby vehicle that sped away.

"Crap," I yelled. "Sam ..."

"I'm not gonna chase her," he said.

"She's not safe. She can't possibly be safe."

"I'll call it in. Get a couple of deputies out here."

"It'll be too late," I said. "You know exactly what that looked like in there."

"Yeah," he said, his tone bitter. "I do."

We rounded the corner. Sam stopped at the traffic light at the corner of Brentwood and Jefferson Street. Two vehicles sped up, coming from behind us. One screeched to a halt beside us on the driver's side. Sam went for his gun.

The other driver rolled down his window. He was white, middle-aged, and wearing a blue golf shirt. He flashed a badge at Sam. Sam let out a deep sigh. The other driver gestured toward the gas station. Swearing, Sam pulled in and parked in the nearest open spot.

"Wait here," he tried to tell me, but I was already out of the car.

"Cruz?" The driver of the vehicle that pulled alongside us got out. He looked furious. A second SUV pulled in behind us. Two men wearing FBI windbreakers got out.

"What's going on?"

"Palmer," Sam said, addressing the first guy who'd flashed the badge. "Mara, meet Lou Palmer."

Agent Palmer stormed up to Sam. "You wanna tell me why you just stepped all over my ops?"

"Your what?" Sam said.

"We've been up on surveillance on that house for two weeks. We were about half a day from running a sting on a suspected human trafficking ring being run out of there. Christ, Cruz. You just pulled up in your cruiser, flashed a badge, now they're scattered to the four winds."

"Wait a minute," Sam said. "You're running a sting in my county, and you don't bother to pick up a phone and let me in on it?"

"These girls are being trafficked across state lines. It's outside your jurisdiction."

"You're standing *inside* my county!" Sam shouted.

The other agents hung back. One shouted into his cell phone. He let out a string of four-letter words, then hung up and walked over to Agent Palmer.

"They completely cleared out," he said. "We're dealing with ghosts now."

"Goddammit," Palmer said. "This was six months of work. About twenty grand in man hours. Poof. You just walked through it like a bull in a china shop, Cruz. And what's she doing here?" He emphasized the word "she" and pointed at me.

"I'm the assistant prosecutor for this county," I said. "Why wasn't my office informed of your operation, either?"

Palmer's face had gone purple. He put a hand on his head as if it were about to pop off.

"We were tracking down a girl I need to talk to about a cold case we've got," I said. "Her name is Leesha Stevens. Did she come up on your surveillance?"

Palmer shook his head. "None of those girls are using their real names."

"She was in there," I said. "I saw her. She ran off with the others and got into a brown sedan just over there."

"They're gone," Sam said.

"She'll be two states away about as fast as you can blink," Palmer said.

"You can drop the attitude," Sam said. "This is your screw-up, not mine. You give me the professional courtesy of letting me know what you're doing in my county."

"I don't answer to you," Palmer said. "And I don't need your permission either. This one's on your head, Cruz. You can be damn sure I'll let the brass know it."

"I am the brass," Sam said through gritted teeth.

Palmer didn't hear it. He made a circular gesture with his index finger. The other agents got into their vehicle. Palmer stomped back to his. He directed a different finger at Sam, then slammed his car in reverse and peeled away.

"Terrific," Sam said. "This headache is getting worse and worse."

"That wasn't our fault. Palmer's guys should have given you a heads-up."

Sam shook his head. "You think that's gonna matter? Nobody cares."

I let out a breath. "They're only gonna care that you followed your girlfriend on a wild goose chase that traipsed right through their sting operation."

Sam didn't answer. He didn't have to. We both knew that would be the gist of it once Palmer wrote his report.

"I'm sorry," I said. "Sam, how could I have known either?"

He went back to the car. I followed him and slipped into the passenger seat.

"Those girls, Sam," I said. "You saw what I saw."

"Yeah," he said, backing out. "I saw."

Then he went stony silent as he pulled out of the gas station and headed back toward downtown.

23

By the time Sam rounded the curve that led to my private driveway, the text tone on his phone had gone off seven times. Mine had gone off once. A quick message from my sister-in-law ... well, former sister-in-law Kat, warning me not to let Sam drive all the way up to the house. Her message was cryptic, saying only that I had a guest who didn't want Sam to know they were there.

"You can drop me off at the end of the drive," I said. "I'll grab the mail and walk up."

Sam pulled in and stopped as I asked him to. He pulled out his phone and read his texts, his frown deepening.

"Sam, I'm sorry," I said. "How were we supposed to know the FBI was set up on that house? It's like you said. Common professional courtesy dictates Palmer should have let either your office or mine know."

Sam slipped his phone in his pocket and turned to me, putting the car in park. I hoped my mystery guest didn't choose now to drive back out.

"I'm not worried about Palmer. That crap back there was nothing but ball-busting. He owes me more favors than he can count on two hands. The problem isn't Palmer. It's Dale Radley."

I paused. "County Commissioner Radley?"

"Yeah. That's who blew up my phone. Palmer called Radley already. Radley's threatening to make trouble over this."

"He can't. He's a blowhard. You're an elected official."

Sam's nostrils flared. "I know. But you're not."

"Me? You think Palmer and Radley are going to make trouble for me? Let them try."

"Mara, you've got to take all this more seriously. Your review hearing is tomorrow morning. This thing with Palmer and now Radley couldn't have come at a worse time for you. I can't be there. That's what's killing me. If I show up, I think it'll do you more damage than good."

"I'm taking it seriously. And everyone seems to want to forget that I haven't done a single thing wrong."

I slipped out of the passenger side. Sam stared after me as I walked to the end of the drive and grabbed my mail. He rolled down his window as I walked back toward him. "Don't worry about me," I said. "Thank you for going out there with me. I'm sorry it went like it did. But Leesha and those girls were in trouble. I'm not going to stop trying to help them."

Sam gave me a begrudging nod. "Neither am I."

"Good," I said. I held my mail to my chest and waved. Sam waved back as he pulled back out onto the main road. I waited until he was out of sight before walking back up the drive toward the house. As I got to my front door, I recognized the tan sedan parked in the circular drive. But not why he'd want to keep his visit a secret from Sam.

I went through the garage and heard laughter as Kat, her wife Bree, Will, and Gus Ritter sat at my kitchen table playing a game of Jenga. Gus had just pulled the piece that toppled the wooden pile. He turned as I walked in.

"A fine mess you've made," I teased. Gus looked chagrined. Will busied himself rebuilding the tower.

"I'll play the next one," Gus said. "I wanna talk to your mom for a few."

"Good luck," Will said. "She won't listen."

Bree and Kat gave me an apologetic look. I had no doubt they'd both grilled Gus when he showed up.

"Come on," I said. "We'll take a walk out back."

Gus followed me off my back porch. I had a sectional outdoor couch, and he took a seat in one corner. I sat opposite him.

"Sam doesn't know I'm here?"

"No. He never made it past the mailbox. Why the need for a clandestine meeting?"

"I'm worried about him. And since I currently can't visit you in your office because you're banned from it, I figured I'd come here. I was surprised to learn you'd taken him on a caper."

"It wasn't exactly a caper."

Gus raised a doubtful brow.

"Okay, it was a little of a caper. It ended badly. I had a tip on this girl I've wanted to question about Hoyt Marvin's story."

"The inmate who Darryl Cox claims told him about Bart Runyon's mystery woman?"

"Yes. She's young, Gus. Marvin's been prostituting her. I just want to talk to her outside of Marvin's influence."

"How'd it go?"

"Terribly." I filled him in on our run-in with Special Agent Lou Palmer of the FBI.

Gus shook his head. "Sam's gonna take heat he doesn't deserve for that."

"He already has. Palmer called Commissioner Radley before we even made it back here. Sam's off putting out fires. He says he's not worried. That it's little more than a pissing contest between them."

"Hmm," Gus grumbled.

"You think it's worse than that?"

"I think Sam's not worried about his own hide. He's worried about yours. That's one of the things I came here to talk to you about."

"My hide?"

"No. What Sam's willing to do to protect it. We're hearing rough stuff, Mara. Stuff Sam doesn't want to tell you. If the FBI makes waves, that won't help."

"Won't help what? And what rough stuff?"

"You're out," Gus said. "Your just cause hearing tomorrow is gonna be a formality. Fletcher's gonna give you an ultimatum. Resign willingly or you'll be fired."

"It's ludicrous. I'll appeal it. I'll sue the county if I have to and win."

"You've stepped on the wrong toes. And you're probably right. These are trumped-up disciplinary charges and you'll eventually be reinstated. You know if I'm given a voice in this, I'll vouch for you."

I touched his knee. "Thank you. I might need to take you up on that."

Gus wrung his hands. I knew there was something even bigger bothering him.

"What is it?" I asked.

"It's this case. Violet Runyon. I've been meaning to talk to you one-on-one about it without Sam around. Mara, you weren't here when this all went down. I was. It wasn't my case, but it nearly destroyed Sam. It nearly destroyed a lot of people. But he took tremendous heat for not being able to find that girl. A lot of people scapegoated him, saying he went too hard on Bart. Made it so he wouldn't talk to the cops at all after it was over. Missed an opportunity to get a confession and the location of Violet's body."

"That wasn't Sam's fault. That was Runyon's or whoever killed her."

As soon as I said it, I regretted it. Not the sentiment, but that I'd said it in front of Gus. Out loud.

"Whoever killed her?"

"Let's not go down that road right now. I'm just saying, Sam did everything right. I know that now."

"This case? Mara, it almost destroyed him. I mean, literally almost destroyed him. He has PTSD from it. For almost two years, it consumed him. He was engaged. Did he ever tell you that?"

"He may have mentioned it once, yes. He said it didn't work out because she wanted to move back near her family in Palo Alto or something."

"He was crazy about Risa. They set a date. He bought the ring. They were under contract on a house over in Cedar Woods. They bought a dog together. Cute little Beagle she named Gorby cuz he had this marking on his forehead that looked just like Gorbachev's birthmark."

"Gus, why are you telling me this?"

"Risa didn't leave because she wanted to move closer to her folks. She would have done anything for Sam. They were that much in love. But then Violet Runyon went missing. Sam became obsessed with finding her. Then with getting Runyon to confess. He started drinking more than he should. Working overtime. Not coming home. And when he did, he was distracted. He was very ... not Sam, you know?"

It certainly didn't sound like the noble man I'd grown to care deeply about. But it was a long time ago. Before I knew him.

"Well," Gus continued. "Risa finally saw the writing on the wall. She gave him an ultimatum. She wasn't going to be married to a guy who was married to his job. And in the end, Sam told her he wasn't going to be married to a woman who expected him to change for her. It was messy. She packed up her stuff and moved out. One day, he came home, and she was just gone. It wrecked him. It was really Carla who helped bring him out of it. She told him it was okay for him to forgive himself. That they both had to if they were ever going to survive Violet's death. She was a good friend to him."

"I know. But Gus, why are you telling me this now? I know how much Violet's case meant to him."

"I'm telling you because I'm seeing it happen all over again. Only this time, it's not Violet he's trying to save. It's you."

"Me?"

"Yeah. He sees you getting sucked under by this case. And as much as it triggers all his stuff, he's seeing you do the exact same thing. He sees you willing to throw your career away over some wild goose chase. And he can't protect you. Not really."

"I don't want Sam to protect me. And if it wasn't this case, it would be something else. Skip wants me gone. He's welcome to try. But I won't go down without a fight."

"Yeah," Gus said. "I'm glad. I really don't want to think about not having you around."

"I'm not going anywhere. And it's very sweet that you came all the way out here to tell me all of this."

"Mara," he said. "I don't know if he's said it, but Sam's in love with you. It's probably not my place to say it. But it's making him do things, take risks on the job he shouldn't. He can't stick his neck out for you right now without risking his own. But he'll do it."

"I told you. I don't need him to. I can take care of myself."

Gus had his phone in his hand. He frowned as he looked at the blank screen.

"Don't worry about me," I said. "Really."

"Violet Runyon's case was a life ruiner for a lot of people. Sam's for a while. Certainly Carla's. Christine Schuler's too. Kenya's. She let a relationship fall by the wayside during it, too. The thing was like plutonium. And I'm afraid it still is. It's happening to you."

"Gus ..."

Gus swiped the screen on his phone.

"I got a message from my contact at NCMEC. They called my office because Sam's no longer in the detective bureau, I am. It was a courtesy call. He said he's got the new age progression photo on Violet Runyon. He was just giving our department a heads-up. You probably have an email from him, too. He said you asked for the thing."

"Yes," I said.

Gus nodded. "He didn't just call me. He also reached out to Carla Gribaldi."

"Dammit. I asked them not to."

"Well, he didn't listen. So now Carla's coming down to the office in the morning to talk to me. She wants to see it. She asked if you could be there too."

"Of course I will."

Gus nodded. "Of course you will. She's probably gonna bring Tony."

That's the last thing I wanted. But there was no longer a court order compelling me to stay away from him.

"Well, I appreciate you telling me. That goes for everything. You're a good friend, Gus. To me and to Sam."

Then Gus Ritter did something he rarely did. He reached across the couch and gave me a hug. Then he rose.

"So come in around ten. If you don't have anything else going on."

It was a joke. He knew I had my review hearing first thing in the morning.

I smiled. "I'm free as a bird."

"Sam will be down in Columbus for a seminar. So at least we can avoid him."

"I'm not trying to."

Gus nodded. "Suit yourself. I'm sorry if I think this whole thing is going to be a waste of time and torture for Carla. But I'll be right there with you."

"Thank you." I smiled. Just then, Will called Gus in for another round of Jenga. As he went back to the kitchen, I had the strongest sensation that tomorrow morning I was about to pull out the piece of this case that would topple my own life over.

24

"You understand this is a formal proceeding, but not a court of law."

I sat at a folding table in front of my tribunal. County Commissioner Radley. Judge Larry Pride from Glanville County, and Herc Manfield, one of the prosecutors who worked in our appellate division. Radley was clearly against me. Pride would be neutral, hopefully. But Herc and I had worked together for years. I prayed he'd be on my side. Beside me sat Olivia Butler, my union representative.

"You're asking me if I know I'm not sitting in a courtroom?" I asked.

Olivia nudged me under the table.

"We just want to get your side of things, Mara," Herc said.

"I've given you my formal statement. I don't have anything to add to it."

Judge Butler looked over the stack of papers in front of him. "You don't deny that you've had issues with Mr. Fletcher?"

"Issues? No. We have no issues. At least not from my perspective. I've conducted myself within the scope of my job and within the code of ethics I'm bound by."

"Mr. Fletcher has concerns that you withheld critical information brought to your attention by a defendant in a murder trial. That you're duty bound to convey all requests for plea deals in cases you're prosecuting," Judge Pride said.

"It wasn't a plea deal request. I had one conversation with Darryl Cox, in the presence of his lawyer. He passed on information pertaining to a different case that I didn't have a chance to vet."

"Before Mr. Cox hung himself in his cell," Commissioner Radley added.

"We appreciate you giving Ms. Brent a chance to speak," Olivia said. "But as you stated, this isn't a court of law. The issue is very narrow, and we don't believe Mr. Fletcher has provided sufficient support for his claim he has just cause to terminate Ms. Brent's employment with the county."

"Shouldn't Mr. Fletcher be given wide latitude to employ assistant prosecutors of his choosing?" Judge Pride asked.

"Of course," I said. "But he can't summarily fire the ones he already has if he doesn't like them."

"Mara," Olivia said under her breath. "Just let me do the talking."

"He's accused you of insubordination," Judge Pride said.

"Ms. Brent was in no way insubordinate. She has a certain amount of discretion in handling her own cases. She acted within the scope of that. She is not facing any disciplinary proceedings before the attorney grievance commission. No complaint has even been filed there. This is, at worst, a misunderstanding. It does not warrant a just cause termination. That's the only statement we'll make here today unless you have any further questions for Ms. Brent."

Commissioner Radley leaned forward. "I do. This goes beyond whatever you think you were allowed to do as it relates to Darryl Cox. I'm concerned Ms. Brent has a serious conflict of interest in light of her romantic relationship with Sheriff Cruz. We've been asked to take that under advisement as well."

"Once again," I said. "There's no conflict. And I've done nothing unethical. Not during the prosecution of Darryl Cox's case or anything else. I resent the implication that I don't know how to keep my personal life separate from my professional one. Especially coming from you, Commissioner Radley. Your wife works for the drain commission. Your son is a lieutenant for the Maumee County Fire Department. Your sister-in-law works for the county clerk's office. Should I go on?"

Olivia nudged me again. Commissioner Radley's face turned bright red.

"I don't have any other questions," he said. Judge Pride and Herc Manfield sat mute.

"Good," Olivia said. "Then I guess we're done here."

"We'll have our formal decision by the end of the week," Judge Pride said. "Thanks for coming in."

I scooted my chair out and tried not to storm out into the hallway. We were on the basement floor of the City-County Building. The virtual bowels. Olivia came out behind me. As I stepped into the hall, I almost ran smack into Carla Gribaldi.

"Carla?" I said, checking my smartwatch. "I thought we were meeting up in Gus's office. That's not for another hour though."

She looked nervously at Olivia Butler. "No. I know. It's not that. I ... uh ... I have an appointment with the panel in there."

"I'm sorry? What? They called you? They dragged you down here?"

"No," she said. "I came voluntarily. Mara, they need to know what you've done for me. They need to know that I didn't put Tony up to that ridiculous TRO petition."

"I don't know," Olivia said. "You being here might do more harm than good."

"I have to," she said. "I feel terrible about what they're doing to you. I can't live with myself if you end up getting fired for your involvement in Violet's case."

The door opened. Commissioner Radley poked his head out. He saw me talking to Carla and frowned.

"I'll meet you upstairs when you're finished," I said to Carla. "And thank you."

She went inside. Radley closed the door.

"Did you call her?" I asked Olivia.

"No. I didn't know she'd be here."

"Do you think it'll help?"

"I suppose it can't hurt."

"Give me the odds."

"The odds?"

"The odds of me getting fired after all of this?"

"I don't know. If they do fire you, I like your odds of overturning it on appeal."

We started for the elevator. "That's not helpful. Appeals take time and money. In the meantime, I'll be out of a job."

"Hopefully it won't come to that."

We rode up to the first floor. I hoped to avoid running into Skip. He'd likely find out soon enough that I was heading over to the Sheriff's Department. Enough people had already seen me in the building.

I thanked and parted ways with Olivia Butler and walked across to the Public Safety Building. Gus wasn't yet in his office, but waiting outside of it was Christine Schuler. "Well, hi!" I said as I approached her. She turned and smiled.

"Mara!"

"Are you coming back to work for the county?"

"Not exactly. I'm waiting for Carla. She asked me to meet her here today. Moral support, I guess."

"She told you why Detective Ritter wanted her here?"

"She said NCMEC did a new age progression photo on Violet."

The elevator door opened across the hall. Kenya stepped out. She looked more like the Kenya I was used to seeing in a designer suit with her hair pulled tightly back. She smiled upon seeing Christine and me.

"Did Carla call you too?" Christine asked. Kenya came up to her and the two women embraced.

"It's good to see you!" Kenya said. "You haven't aged a bit!"

"Look who's talking," Christine said. "Kenya, you're luminous. Unemployment agrees with you."

Kenya turned to me. "On that note, how'd it go with the firing squad this morning? I'm still sick about all of that."

"It went. Our union rep seems to think I'll have better luck on appeal after Skip successfully fires me."

Kenya had a pained expression. She hissed through her teeth. "Oooh. That's not good. That's not good at all."

"They're firing you?" Christine said. "For helping Carla?"

"They're firing her because Mara has her own brain. Skip Fletcher apparently can't handle strong women."

"Well, that's a problem. Can you go to the EEOC? Or the Ohio Department of Civil Rights? I have a good friend over at ODCR. You should at least talk to her."

"One battlefield at a time," I said.

"Christine's right," Kenya said. "That's good advice. Raise a stink. See if Skip will back off."

Gus stepped off the elevator. He was holding an oversized file under his arm. He paused when he saw the group of us.

"Dr. Schuler!"

"I'm still not a doctor, Detective," she said. Gus gave Christine a hearty handshake. He took out the keys to his office and led the three of us inside.

Gus set the envelope on his desk and started pulling piles of files and other items off the chairs surrounding the table he kept here. Back when he shared the office with Sam, Sam used to keep it tidy and pristine. He always said left to his own devices, Gus might become a hoarder. He had a point, but I also knew Gus had a method to what looked like disorganization to everyone else.

"Have a seat. Anybody need any coffee?"

"Not if it's still that swill I remember," Christine said.

"How do you like working for the private sector?" Kenya asked her.

"It's fantastic. The equipment works. I can make decisions on my own cases without having to go through a committee, and we always have office supplies."

"Sounds like heaven," Kenya said.

"I was hoping you'd say that. Kenya, we could use you. New Hope's parent agency is always in desperate need of administrative law judges. As an ALJ, you'd work from home ninety percent of the time. You'd set your own hours. You'd have full discretion over which cases you want to take. They pay very well, too."

Kenya cocked her head to the side.

"You should do it," I said. "It'd be good for you to get out of the house. You can't build puzzles for the rest of your life."

"Never you mind," Kenya said. She was about to say something else, but there was a light knock on the door. Then Carla Gribaldi poked her head in.

"Is it okay if I come in?"

"Of course," Gus said. "We were just waiting for you."

Christine crossed the room and put her arms out, pulling Carla into an embrace.

"It's so good to see you. I just hate that it's for this. We need to go get lunch. Are you free today?"

"Maybe," Carla said, then she turned to me. "I did the best I could. But Mara, I really think Commissioner Radley has it out for you. Or he's too buddy-buddy with Skip Fletcher."

"I appreciate your going to bat for me," I said. "You didn't have to."

"Well, I at least think I convinced them not to consider that stupid TRO Tony tried to get. I'm so sorry you had to go through that."

"You wanna do this?" Gus said, ever blunt.

"Sorry," I said. "We're cutting into the middle of your day."

"I don't mind," he said. He grabbed the envelope off his desk and opened it. He pulled out an 11x14 photograph and laid it face down on the table. Before any of us could react, Carla reached for it. She picked it up and held it to her chest.

"Carla," Christine started. Carla put up a hand, gesturing that she was okay. Then, she flipped the photograph over and laid it on the table.

I held my breath. NCMEC did such a good job with age progression photos. You couldn't really tell that it was computer generated. It looked just like any other high school girl's yearbook photo. In one corner of the photo was Violet Runyon's real kindergarten photo. In it, she had a crooked smile and a purple ribbon in her hair.

I stared down at the rendering of what Violet might look like now at the age of seventeen.

Brilliant blue eyes. Straight blonde hair parted down the middle. They'd chosen a style popular with teenage girls today. The rendering was beautiful. Luminous. And it looked so very real.

Carla put a hand to her mouth. Christine and Kenya moved in, standing on either side of her like pillars, ready to step in if she started to crumble.

"Violet," she whispered. "Do you really think ..."

"No," Gus said, his tone gruff. "But we can make this public anyway."

I leaned in. Gus caught my eye. I wished Sam were here. It had been admittedly brief, but he'd seen Leesha Stevens for a moment right before she slipped into that car.

Could it be her? I stared at the smiling image. I closed my eyes and tried to picture Leesha. I couldn't say it out loud. It seemed cruel. But yes. Yes. Leesha Stevens looked very much like the age progressed photograph of Violet Runyon. And as of two days ago, Leesha was still very much alive.

25

"You see it. Tell me you see it."

Sam sat across from me at a back table at the Blue Pony Bar and Grill. It was Saturday night. We'd taken a rare night out together. One we both needed. Will played pool with Gus at the front of the bar. If they'd been playing for real money, Will would have wiped out Gus's pension so far.

Sam had the age progression photo of Violet Runyon open on his phone. I'd stared at it for more time than I'd wanted to admit. It haunted me now as much as Christine Schuler's recorded interview with the five-year-old Violet. A freeze frame. A moment in time.

"Sam," I said. "It could be her. You can't rule it out."

He put his phone down. "I was hoping we could talk about something else besides work."

"This isn't work. This is ... important."

"I saw her for a split second. You saw her for maybe thirty seconds."

"Hoyt Marvin says he got information about this Ginger Ivan. It makes sense that it would have come from the woman he was living with. From Leesha. Maybe she knew Ginger Ivan because she had firsthand knowledge of her."

"Except she's not real," Sam said. "That's the part you keep conveniently forgetting. Bart Runyon admitted he made her up."

"What if Bart Runyon is changing his story now because he's scared? Darryl Cox died right after he told me Hoyt Marvin's story. Why wouldn't Bart think he might be next? I told you; he was terrified of something."

"Darryl hung himself. Mara, I know you want this girl to be Violet Runyon. But ..."

"Don't you?"

"What?"

"Don't you want it to be her, too?"

He threw his napkin down. "Yes. Okay? Yes. I'd love it if this thing would have a happy ending. But the world doesn't work that way. You're the last person I thought I'd have to say that to."

"I just want to find her. I need to find her. Leesha, I mean. I know the odds of her actually being Violet Runyon are, well, fantastical. I know that. I hear what I sound like when I say it. It's just, it feels like a loose end. And I promised ... we both promised Carla Gribaldi that we wouldn't leave any of those untied. You know?"

He looked at me. The corner of his mouth curled up and I knew he wasn't mad at me. Frustrated. Exasperated. But not mad.

"You're gonna be the death of me," he said.

"Come on," I said, reaching across the table. I stole one of his French fries. "I make you better."

"You make me better?"

"Yes. Bring you out of your shell."

Sam laughed. "Is that what you call it?"

"Where would you be without me? You'd be all alone in your sad little apartment. Feeding your fish."

"I happen to like my fish. They're quiet. They don't tell me how to do my job."

My smile faded. "I'm not trying to tell you how to do your job."

"No," he said. "I didn't mean it like that. It was a bad joke." He reached across the table and put his hand over mine.

"I am sorry. I've been worried about you, you know. I'm aware how much this case means to you. Has meant to you."

We heard a shout from the pool room as Will sunk another ball. Sam turned toward the sound.

"Kid's cleaning me out!" Gus yelled.

"He's worried about you," I said. "Gus."

Sam turned back to me. "Gus worries too much about everything. He's worried about you, too. He knows what's about to happen to you and wonders why you aren't more worried."

"Is that Gus talking or you?" I asked.

Sam's face fell. "Both. When are you supposed to hear back from Skip's little witch hunt?"

"They told me by the end of the week."

"Mara, what are you going to do if Skip gets you fired?"

"Collect unemployment."

"With a just cause firing?"

"I've got some money saved up. I've got time if things go belly up for me at the prosecutor's office."

"Will you stay?" he asked, his voice dropping an octave.

"Yes," I said. "I'll stay. I'm not that easy to get rid of. Not even for Skip."

"Do you want it that bad?"

"What?"

"Your job. Have you entertained the possibility of maybe just, I don't know, giving up?"

"Roll over? Let Skip win? Is that what you're suggesting?"

"No. Not letting Skip win. But maybe, Skip notwithstanding, you've outgrown being an assistant prosecutor. Maybe your mother has a point. You could make a lot more money in the private sector."

"Ugh. Doing what? Corporate law? Real estate closings?"

"You could still litigate. And no, I don't see you in the business sector. Not like that. But Mara, you're a champion. You know that, right?"

"What do you mean?"

"I mean, you could make a name for yourself doing something you're passionate about. Special education law. You could be an advocate for other kids like Will. For their parents. Or other types of discrimination law. Employment law. Workplace harassment. That sort of thing."

The idea wasn't without appeal. Especially the education law piece.

"To be honest," I said. "Yes. I have thought about that. It's an area that interests me. But I'd have to start from scratch. Completely reinvent myself. That's not easy at my age."

"You sound like you're a hundred. You're not even forty."

"There are no good jobs in that field here, Sam. Not in Maumee County. I'd have to go to a bigger firm. Columbus, probably. I'm not willing to uproot Will."

"Have you asked him about it?"

"He's thirteen."

"Mara, he's worried too."

Sam's expression went grim.

"Has he said that to you? You've talked about it with him?" I asked.

"Don't be mad. He brought it up to me the other day when I had him outside shooting hoops."

"Will you tell me what he said?"

"Not all of it. Some of it was guy talk."

In the last two years, Sam had become a male role model for Will. I was grateful. No matter where things went between Sam and me, I hoped both Will and I could always count Sam as a friend.

"What can you tell me?" I asked.

"He said he wants you to be happy. He's not sure being a prosecutor always makes you happy. And he worries about the money."

"He shouldn't. This is something we've talked about. A lot. I blame Jason for it to some extent. He wanted Will to be literate in personal finance. So do I. But Jason wasn't always good at understanding what Will could handle. He assumes that Will's brain works the same way his does."

Sam smiled. "Will's brain works his own way."

"I'm glad you see that. And I'll talk to him. I have been talking to him. Whatever the review board decides to do with me, I'll handle it."

Gus and Will came back from the pool room. Gus carried a giant basket of curly fries. Will grabbed a handful.

"Boy, I don't know where you put it all," Gus said.

"I know. He ate a double cheeseburger and onion rings already."

"You're growing like a weed," Gus said. "By the end of the summer, he's gonna be taller than me."

"I grew two point eight inches in six months," Will said. "How tall are you, Uncle Gus?"

"Five nine," he said.

Will scrunched up his face. "You might want to stop eating the fries. I'm guessing your BMI is hovering near thirty? That puts you in the obesity category. At your age, the heart attack and stroke risk increases. When's the last time you had your cholesterol checked? Or your A1c levels?"

Gus reached across the table and grabbed a handful of fries. "I'm healthy as a horse, kid."

Sam and I both covered our mouths to suppress a laugh. Had anyone but Will said something like that to him, Gus would have ripped them a new anus.

"I've been swimming at the YMCA," Will said. "It's part of a program at school. I want to add a day to my workout though. Will you pick me up on Saturday? We can work out together. Laps would be good for you. Less stress on your joints. I heard it's good for sciatica too. You said your right leg's been bothering you. It's probably from how you wear your gun belt."

Sam's eyes widened. I was afraid to take a breath.

"How about you pick me up at eight?" Will said. "They also do water aerobics for the Silver Sneakers club. It'd be good for you."

"Silver Sneakers?" Gus said. I gave him credit for not adding the four letter word I knew he was thinking of.

"Sounds like you've got a date," Sam said. "Unless you're planning on disappointing Will."

Gus actually growled. But he didn't say no. Sam reached across the table and knocked knuckles with my son.

We finished our meal and drinks. Despite my offer to pick up the check, Gus wouldn't hear of it. He paid for everyone. I thanked him and we started to make our way to the parking lot. Gus hung back. He and the bar's owner, Paula, had an on-and-off-again fling. They were currently off, but Gus was trying to rectify it. I caught Paula smiling while he played pool with Will.

Sam walked Will and me to my car. As we started to say our goodbyes, Sam's phone rang. Will slipped into the passenger side as Sam held up a finger to me and answered.

I waited by the driver's side door as Sam's face went through a series of expressions, settling on a deep frown.

"Okay," he said. "Thanks for giving me a heads-up. I'd like to see for myself if you don't mind. Right. I'll let her know."

I looked back. Will had his face in his phone, oblivious to us. Sam gestured for me to step away from the car out of earshot anyway.

"What is it?"

Gus walked out of the bar. He was also talking on his phone, his expression just as sour as Sam's. He hung up and jerked his chin at Sam. From all their years working as partners, the two of them still shared a special unspoken language.

"That was Detective Tara Langley. Over in Holden County. Hoyt Marvin was found shot to death in his car. He was in a park just near an overpass along the Maumee River."

"What?"

"They called Kevin Barnum to head over and make a positive identification. Hoyt doesn't have a next of kin."

"Shot to death," I said. "Hoyt was murdered. Or did he do it himself?"

"Unclear," Gus said. He'd obviously taken a call on the same matter. I didn't like the way Gus and Sam looked at each other.

"What is it? You guys?"

"Mara, he wasn't alone," Sam said. "There was a woman in the car with him. No positive identification, but the ME says she's young, blonde, thin, blue-eyed."

"Oh God. Sam. Leesha?"

"We don't know that. Not yet," Gus said. "I'll head out there."

I turned back to the car. "I want to go with you."

"Mara ..."

"I know what Leesha looks like. I'll know if it's her. Let me drop Will off with Kat and Bree. Will you let me come with you?"

Sam turned to me. I knew he wanted to say no. But he also knew I was right.

"Yeah," he said. "We'll all go together. Gus, let them know we'll be there within the hour."

26

Detective Tara Langley was a female version of Gus. She'd been a one-woman band in Holden County, one county over from us, for over a decade, handling every homicide, mugging, and sexual assault solo. She stood five feet in comfortable shoes and had a head of wiry silver hair she wore closely cropped.

"Thanks for getting down here so quickly," she said.

"Thanks for giving me a heads-up," Sam said. Langley pointed to the gold badge hanging from his neck.

"Congratulations on that. I was sorry to hear about Bill Clancy, but they couldn't have put a better guy in to replace him."

"I appreciate it," Sam said.

We met at the Holden County Hospital. Tara used her ID badge to key us in a side door. We went down a long hallway, passing the pharmacy and blood lab. When we reached a black metal door, Langley banged on it. We heard a click. Langley turned the handle and the three of us went inside.

I heard two voices. One I recognized as Kevin Barnum. He'd texted me he was twenty minutes ahead of us. We walked down a smaller interior hallway to an office across from the main examining room. The shades were drawn to it.

"Dr. Pulaski?" Tara Langley called out.

"In here, Tara," a gruff male voice answered. We walked in together, crowding Dr. Pulaski's small office. He sat behind his desk. Kevin stood leaning against one wall. He pushed himself off it and shook hands with Langley and Sam.

"You all know each other?" Pulaski asked.

"We do," Langley said. "Oh. But this is Mara Brent. She's the prosecutor down in Maumee County ... er ... are you still?"

"Assistant," I said. "And as of this moment, yes."

"They're trying to get rid of her," Kevin offered. "Completely bogus."

"I heard something about that," Pulaski said. He was maybe sixty, dyed brown hair and taut, tanned skin that I surmised had been surgically lifted.

"She won't go down without a fight," Sam said. "And Mara's got more people in her corner than Skip Fletcher does."

"I worked with him some," Tara said. "He was an assistant pros here for about ten minutes. Practically incompetent. Could barely figure out how to introduce evidence at trial. Of course, that was a while ago. He was fresh out of law school. Still, he had a shitty attitude. The kind that felt ingrained."

"Nothing much has changed then," Sam said.

I didn't want to go too far into the mud on Skip Fletcher. I didn't know Pulaski or Langley well at all. I also felt a buzz of emotions, wondering what we'd find on the other side of those blinds in the lab across the hall.

"I really appreciate you indulging me coming down here," I said. "Kevin, have you had a chance to make a positive ID?"

Pulaski rose from his desk chair. "We got to shooting the breeze. Kevin and I used to play in a golf league together a hundred years ago. His wife's my second wife's second cousin or something like that."

"Small world," I said.

"Big family," Kevin answered.

Pulaski picked his ID badge up from the desk and led the group of us across the hall to his lab.

"Haven't had a chance to do the full postmortem on either of the victims yet. It's just me tonight. I've got my assistants coming in first thing in the morning. Is that soon enough for you, Tara?"

"It'll be fine," she said.

Pulaski unlocked the lab and led us in. It was pristine and clean. He led us down another short hallway to the cold room with a wall of drawers. Pulaski went to one right in the center and opened it. A black body bag lay on a metal slab.

I moved in beside Kevin Barnum. Pulaski carefully unzipped the bag and pulled back the plastic, exposing the body from head to the top of the chest.

Sam came in right behind me. I'd seen dead bodies before. The pungent smell of death hung in the air. Sticky. Sour. Metallic. There's no mistaking it.

"That's Hoyt Marvin, all right," Kevin said.

Marvin's brown hair was slicked back, wet with blood. His eyes were still open, pearled, and staring vacantly at the ceiling. Even I could see one pupil blown. His left temple had a gaping hole through it. I didn't look too closely at it.

"Entrance wound through the left temple," Tara said. She peered in closer. "Exit through the right."

"Close range," Pulaski said. "Powder burns to the left temple."

"The weapon was held right against his head," Sam said.

"Could he have done it to himself?" I asked.

"I don't want to draw conclusions yet," Pulaski said. "I'll know more after my full exam. His hands were bagged at the scene, but there were no visible signs of powder residue on them."

"And no weapon was found at the scene," Tara said. "Doesn't seem self-inflicted. At least not on the face of it."

"Did you find his cell phone on him?" Sam asked.

Tara shook her head. "No. No wallet either."

"Could have been a robbery," Sam said.

"It's a good guess. I'm just getting into it though."

"The woman," I said. "There was a woman in the car with him?"

"Not in the car," Tara said. Kevin and I stepped back. Pulaski closed the drawer, locked it, and walked further down the row.

"She was found about twenty yards away from the vehicle, face down in a ditch. Shot in the back."

"She was running away?" Sam said.

"Could be. I mean, probably," Tara said.

"If it was a robbery," I said. "She tried to escape. Ran out of the car?"

"That's my working theory," Tara said.

I tried to keep myself from imagining it. If it was Leesha. If Leesha was really Violet. I knew how farfetched it all sounded. But after all of this. All these years. To die like that.

And even if it was the more likely scenario having nothing to do with Violet Runyon. Hoyt Marvin was bad news. He was involved with trafficking young girls and no matter who was in that drawer, she met her end because of her association with him. She was someone's daughter.

Pulaski unlocked the drawer. "She's pretty," he said. "Or might have been at one time. This girl had a hard life and a hard death. She's got some fresh injuries that probably aren't related to the way she died. She was sexually assaulted probably within the last couple of days."

He opened the drawer. I felt a little lightheaded and I was never one to get queasy in these situations.

She was someone's daughter.

Sam sensed a change in me and moved closer. I put my hand up, indicating that I was all right.

Pulaski reached for the zipper on the body bag and slowly pulled it down. A tuft of blonde hair poked out.

I didn't know what to wish for. That it was Leesha? That it wasn't? I found myself wanting to be anywhere but here. At the same time, I knew in my soul it was my job to bear witness. It didn't matter what Skip Fletcher did to me. It didn't matter what Tony Gribaldi or even Bart Runyon wanted. Darryl Cox had set me on this path. I would see it through.

She was still pretty. Waxen, bloodless. She might have had full lips in life, but now they were parched and white.

I stepped closer. One of her false eyelashes had come unglued. It rested against her swollen cheek. The mother in me rose up. I wanted to wipe it away.

"Do you recognize this girl?" Tara Langley asked me.

I looked closer. She had a chipped front tooth and a slight overbite. She was fine-boned like Leesha Stevens. Her wispy blonde hair rested against her shoulder on one side. From here, I could see it going all the way down to almost the top of her breast. There was a coarseness to her features. A broad, flat nose. Her left ear was pierced multiple times. She wore pink rhinestones in each hole, all the way from the lobe to the curve near her temple.

"It's not her," I said. "This isn't Leesha Stevens."

Sam moved in closer. He cocked his head to the side.

"You're sure?"

"I'm sure. Leesha's hair was shoulder length at best. This girl's is longer. And her nose is different."

"They sure do have a similar look though," Sam said. "Hoyt Marvin had a definite type."

"They usually do," Tara said. "You sure you've never seen this girl before? Any of you?"

Kevin got closer. "I've not seen her before. But I'll agree every girlfriend I ever knew Hoyt Marvin to have ... looked like her. Blonde. Blue-eyed, no taller than five three."

"This one's maybe five foot two," Pulaski said.

"It's not her," I repeated. Once again, I didn't know how to feel. She wasn't Leesha. But she was someone. And I had no doubt in my mind that if she hadn't hooked up with Hoyt Marvin, she might still be alive.

"What a waste," I whispered. "Do you have a theory as to how old she might be?"

"Rough guess, between eighteen and twenty-five."

"We'll find out who she is," Tara said. "We'll take care of her."

I looked more closely at Tara Langley. I didn't know her well at all. Had only met her once before, years ago. But she was choking up. It wasn't just me. There was something about this girl.

"I really appreciate you letting us come down," I said.

"As soon as you know more, give me a call," Sam said to Langley.

"You think this has anything to do with your inmate's death?" Langley asked.

"It's hard to say."

"Hoyt was on borrowed time," Kevin said. "He was back in the life. For a while, I thought he'd maybe turn himself around. Unfortunately, I think he met the end he was always destined for. Hoyt was a big talker. He got mixed up with dangerous people and always thought he knew better. I tried to warn him."

"I just wish he didn't take this girl down with him."

There was nothing left for us to do. Pulaski and Langley thanked us all again. Sam and I walked out to the parking lot. Kevin had parked a little further away.

I climbed into the passenger seat. Sam pulled out. He didn't say much the whole way back. When he stopped in front of my house, I could still see lights on in Will's room. It was past ten o'clock.

"Thanks for doing this," I said. "All of this. I know how far this all is from any active case in Maumee County."

Sam stared straight ahead. He gripped the steering wheel.

"What is it?" I asked.

He gritted his teeth.

"Are you mad at me?"

Sam turned to me, his expression pained. "No. God. No. It's just ... I think ... dammit. I think you're right. God help me, I think you're right. About all of it."

"What do you mean?"

"I mean, there's something going on. I can feel it. I don't know if it has anything to do with Violet Runyon. But ... my gut instinct is telling me it's worth another look."

"You're reopening her case?"

"It was never officially closed. That girl in there. She's not Violet. But maybe Leesha is. Or maybe you're right that she's the one who knows something about this stupid Ginger Ivan."

"You said she doesn't exist. Runyon made her up."

"Runyon is a liar. Who knows if anything he said is true? But ... there's something going on. I feel it too. I finally feel it too."

I leaned over and kissed him. "I'm sorry. Well, I'm not sorry. But thank you for believing me."

Sam nodded. "I'll talk to you tomorrow."

We said our goodbyes. I walked through the garage. I heard voices coming from upstairs. Will was upset about something.

I found him and Kat in Will's Lego room. He was standing over a partial model he'd built of a *Titanic* lifeboat. He was agitated, hitting his fist against his left leg.

"Thank God you're back," Kat said. "Will, it's okay. See? Your mom is okay."

"Will, honey? What is it?"

Will turned to me. "It's not right. Something's not right."

"What's not right?"

Will went to the window. He opened the shade. We could just see Sam's tail lights as he made his way down the driveway.

"They were here," Will said. "Someone was here."

"No one was here," Kat said. "He's been like this for an hour."

"Who was here?" I asked.

"You don't understand. Neither of you understand. But I do. I know. Someone's been in this room. In this house. Things are different. I know it."

A cold chill went down my spine. "What are you talking about?"

"They've been moved. The pieces have been moved. You both know not to touch them. But someone's been in this room. Someone who wasn't supposed to be."

Kat threw up her hands. "There's an alarm. We checked the whole house, Will. No one is here."

Will shook his head and looked at me. "Mom, I'm telling you. Somebody's been in the house. Get Sam. Get the police."

My throat ran dry. I pulled my cell phone out of my pocket and dialed Sam.

27

"They won't listen," Will said to Sam. "They think I'm crazy."

"Nobody thinks you're crazy, buddy," I said. For the last hour, Sam sat with Will while two deputies searched the house and the woods behind us. I had a secluded lot at the end of a country road. It's why Jason wanted the place. Acres of natural woods. Complete privacy. At the time, he said he never wanted to have a neighbor again for as long as he lived. Now he'd spend the next twenty or so years living in a 7x12 foot double cell.

Deputy Pam Pappas came in through the back slider. She carried her Maglite flashlight in one hand and quickly switched it off. She wiped her feet on the mat.

"All clear, boss," she said. "Looks like you had some raccoons upend your garbage can, but there's no sign of anybody back there. It's pretty dark though. If you want me to come back first thing in the morning, I can do another sweep."

"Sam," Will said. "I know where I put my Lego pieces. They were moved. Knocked over. Mom didn't do that. Aunt Kat didn't do that. The cleaning lady comes on Mondays. This happened today. It happened tonight while we were gone."

Sam and Deputy Pappas exchanged a look.

"There's nothing missing in the house?" Sam asked me for the third time.

"Nothing," I said. "The door to my study wasn't locked. My computer's still there. I've got a jewelry box sitting on my dresser in the bedroom. Everything's still there. I keep my engagement ring in the top compartment."

Sam made a silent gesture. "Show me."

He left Will sitting at the kitchen table with Kat. I led Sam upstairs. My bedroom was the first door on the left.

"Right here," I said, pointing to a small cedar jewelry box I got from my mother.

"You really need a safe for that stuff, Mara."

"I have one. I put the stuff I care about inside of it." I opened the box. My two-carat engagement ring sat nestled in its velvet lining. I hadn't worn the thing in almost two years.

"What about your alarm system? I didn't want to ask you in front of Will. He's upset enough. You set it, right? Please tell me you set it before you left for the Blue Pony."

Sam went to the control panel for the elaborate alarm system he'd recommended for me. He'd supervised its installation. He flipped up the cover and punched a few numbers in.

"I don't know," I said, feeling a sick ball of dread form in my stomach. "I might have forgotten to arm it when we left. We were in a hurry. Will was working on one of his models and I had trouble getting him out the door."

"What's the code?" Sam asked.

"Same one you programmed," I said.

Sam scowled. "You were supposed to change it." He punched the code in.

"Last armed at ten p.m.," he read from the panel. "Disarmed this morning at seven."

"I disarmed it when I took Will to school. Ugh. Sam, I forgot. I totally forgot."

Sam flipped the panel closed. "Don't beat yourself up over it. You said nothing's been taken."

I sat on the storage bench I had at the foot of my bed. "Will's going to figure that all out, too. He'll read the alarm system data just like you did."

Sam turned to me. "Do you think he's right about the Lego pieces? It was just so specific."

I met Sam's stare. "You know him. Will's particular about that stuff. If he says the pieces were moved, they were probably moved. But that doesn't mean someone was in here who shouldn't have been."

"No sign of forced entry anywhere. Your system was disarmed, but the doors were all still locked. Your furnace is still on. You don't have any open windows."

"Not that I know of. The window to Will's model room is always locked."

"It's on the second floor," Sam said. He walked back out into the hallway. I followed him. We went to Will's model room across the hall.

"It doesn't make any sense," I said. "Let's assume for a second someone did break in ... why on earth would they just mess around with a bunch of Legos and leave everything of value untouched?"

"I'll say it again ... do you believe him?"

"Yes," I said. "I believe the pieces he said were moved, were moved. I'm just not convinced it was because of some sinister reason."

"That's where I'm at with this, too."

Kat walked into the room. "He's a little calmer," she said. "Deputy Pappas took him outside to walk the perimeter with her again."

"That's a good idea," I said. "Let him see for himself."

"Mara, Will's not acting like himself. He knew where you were going tonight when you dropped him off."

"I told him," I said. "He was there when Gus and Sam took the calls."

Kat nodded. "You know how he gets. He can become a little obsessed with whatever cases you're trying. He's been doing a lot of online reading about what happened to Darryl Cox. He's convinced Gus is wrong. That it wasn't a suicide."

I let out a sigh and stared up at the ceiling.

"I'll talk to him again," Sam said. He gave me a light touch on the elbow, smiled, then went downstairs to find Will.

"It's getting bad again, isn't it?" I said to Kat. I'd been down this road with my son before. He could obsess over the more morbid aspects of some of the cases I worked on.

"It's been worse," she said. "But you know Will. He's taking this ... um ... flux in your career pretty hard. He's worried about what happens if you lose your job."

I put my hand up. "I can't keep having this conversation."

"I know. I know. And look, I don't have an explanation for whatever's going on with his Lego pieces ..."

"You think he's wrong about it? I mean, it's Will we're talking about."

Kat shrugged. "I think ... well ... I believe that Will believes he saw something strange. I'm just wondering if maybe his mind is playing tricks on him with all the stress he's taking on for himself."

"Kat," I said. "I forgot to turn the house alarm on when we left to go to the restaurant tonight."

"I heard. But you said nothing's been stolen. Mara, nothing else has been disturbed in the house except for Will's stuff in here. Like I said. I believe *he* believes things were messed with. It's just ..."

"You think it's in his head?"

She bit her lip. Worry lines creased her forehead.

"It's okay," I said. "You can say it."

"He's not lying. I wanna be very clear about that. I just think he's letting his mind run wild. I've seen this coming on for a while."

"Me too," I sighed.

"It's going to get better. You'll sort out your stuff at work. That'll help. If Will knows there isn't going to be some major lifestyle upheaval, he'll settle again. It's going to be fine. Look. He's got spring break coming up. Bree and I were thinking of heading down to Orlando. I was going to ask you about it. See if you'd be okay with us taking Will. He's been wanting to go to Disney World. If you're still in work limbo, maybe you could come too."

I went to her. I opened my arms and hugged Kat.

"I honestly don't know what I'd do without you. That's a fantastic plan. I can't say for sure what my schedule will allow. But yes. If you're serious. If you wouldn't mind having Will with you ..."

"We'd love it!" Kat said. "It'll be a blast. Bree will have someone to stand in line with her at the rides they both like. I hate that stuff. I'd rather find an air-conditioned restaurant at Epcot and tour the different countries."

"Well, if I go down with you, that sounds like my speed, too. Why don't you go tell him? Maybe it'll take his mind off all of this."

"It's going to be okay," she said. "I promise. You've gotten through a hell of a lot worse than one crappy boss."

Kat and I walked back down to the kitchen together. Sam sat at the table with Will. My son was still frowning, but somehow seemed calmer. He'd just finished his walk outside with Deputy Pappas. Once again, she found no signs of anything amiss out there.

"Will," Sam said. "If you'd feel better, I can have a crew stay right outside tonight."

"You can't use county resources for that," Will said. "They'll tell you you have a conflict of interest. It won't be good for my mom."

I opened my mouth to argue. To tell him he shouldn't worry about things like that. But my almost thirteen-year-old son had a point. "We'll be okay," I said. "I'll arm the alarm system as soon as you leave. The front and back door cameras are good to go."

The deputies left through the front door. Kat said a brief goodbye. As Will made his way back upstairs to check on his model room, Sam and I had a brief moment alone.

"Sorry for all the trouble," I said.

"It's no trouble. I'd rather come out here for a false alarm a thousand times than be wrong."

"Kat says Will's internalizing everything that's going on with my career situation. She thinks that's what's driving this."

"She's probably right."

I walked with Sam out the side door. He'd parked his car at an angle in front of my garage.

"I'm going to have to come up with a game plan," I said. "If Skip gets his way."

"You'll appeal. And you'll win."

"I know. It's just ... I hate what it's doing to that kid up there."

"Do you want me to stay tonight? I can sleep in the guest room."

It was a bridge Sam and I had yet to cross. The truth was, I did want him to stay. But it wasn't the kind of thing either of us wanted to spring on Will. Not yet. My career wasn't the only thing in flux, it seemed.

"We'll be okay. Really. And thank you."

Sam pulled me into a brief embrace. "I'll call you first thing in the morning. Langley should have more information on Hoyt Marvin's murder. We're going to figure out who that girl was and get her back to her family."

"What a nightmare," I said.

Sam kissed the top of my head. "Try to get some sleep. We'll all have fresher minds in the morning. I meant what I said. I'm all in, Mara. Wherever this thing leads us. We're going to find Leesha Stevens and figure out what she knows about Violet's case."

"If anything," I whispered.

"If anything."

Sam let me go. I walked up to the front porch and waved as he drove off one more time.

It was late. Past midnight. As I walked in, I could hear Will running the bath upstairs. His nightly ritual. It didn't matter how tired he was. How late it got. He would take a bath every night before going to bed.

I went into the kitchen and poured myself a glass of wine. I drank it right there at the kitchen sink, staring out the window into the woods.

Deputy Pappas had left the floodlight on. A thousand tiny flying insects swirled around the bulb. She'd put the trash bin on the wrong side of the porch. I'd move it in the morning.

The wine went down easy. I poured myself another glass. Then I went to the wall next to the slider and turned off the floodlight.

As I turned away from the window, something caught the corner of my eye. Movement.

I turned back. There was nothing there but the thick, dark woods. Early April and the leaves were springing forth on every branch. In another week or two, they'd be fully green.

I heard the water draining from the tub directly above me. I finished my wine and headed up to tuck Will in.

There. Again. A flash of movement from the corner of my eye. I turned back to the wall and hit the floodlight.

A breeze kicked up, making the branches shimmer. That's all it was. I was just jumpy. I flicked off the light and headed upstairs.

28

He didn't want to leave me. Will was agitated as I drove him to school on Monday morning.

"I should stay home with you," he had said. He listed a dozen reasons that made no sense. He could help me clean. He would make me lunch. He would help me balance the checkbook.

"I barely write checks anymore, Will. There's nothing to balance," I told him. It tore at me as we sat in the drop-off line. But I knew what his therapist would say. Will thrived on routine. We had to set boundaries around his obsessions.

"I'll pick you up at two thirty," I said. "You don't have robotics today. Think about what you'd like for dinner. I can make something. We can go out. Whatever you like."

He had stared out the car window, his backpack in his lap. Finally, without further warning, he launched himself out of the car and walked into the building, never looking back.

Now, I sat at the kitchen table, my oversized coffee mug almost empty. My doubts plagued me. Had I done the right thing?

Should I call Dr. Vera, his therapist? Was this the beginning of a crisis for Will? For me? He'd handled so much upheaval in the last couple of years. My divorce. His father's move to D.C. Then his arrest and conviction. Will had made the recent and very grown-up decision not to visit Jason or correspond with him for the time being.

I jumped when my phone rang. It skittered across the granite countertop as it vibrated. Sam's caller ID popped up.

"Good morning," I answered. Leaving the phone where it was, I clicked the speaker button.

"How was he this morning?"

"Unsettled. I just hope he has a decent day."

"He will. I can stop by later after work. Shoot some hoops with him."

"He'd like that. I'm leaving it up to him what he wants to do for dinner. But you're invited. We might go out or I might cook."

"Spaghetti then," Sam teased. Then he switched gears.

"I heard back from Tara Langley. They made a positive ID on the female shooting victim. She's a runaway. One of ours. Her name was Courtney Mack. Nineteen years old. She went missing from her mother's house six years ago. There was a custody dispute between Courtney's paternal grandmother and her mom. The kid ran away constantly. The mother had a drug problem. There was an abuse and neglect case opened when she was eleven. The last time she ran off, she never came back."

"How awful," I said. "Has her mother been notified?"

"No one to notify so far. Her mother passed away four years ago. Her father died a couple of years after she was born. That's why the grandma was in the picture. She's gone now too. Died last year. Neighbor said it was a stroke."

"So, she has no family at all?"

"Not that I can find."

My heart hurt just thinking about it. "She had nobody. She never had a chance."

"No," Sam said. "I'm trying not to think too hard about what that kid's life must have been like these last six years. Tara said Dr. Pulaski found evidence of past abuse. Multiple old bone fractures. Some healed burn marks."

"Oh Sam," I said. My thoughts immediately turned to Violet Runyon. "It makes me not know what to wish for in terms of Violet. If the best-case scenario is that Bart really did hand her off to someone ... you and I both know what could have happened."

"I know. And look, there's nothing so far to connect this case with Violet's in any way. I just wanted to let you know where we're at with it. I'm working on getting the court records on Courtney Mack over to Langley."

"I'm sure she appreciates it. And so do I."

"I'll see you later, okay? Don't beat yourself up about Will. He's okay."

"I know."

I clicked off the call and stared into my coffee mug. In my imagination, Courtney Mack's lifeless face superimposed itself over the age progression photo I had of Violet Runyon. It was like I said to Sam. I didn't know what to hope for.

Was it better if Violet's father had killed her all those years ago? Or that he'd really done what he claimed. Handed her off to some monster to lead a life like Courtney's. Or Leesha Stevens. Or any number of other lost girls I couldn't save.

I took my mug to the sink and rinsed it out. The dishwasher was full. I'd meant to empty it after I got home last night but everything had gone sideways. I looked out at the woods. Blades of grass glittered with fresh dew and I could see the depressions of Deputy Pappas's footprints.

She'd left her smaller Maglite, the one she'd let Will borrow when the two of them went back outside. I made a mental note to give it to Sam tonight so he could get it back to her.

I upended my mug and put it in the drying rack next to the sink. When I looked back out the window, I saw a shadow behind me, reflected in the glass.

My nerve endings caught fire. Slowly, I reached for the flashlight. It was small, thin, but hard. The knife block was too far away.

The alarm hadn't tripped. I'd set it when I came back home. I knew it. Will made me promise. The cameras were pointed to the front and back door. Had I left the garage door open when I came back from dropping Will off? I must have. The alarm wouldn't have gone off if someone came through the open garage. All these thoughts raced through my head at lightning speed in the span of one second.

Then slowly, gripping Deputy Pappas's flashlight, I turned around.

She stood at the doorway to the garage. Her face smudged with dirt. Her tee shirt wrinkled. Grass stains smeared over the knees of her light denim jeans.

"Leesha," I said.

She took a step toward me. She hugged herself, holding one arm tightly around her waist with the other.

"I won't hurt you," she said, her voice ragged. "That's not why I'm here."

"You broke into my house last night, didn't you?"

"I didn't break in. You keep your garage door unlocked."

"You broke into my *house!*"

"You said you could help me. You gave me your card. I waited. I saw you leave with your son this morning. I didn't want to scare him."

The tension went out of me. This wasn't a woman standing in front of me. This was another frightened child. She trembled as she took a step toward me. Her eyes went to the basket on my counter. It was filled with blueberry muffins Kat had brought over the day before yesterday.

"Are you hungry?" I found myself asking.

Leesha froze. I thought of Courtney Mack. No mother. No family. Alone. As angry as I was that this girl had come to my home. As worried as I was about what it could have meant for Will. He had been right this whole time. And yet ... this was a child before me. A trauma survivor. She was lost. And I had offered her my help.

"Here," I said. "Come sit at the table. Do you like orange juice?"

With halting steps, Leesha did as I asked her. I put the muffin basket in front of her. I went to the fridge then poured her a glass of juice.

She kept one hand under the table but inhaled both the juice and the muffin, her fingers shaking.

"Have another one," I said. "Eat the whole basket if you'd like. Can I make you an egg or something?"

Leesha shook her head. A slow tear made its way down her cheek. "Thank you," she said.

"Can I call someone for you?" I asked. "What is it that you wanted me to do for you?"

She met my gaze. Those piercing blue eyes of hers cut through me. The question swirled in my mind. Could it be her? Was this Violet?

"Is he dead?"

"Who, honey?"

"Hoyt. Is he dead?"

I let out a breath. "Yes."

"You're sure?"

"I'm very sure. Yes. He was shot. There was a girl with him. Courtney Mack. Did you know her?"

Leesha was small to begin with. Maybe five foot one, one hundred pounds. As she sat at my kitchen table, she managed to make herself even smaller.

"Did you know Courtney?"

Leesha closed her eyes. "Hoyt knew a lot of girls. He was ... it's not like you think."

"What's it like, Leesha?"

"He tried. You know. To get me out."

"Your neighbor said she saw you covered in bruises. Saw you thrown out of a moving vehicle. Hoyt couldn't really protect you. And he didn't protect Courtney Mack."

Leesha met my eyes. "What do you mean?"

"She's dead too, honey. Courtney Mack was shot with Hoyt."

She went very still. Then she pushed the muffins and juice away.

"I shouldn't have come here."

"But you did. Leesha, do you have someone? Family? Anyone I can call for you?"

She shook her head. "There's nobody. There's just me."

"Hoyt was murdered," I said. "So was Courtney. I met with the detective who's handling the case. Her name is Tara Langley. She's very good at what she does. Will you talk to her?"

"I don't know anything. I haven't seen Hoyt in a few days. He was ... he threw me out. He said I was going to get him killed."

"Why?"

Leesha closed her eyes. She drew her legs up to the seat of the chair and hugged them against her body.

"Honey, you came here for a reason. You want my help. I told you the first time I met you, there are places you can go. Places where girls like you can get a fresh start. Resources. Support."

"I'm not going to some shelter. Or some group home. I won't do it."

"Do you know who might have wanted to hurt Hoyt?"

"Everyone wanted to hurt Hoyt."

"Right. What about Darryl Cox?"

She blinked. "I don't know Darryl Cox."

"Hoyt did. They were cellmates. I know you know that. I know you were in the house when I came out to talk to Hoyt. You heard everything. You ..."

"This was a mistake. I should go."

She started to get up. I resisted the urge to reach for her. If she ran, I couldn't physically restrain her.

"Leesha! You came into my home. Why?"

"I don't know! I just thought ... you seemed different."

"Different from what?"

"You want me to talk to the cops?"

"You know who I am. What I do for a living?"

Leesha turned to face me, dropping her feet back to the floor. "I read what they're saying about you. You're asking a lot of questions. You got in trouble for not reporting what you knew to your boss. I figured maybe that means you know. You do, right?"

"Know what?"

She rubbed a hand across her face hard. She kept her other arm behind her. "I don't know where else to go. Hoyt kicked me out. I can't go anywhere because you came looking for me. Because you started asking all those questions. Saying her name. Now everyone thinks I'm working with the cops anyway. If Hoyt's dead, what chance do I have?"

"You did the right thing coming here. I can help you."

"You'll let me stay?"

"What?" It dawned on me then what she intended. "Leesha, no. I can't hide you here. This is my home. I live here with my son. But there are people. Good people that I trust. Let me reach out for you."

"Don't you get it? Don't you see what's been happening?"

"It was you," I said. "Hoyt had what he thought was an ace in the hole. Information about a trafficking ring that went all the way back to a woman. Ginger Ivan. She's real, isn't she? That's what this is about. You heard me talking to Hoyt. You know this has to do with that missing girl."

Leesha froze. Her face went white.

"He shouldn't have said that."

"You know something too, don't you? Do you know who Ginger Ivan is? Leesha, you can tell me. It's time."

"This was a mistake."

"It wasn't. It's the first completely right thing you've done. How do you know Ginger Ivan?"

"I don't. You don't know what you're talking about."

"Hoyt blabbed. He got scared in jail and blabbed to Darryl Cox. Then Darryl tried to bargain with the information Hoyt gave him. To me. Darryl thought I could get his charges dropped. So, what else did Hoyt tell Darryl about Ginger

Ivan? You know. I can see it in your face. You know something, too."

Leesha rose out of her chair. She started to pace in front of the kitchen island. The girl tore strands of hair out.

"I can help get you somewhere safe. I promise. Tell me what happened to you. Did she take you too? Ginger? Someone you trusted gave you to her. Is that what happened?"

Leesha stopped pacing. We both froze, staring at each other.

"You don't know what you're talking about," she said. "You have no idea what you're messing around with."

"So, tell me. What happened to you, honey? Where is your family?"

"I never had a family. Not a real one. I ran away when I was twelve years old."

"Where'd you run away from? How old are you now?"

"Eighteen," she answered. "I was in foster care down in Allen County. It was horrible. I wouldn't even put a dog in the houses I lived in. That's why I'm telling you. I won't go to another group home. Never again. I'd rather someone shoot me like they shot Courtney."

I thought about what Sam had said on the phone. Courtney Mack's body bore signs of systematic and long-standing physical abuse. I caught myself looking at Leesha's arms. I saw nothing obvious, but that meant nothing.

She walked back over to the table and sat down.

"You don't have to go anywhere like where you've been," I said. "You're eighteen. You can choose your destiny. But I can put you in touch with people. The right people. You can go to school. Have a fresh start. Live in your own place."

"I never had that. My own place. My mom? She was strung out as far back as I can remember. My fourth birthday party, she passed out in the middle of it. I had to call 9-1-1. I was four! That's the first time they put me in foster care. She got me out, but it never lasted long. Then she died. I was seven. I was the one who found her. She wouldn't wake up."

Seven years old. Leesha remembered her mother.

"What about your dad?" I asked.

Leesha shook her head. "I met him once. I think I was five. He and my mom got back together for a bit, but it didn't last. He hit her a lot. Then he hit me."

She wasn't Violet Runyon. If she was telling the truth, she couldn't be.

"I'm sorry that happened to you," I said.

"There were some nice places," she said. "One family I stayed with wasn't so bad. But they had to move. The dad lost his job."

"Leesha, will you tell me about Ginger?" She hadn't mentioned Violet. I had to be careful not to put words in her mouth.

"We called her Aunt Ginger. She owned one of the houses I lived in with some other girls. I ran away from one of the foster homes they put me in. I was on the street for a few weeks. Then I met some other kids, and they took me home. To Ginger's house. It was nice there, at first. She was nice. Then ... she wasn't. Some very bad men came on motorcycles."

"How old were you?"

Leesha shrugged. "Right after I turned thirteen. One by one, the girls at the house started coming back with bruises. And stories. Then they stopped coming back at all. Then, they came for me."

"Who came for you?"

"Bad men. She told me it would be fun. That they were just going to take me for a ride on their motorcycles."

"Motorcycles. A biker gang?" Bits and pieces of what Kevin Barnum knew about Hoyt came to my mind. Hoyt had tried to join a motorcycle club. They wouldn't have him. He'd been thrown out and beaten.

Leesha froze.

"What about Hoyt?" I asked. "Was he a member?"

She shook her head. "They'd never have somebody like Hoyt. Small potatoes, they used to say. But he was nice to me. Hoyt took care of me after they ... after it got bad sometimes. Then one day, there was a raid and Aunt Ginger stopped coming. For weeks. Everyone stopped coming around. We had no money. No food. Hoyt came. He said I could come live with him. I told you. He took care of me. He was the only one who ever cared."

My blood curdled, knowing exactly how well Hoyt had taken care of this girl.

"I know what you're thinking. But I had a roof over my head with Hoyt. We had food on the table. I told you. There were worse things than Hoyt."

"He saved you from Ginger's house. From the motorcycle club."

She nodded. "I knew he'd get killed for it. I told him. Warned him. I belong to them. We all do. Nobody gets out. Me and the other girls. Aunt Ginger told us she'd protect us. But she was a liar. She was the one who let them take us away on their bikes."

"Leesha, who were they? The bikers? If it was a gang, I know you know their name. You have to. You can tell me."

Nothing. She clammed up.

"Where was the house, Leesha? Aunt Ginger's house. Do you know the address? Could you find it again?"

"I'm not sure. I was only thirteen. I was the youngest girl there."

There were other things she wasn't saying. I could guess. Aunt Ginger's house was likely a brothel of sorts. God. This poor girl. All those poor girls. I couldn't help but wonder. If this were all true. Could Violet Runyon have been one of the other girls?

"Leesha, I know you know I'm looking for the truth about Violet Runyon. Did you know her? Was she one of the girls at Aunt Ginger's?"

She shook her head. "I didn't know anyone named Violet. I don't know where Hoyt came up with that. I never told him about anyone named Violet. He's lying. He had to be lying. I can't talk about this anymore. You don't understand."

"So, make me. What can't I understand?"

She just kept shaking her head back and forth.

"I feel sick," she said. "I feel like I'm gonna puke."

"Let me get you a glass of water." I went to the sink and grabbed a glass from the cupboard. I filled it with cold water from the tap. Before I could turn. Before I knew what was happening, I heard a faint whizzing sound then a pop. The glass exploded in my hand.

It took a moment for my brain to catch up to what my eyes were seeing. There was a perfect round hole in the window glass in front of me.

Then, I heard another crack.

"Leesha!" I screamed as I dropped to my knees. "Get down! Get away from the windows!" The house alarm went off, blaring, filling my head.

I crawled toward her. With panic on her face, Leesha rose. I hadn't seen it before. She'd hidden it behind her. But as Leesha walked toward me, she held my sharpest kitchen knife in her hand.

29

"Leesha, get down!" I covered the back of my head with my hands, as if that could stop a bullet. But there were no more shots fired. It was hard to hear. Hard to think with my house alarm blaring. But I thought I heard tires screeching in the distance.

"They'll come," Leesha whispered. "They're always going to come. I can't hide. Not here. Not anywhere."

"Who?" I shouted. "Leesha, who's coming for you?"

She shook her head. "I won't go!" she shouted at the top of her lungs, her face beet red, her hands trembling, but she held the knife with a firm grip. "You hear me! You'll have to kill me! I won't go!"

"Leesha," I said, crawling toward her. "Put the knife down."

Over the chaos, I heard someone call my name. "Mara! Mara!"

"Did you call someone? Did you call the cops?" Leesha asked.

"No. You've been with me the entire time. You know I didn't call anyone. But that alarm ... it sends a signal to the security company. They call the police when it goes off."

It was hard to think. The alarm kept blasting. It felt like my ears would start to bleed.

"Then they're out there! They're going to kill me!"

"Who's out there?"

Leesha kicked the chair out from under her. She kept my kitchen knife pointed straight at me and started to back up into the living room.

"Leesha," I said. "If I don't turn off that alarm, the cops *will* be here in about five minutes. They can help. I have to go to the foyer. I have to come toward you. Do you understand?"

She was ghostly white. Her hand trembled as she held the knife.

"Who's out there? Who shot a bullet into my house?"

My head began to throb in time with the house alarm.

"You think Darryl Cox just decided to kill himself? You think Hoyt just got shot from some sideways drug deal?"

I held my hands up and went to my knees. I kept away from the windows but crawled toward her.

"We can talk," I shouted. "We can work all of this out. You did the right thing coming here. I promise. I can help you."

Tears streamed down her face. Leesha's whole body trembled as she backed up. She nearly tripped on the step leading down into my sunken living room. Over the piercing sound of the alarm, I thought I heard a car door slam.

There was nowhere safe to go. Whoever was out there was armed.

I couldn't get to the alarm panel to see who was on the front door camera without walking right past Leesha or potentially putting myself in the line of fire. I tried to call her. But whatever fragile trust we'd built shattered the moment those shots were fired, and the alarm began to scream.

"I can't," she shouted. "I can't."

Then she turned and ran. With lightning speed, she vaulted over my ottoman and got to the back slider.

"Wait!" I shouted. But she threw the door open and ran out toward the woods.

"Shit," I muttered.

Staying low and away from the windows, I went to the foyer and pulled up the panel on the alarm console. I couldn't see anyone at the front door. I swore I heard a car door slam but couldn't see any vehicles on any zones around the house in the cameras.

Was she right? Had Leesha inadvertently led whoever killed Courtney Mack and Hoyt Marvin right to my own front door?

I said a silent prayer that I'd made Will go to school today. I kept the alarm on. It had been long enough to send the alert to the security company. What I'd said to Leesha was true. In about five minutes, they'd send a squad car out. By then, it might be too late ... for what, I wasn't sure.

I grabbed my cell phone off the table and ran to the back slider. Leesha had left it wide open. I couldn't see her anywhere out there. Should I run? Should I try to get to my car? There was danger out there, for me and for Leesha.

I wanted to look for her, but wasn't foolish enough to leave the protection of my house. Please, I thought. Let the cops get here soon.

A shadow moved in front of me. It seemed to come out of nowhere. Then strong arms enveloped me and hauled me back away from the door and into the house.

I kicked backward, then remembered what Sam had told me to do. I went limp, dropping to my knees. I'd have just a split second to wriggle away if I were very lucky.

My ears still rang from the alarm. I almost didn't hear my own name as he called it.

"Mara!"

I whirled around, fist raised. One punch. One chance. My heart nearly thundered right out of my chest.

A hand shot out, encircling my wrist with vice-like force.

"Mara!"

My eyes finally caught up with my brain. Sam held me against him.

"Mara!"

"Sam." I choked out his name. He pulled me back, away from the windows. It was then I noticed he had his gun drawn.

"Where is he?" Sam whispered. He pulled me down, so we were both behind the couch in the living room.

"What?"

"Which way did he go?"

"He? What?"

"Mara!"

I shook my head to clear it.

"They shot through the kitchen window. I didn't see anyone. Leesha was here. She broke in. She just ran out the back and into the woods."

Sam led me to the alcove under my stairs. It was a protected position away from all the first-floor windows. "Don't move!" he commanded.

He left me, went to the alarm panel and shut the thing off. Then, he barked into his radio. With the house alarm silenced, I could hear sirens all over the house. Sam had come with reinforcements. Thank God.

Within seconds, my house and yard swarmed with deputies. I stayed where Sam put me, under the stairs. Finally, after a while, he came to me.

"It's all clear out there," he said. "No sign of whoever shot through your window. I'll have the crime scene guys out. Are you okay? You sure you're not hurt?"

I nodded. "I'm fine. But Sam, you have to find Leesha. She ran out there. Didn't they find her?"

"No. Tell me what happened."

"I think she was here last night. She's the one who came into the house and messed with Will's things. She was waiting to talk to me. Waiting until I was alone."

Anger flooded Sam's face. He holstered his weapon and slowly rose.

"She went out that way after the shots were fired."

Sam walked with me back to the kitchen. His face went white as he saw the round hole through my window glass. He pulled me to him, holding me tight.

"Leesha pulled a knife on me. She was scared. Sam, we have to go after her. We have to convince her she can trust us. She told me everything. She's real, Sam. Ginger Ivan is real. Hoyt Marvin was telling the truth."

Sam's face went slack. We'd suspected it. We knew it. But to have Leesha Stevens confirm it had to feel like a blow to the solar plexus for him.

"Come on," I said. "She can't have gotten very far on foot."

"You said she's got a knife. And I'm sure as hell not letting you out of my sight. Whoever shot that hole in your kitchen is still out there somewhere. In fact, I want you to pack some things for yourself and for Will. You're not staying here tonight."

"Leesha wasn't going to hurt me. She's just scared. Sam, this girl has been through horrors I don't want to imagine. She needs our help. She said ... she said this Ginger Ivan person was connected with a biker gang. She was trafficked by them. For years before she finally ran off with Hoyt Marvin. Sam, I think he got close enough to hear something he shouldn't have heard. I think that's why they killed him."

Sam closed his eyes. "She's not out, Mara. I got a call from Special Agent Palmer. They've been trying to make a case against a club called the Shadow Brotherhood, MC. That's what that surveillance was all about that day we stumbled into it. That house is one of their known hangouts, Palmer told me."

Deputy Pam Pappas came back through my slider door, breathless. "It's all clear out there. We've got crews all along your property line, Mara."

"She's out there still," I said. "Leesha's got to be out there. She couldn't have gotten past your deputies on foot. We have to find her. Let me go out there with you. I know the nooks and crannies of my property better than the rest of you do."

Pappas nodded. Sam grumbled, but didn't argue. He knew I was right.

Sam insisted on taking the lead but didn't try to prevent me from following.

I had a hunch where Leesha might have gone. It was old. Rickety. Will had long since stopped using it and since he and Jason had become estranged, he never went back there. But it was still there, high in the branches of the sturdiest oak tree Jason could find.

"There," I whispered to Sam, pointing to the tree about twenty yards away from the house. He saw the treehouse ladder. There were broken branches along the way. If Leesha weren't there now, I guessed she'd stayed there last night.

"Leesha," I called out. Sam looked back, concerned. I put my hand up.

"Leesha, it's okay. No one's here who shouldn't be. You're safe. I promise. All these deputies want to help you, not hurt you. You know you don't have anywhere else to go. You can trust us."

Nothing. But as we edged a little closer to the oak tree, Sam put a finger to his lips and pointed upward.

I saw it. A dirty converse sneaker poking through one of the slats of the treehouse.

"Leesha, I'm gonna make you a promise," I said. "I won't lie to you. I'm here with a friend. Sam Cruz. He's a cop. Leesha, he's the sheriff."

I stopped myself from saying that everything would be okay. It hadn't been okay for Leesha Stevens for a very long time. She wasn't Violet Runyon. Unless she'd lied about her entire history. It was possible. But there were thousands of Violet Runyons and Leesha Stevenses in the world. All of them needed help to find their way back.

"I know you're up there," I said. "I can see you. Listen to me. There's nowhere else for you to run. You don't have to run anymore. Let us help you."

She didn't answer, but a flock of sparrows lifted off at once, rattling the branches. Sam put a protective arm around me, pulling me back.

"Leesha," I said. "I'm going to climb up."

"Not a chance," Sam whispered. "Not until she drops that knife."

We took a step closer together. The wind died down a little, making the woods fall silent. It was then I heard a sound that cut through me. Up in that tree, Leesha Stevens was crying.

"Leesha?" I said. Sam and I looked up. Together, we saw something that made my heart turn to stone.

A thin river of red ran down the bark. "Oh my God," I whispered.

"Stay back," Sam said, then he sprang into action. He ran forward and vaulted up the ladder, two rungs at a time.

"Leesha!" he shouted. I wanted to follow but knew the ladder would never support both of our weight.

"Sam?" I called out.

"No!" he shouted. "God, no! Mara ... call 9-1-1. Tell them to send an ambulance!"

30

Four hours later, I sat at Leesha Stevens's bedside at the Waynetown Hospital. Her lips were stark white and waxen. Her throat was heavily bandaged where she had tried to slice her own jugular. She had missed it though. My kitchen knife had been mercifully too dull for the job. I had never been the one to sharpen them. Jason did that. Cause for an argument we often had. He kept them too sharp. Every time he used them, he nicked his finger. I never wanted Will to accidentally do the same.

And so ... they hadn't been sharpened in almost two years. Not since Jason finally left the house.

Leesha stared at me. Her eyes were blank and swollen from the tears she cried. But she'd let me sit beside her. Now, she let me hold her hand. It broke my heart when a nurse asked her whether she had anyone she could call. Someone who could come for her. So, I did the one thing I could for her. I answered and said, "I'm here for her."

Sam had posted a deputy outside Leesha's hospital room. He'd pulled a few strings and got her into a private room. Within the hour, a social worker would come in. She had a very long road ahead of her. But tonight, at least, I felt it in my heart that this girl had a fighting chance.

I stayed with her through the night. Not talking. Making no demands of her. Kat and Bree picked up Will and kept him at their place. Kat filled him in on what had happened. He took it well. Satisfied that everyone believed him now. He had been right. Tomorrow, he asked if he could come in and visit our mystery intruder. I hadn't decided yet whether I thought that was a good idea.

At eight the next morning, after Leesha had eaten her first hot meal in more days than I wanted to fathom, she finally allowed Sam to come in and ask her some questions.

"Do you know if Ginger Ivan was this woman's real name? The one who brought these girls to the house you were staying in?" he asked.

"I'm not sure. I only heard her called by her full name once. Most of the girls just called her Aunt Ginger."

"If you saw her again, would you recognize her?"

Leesha shrugged. "I don't know. Maybe. But it's been at least five years since I laid eyes on her. It was only a couple of times. I wasn't one of her girls."

"Would you be able to describe her?" I asked. "We have sketch artists. They're very good. They could maybe help draw a picture of her, so we had at least some idea of who we were looking for."

Leesha's eyes wandered to the window. "Maybe. I think so."

"You'd be willing to try?" Sam asked.

It took a moment. Leesha closed her eyes. For a moment, I thought she'd fallen asleep. But then, in a tiny voice, she answered, "Yes."

Sam had tried to ask her questions about the biker gang she'd been passed off to under Ginger Ivan's roof. But Leesha withdrew every time. She was still terrified. She would only talk about Ginger. No one else. She denied knowing anything about Violet or ever hearing her name.

"Do I have to stay here?" she said, still tightly holding my hand.

"In the hospital? Yes," I said. "They're going to want to keep you here for a couple of days. You'll need to talk to someone."

"A shrink?"

Though I didn't like the term, I nodded.

"It's okay," she said. "I'm not going to do it again. I don't want to die. Not ... today."

"You could be very helpful," Sam said. "You *have* been very helpful. But more than that, Leesha, you survived."

She looked back out the window. "You think I can help you find that little girl? Violet. What if I can't?"

"It's not your responsibility," Sam said. "It's enough that you tell your truth. The rest of it is for me to worry about."

There was a soft knock on the door. Leesha's nurse and another woman walked in. I recognized her as one of the hospital social workers. Her name was Tonya McDevitt. She specialized in survivors of sexual abuse. With her, I knew Leesha would be in good hands.

"Do you want me to stay?" I whispered to her. Leesha shook her head.

"I'm okay," she said, but she looked back at the window. She let go of my hand. Tonya gave me a kind smile. I knew she knew what to do.

"I'll just be outside," I said to Leesha. "Sam and I are going to grab a cup of coffee."

Leesha nodded. Sam put a gentle hand on my back, and we walked out together.

"You should go home," he said once the door shut. "You've been here all night."

"I will. I just had to make sure she made it through, you know?"

"Detective Langley is going to want to talk to her about Hoyt and Courtney Mack. Do you think she's up for it?"

I looked back at the closed door. "I don't know. But something broke in her overnight. Not necessarily in a bad way. She just seems like she's surrendered to all of this. I think she wants to help. I think she's starting to realize it's a way to take back some of her power."

"Tonya McDevitt is good. I'm glad they sent her."

"Me too."

"Your idea about the sketch artist was a good one, too. I just don't want to put too much on that kid all at once."

"Violet's dead," I whispered, closing my eyes. "It was ridiculous of me to think Leesha could be her."

Sam put his arms around me. "Leesha's alive. And that's because of you. You threw her a lifeline. Thank God she took it."

I hugged him. Sam felt so strong and solid.

"The feds are going to want to talk to her, aren't they?" I asked.

Sam nodded. "There's something else I didn't get a chance to tell you. Detective Langley said Dr. Pulaski found some tattoos on Courtney Mack's body. On her sacrum. Another on her hip. They were distinct. A scythe. Some lettering. Insignia that's associated with the Shadow Brotherhood MC. They're bad, Mara. The worst. Palmer says they're a known affiliate of the Aryan Brotherhood."

"And they're involved in human trafficking?"

"Yes."

"I just can't stop thinking about those other girls that ran out of that house that day. Where are they? Are they safe today too?"

Sam couldn't answer. It made me heartsick.

"Mara, there's one more thing."

His face turned to stone.

"Sam ..."

He put a hand on my shoulder. "A guard came forward at the county jail. He talked to Gus last night. It's about Darryl Cox."

I felt unsteady on my feet. "Sam, what?"

"With what Palmer said to me last night and the ink on Courtney Mack, now with what little Leesha has told you ... it's all starting to fit together. But Gus has had a second look at some of the surveillance footage from the jail in the hours before Cox hung himself. He was visited in the yard about two hours before he died. It was a brief conversation. Nothing that aroused any suspicion or would have otherwise been out of the ordinary. But he was approached by two inmates. Both members of the Shadow Brotherhood MC."

"You think they threatened him?"

"We may never know unless one of them starts to talk. Which is unlikely. But there was another incident about ten years ago. On Clancy's watch. Two inmate members of the Shadow Brotherhood got to an informant in a murder case. Guy was about to rat out another member of the club. He also hung himself in his cell and it was ruled a suicide. It *was* a suicide. But later, one of the club members confessed that they threatened the guy ahead of his hanging. Told him either he offs himself voluntarily or they'd do it for him ... through torture. There was a similar incident in Florida. Same MO. Informant was visited by club members, then hung himself the next day."

"You think that's what happened with Darryl Cox?"

"I think it's a distinct possibility. Exact same MO. Gus is looking further into it. Seeing if he can get one of these inmates to talk. Maybe he never will. It just seems too similar to be a coincidence. It means you were right, Mara. You've always been right."

It was almost too much to process. "God. Sam. If this is what happened to Violet Runyon. I told you, her father seemed terrified. What if members of the Brotherhood got to him, too? It would explain why he clammed up when I met with him. He's scared of them, too."

"Maybe."

"That poor girl in there. I just don't know if Leesha can ever come out the other side of this."

"We're all just doing the best we can," he said. "Leesha might come around, I think. If we give her some time, she might be willing to get more specific about the Brotherhood."

"I want to help her find somewhere safe to go. I'm not sure she can handle being placed in another group home."

"She's over eighteen," he said. "We can't force her to go anywhere."

"I know."

"Seriously. Let me take you home. Get some sleep. Leesha needs it too. Check in on Will. He's worried about you."

"You talked to him?"

"I stopped over at Kat's before I came here. He's good. I told him how proud I was of him that he was so observant at the house. He's doing okay. Though he came at me with some rapid-fire ideas about building a panic room at your house."

"Oh Lord. Did you talk him out of it?"

Sam gave me a sheepish smile.

"Great," I said. "You gave him tips. The two of you are a menace when you put your heads together."

A little while later, Tonya McDevitt came out. She told us Leesha said some encouraging things about her own future. And she had finally fallen asleep. After assurances from the nursing staff that they'd call me the minute Leesha woke up or asked for me, I let Sam drive me home for a while.

As we sat in my driveway, he looked at me. "You're not gonna go to sleep, are you? You've got that look on your face."

"What look?"

"You're making plans of some sort. You know, Will is more like you than you think."

"I'm just trying to think of somewhere Leesha can stay after she's discharged. I'm worried about her being around bad influences. She's vulnerable."

"You're not thinking of bringing her here, are you? Mara, you can't ..."

"No," I said. "I can't. Not with Will. It wouldn't be good for him. But I think I know who can help."

"All right," he said, leaning over to kiss me. "But try to get at least a nap in before you solve the rest of the world's problems, okay?"

I laughed and gave him a salute.

31

Two days later, I met Christine Schuler in her office. Since the last time I was here, she'd unpacked all her boxes and decorated it in homey, muted beiges and pinks. She had two overstuffed chairs in one corner and brought me to them instead of her desk.

"Thanks so much for making time for me," I said.

"Oh, honey, you didn't even need to ask. You have walk-in privileges as far as I'm concerned. You've been doing the Lord's work this year, haven't you?"

"I don't know about that. I'm just trying to facilitate what I can."

Christine had a tablet in her lap. She swiped the screen, then smiled at me. "So, tell me what happened?"

I had already told her the highlights on the phone. Leesha Stevens was doing well and was due to be discharged from the hospital today.

"This girl's been through hell, Christine. She's just beginning to process some of it."

"Do you know who she's met with?"

"Tonya McDevitt has been in to see her yesterday and today."

"She's the best. I'm glad you said that. But this poor kid's going to need major counseling. The hardest part is yet to come for her."

"That's my fear. I want to do whatever I can to get her somewhere safe while she starts to recover."

"It's almost a deprogramming some of these people must go through. I have to be honest with you. A lot of them like her don't make it. More than you can imagine end up back in the life. It's important to get her away from the people who want to hurt her."

"Hoyt Marvin was the main influence in her life lately. He's dead now. I'm not saying that to sound like I'm glad about it. But ..."

"But she's better off without him. If Marvin were still alive ... if he were still out there, her temptation to go back to him would probably be too strong for her to resist."

"Can you help? I know your caseload must be huge ..."

Christine reached across the desk. "Honey, I can help. At least, I'll do my damndest."

"I appreciate that. More than you know."

Christine sat back and crossed her legs. "You were hoping she was Violet, weren't you?"

"I knew it was a long shot. A pipe dream, really. But yes. I was hoping she was Violet. It doesn't matter now. She's Leesha. If I can help keep her safe, that has to be enough."

"That's why I do this. And I know how damn hard it is. But Leesha Stevens is one of the lucky ones. She's alive. She has an advocate in you. She has a chance."

I brought a file with me. There was another girl in this. One whose last chance had already run out.

"Have you been contacted by a Detective Langley from Holden County?"

Christine blinked. "No. I haven't. Is this about Hoyt Marvin's murder? I read online that's where his body was found."

"Yes. Christine, he wasn't alone. There was another girl with him. One of the unlucky ones, you can say."

I pulled out the copy I'd printed of Courtney Mack's last mugshot. She'd been picked up for solicitation just six months ago. I handed the photograph to Christine.

"Her name was Courtney Mack. Hoyt Marvin was pimping her out just like Leesha. The running theory is she witnessed Hoyt's shooting then tried to run away. She was shot in the back. Does she look familiar to you?"

Christine covered her mouth with her hand. "She looks like a million girls I've seen and tried to help. What's her name again?"

"Courtney Mack. She was also a runaway. Like I said, you'll probably get a phone call from Detective Langley. She's investigating the homicide."

"Why would she be calling me?"

"Courtney Mack was on your service back in Maumee County, it turns out. It would have been about ten years ago."

She stared at the photograph. "She looks a little familiar. I'll have to check my records."

"That'd be great. I'm sure Detective Langley will appreciate it."

She put the photograph down. "What do you know about Leesha's story? Does she have any family to speak of?"

"None. All dead. She's been on her own since she was twelve years old basically."

Christine shook her head. "She never had a chance."

"Not much."

"Was she able to give the police any solid leads about who might have killed Hoyt Marvin?"

"I'm not sure. Questioning her has been tricky. She's fragile. But we have reason to believe that Hoyt was mixed up with a biker gang called the Shadow Brotherhood. Sam's contact at the FBI says they've been involved in human trafficking for a long time. We believe they have a hand in what happened to Darryl Cox as well. Somebody found out Hoyt was trying to bargain with what he and Leesha knew. I'm just trying to help find her a safe place to land. She's been adamant that she doesn't want to go into another group home. She's had some bad experiences there. It's going to be a long time before she's able to tell her full story, but at least she's talking now. We've developed a rapport. She's cooperating with law enforcement."

"That's great. Mara, that's really great. Most of these girls never do. They become so conditioned not to trust. Did she say anything useful about Violet's case?"

"She has information about the woman Bart Runyan once claimed he handed Violet off to."

"But the police discounted all of that. I thought he kept changing his story depending on which way the wind blew."

"Well, she knew things," I said. "Leesha has been able to corroborate parts of his story. That's the first time that's happened. They're reopening the investigation into her disappearance, at least."

"Has anyone told Carla yet? I don't know how to feel about that. The last thing that woman needs is to have her hopes crushed again. Mara, I was there. I know what this whole thing has done to her. She might come off as strong and able to handle it. I'm telling you, she's not."

"It's all preliminary. I trust Sam and Gus Ritter."

"Me too," she said. "I'd like to talk to her."

"To Leesha?"

"If I'm going to find her the right placement, I'd like to include her in the process. Trust me, it'll make her feel more empowered. She can start taking back some of her own agency. That's going to be critical to her recovery process."

"That makes sense. She's due to be released today. For the interim, she's going to be in protective custody."

Christine swiped her table screen. "I've got a couple of appointments later, but I can swing by this evening. I'll coordinate with Tonya. She and I go way back. I have a couple of ideas about some therapists who might be a good fit for Leesha."

"You're a godsend," I said.

"It's going to take a village and all that."

My phone rang. It was Gus Ritter.

"Why don't you go ahead and take that," she said. "I'll step out and make a couple of calls on Leesha's behalf myself. There's a woman I know who might be able to take Leesha in. She's over eighteen, right?"

"She is."

"That presents a different set of problems. You understand we won't be able to force her to go anywhere she doesn't want to go."

"Hang on a second, Gus," I said, answering my phone.

Then to Christine, "I'd never want to force her to do anything. Never."

Christine smiled. She made a circular gesture with her finger then took out her own phone. She stepped into the hallway and left me to finish my call with Gus.

"Hey, Gus. What's up?"

"I just finished interviewing Leesha Stevens. Tara Langley came down. She didn't have much actionable intel on Hoyt Marvin. She hadn't seen him in almost a week. She's reluctant to identify his associates or any members of the Shadow Brotherhood by name."

"She's scared."

"I'd say terrified. But the nurses are saying she's in a way better mindset than she has been."

"I appreciate you calling me."

"That's only part of what I'm calling you about. Mara, Leesha's story about this Aunt Ginger person has stayed consistent. I had our sketch artist come out. She's still in there with him. I'm leaving them alone to do their thing, but the bit I heard ... she had some distinct features she could give to the guy. Once she started talking about this woman, it was like a valve opened. She's animated. Actively involved in making edits to the drawing. I don't know what good it's going to do. But I think they're going to have something soon."

"That's fantastic. I'm so glad. Has anyone gone back to question Bart Runyon about any of this?"

"Sam wants me to wait until the sketch is done. Same thing with Carla Gribaldi."

"Actually, I'm with Christine Schuler now. Violet's social worker. She thinks she might be able to get Leesha into a safe house when she's ready for it. She's been a valuable resource."

"That's good. Christine's good people. It was a real loss when she left the county. If you can get the kid to go. She's got trust issues, to say the least."

"I know."

"Hang on a second, Mara," Gus said. "They're calling me back into the room."

Gus must have muted his end. I couldn't hear anything. I looked out the door. Christine stood at the desk in the lobby, talking on her phone. She caught my eye and smiled. She raised an index finger, gesturing that she was almost done with her call. Then she gave me a thumbs up. I hoped that meant she would have good news to share.

A moment later, Gus came back on the line. "Mara, where are you right now?"

"I'm sitting in Christine's new office. I'm telling you. I think we're doing this all wrong, Gus. The private sector is like a fantasy land. She's got new furniture. A computer that works. They offered me muffins when I walked in."

"Mara, I'm going to send you something. Leesha finished with the sketch artist."

"Okay?" His tone had gone flat. He sounded off.

My text alert went off. I pulled the phone away from my ear for a second.

"Hang on," I told him. "It's downloading now."

"Mara, what's the address?"

"What?"

"The address. Where you are."

"What?"

It took another second. The picture text Gus sent came through in a choppy chunk, then finally loaded.

I stared at it. The air went out of me. I blinked hard.

"Don't hang up the phone," Gus was saying. But I couldn't bring it back to my ear. I stared at the drawing.

The woman was pretty. Reddish hair. A dusting of freckles across her cheeks. A bit younger than she was now, but that made sense. Leesha hadn't seen her in a few years.

"Mara?" Christine stood in the doorway to her own office. She smiled at me, tilting her head to the side.

Pretty. Reddish hair. Bleached blonde now. A dusting of freckles across her cheeks and lines in the corner of her eyes.

It was madness. Impossible. But the sketch Leesha Stevens had worked on was the spitting image of the woman standing before me.

The woman who gained Violet Runyon's trust. Perhaps Courtney Mack's as well. Ginger. For her red hair before she bleached it. Even now, I could see her roots starting to grow in.

Ginger Ivan was Christine Schuler.

"Mara?" Both Gus and Christine called my name at the same time.

"Mara," Gus said again. "I need you to get out of there. Now!"

32

"Do you think she'll talk to me?"

I stood frozen, Gus talking in my ear. He wasn't on speaker, but he was loud enough there was every chance Christine could hear him.

"Leesha?" I said, keeping the phone up. Hoping Gus would stay on the line and stop talking. "You're asking if you could talk to Leesha, Christine?"

"Keep her there," Gus said. "Are you alone with her? Does she know?"

"Yes," Christine said. I plastered a smile on my face and prayed it looked genuine. "If you think it would help. I can tell you about the placement I think might work best for her. The issue is she's over eighteen. I can't legally make her go anywhere."

"I think if I went with you," I said. "As I told you, I've developed a rapport with her. She's got major trust issues, as you can imagine."

God. What if Leesha hadn't been able to help with the police sketch? Could she be wrong? Could it just be a coincidence?

"Keep her talking. Keep her there," Gus said. "Mara, I've got a unit on the way. We're going to bring Christine in for questioning."

"Mara," Christine said. "I'm the last person you have to say that to. I've dealt with hundreds of young people in Leesha Stevens's same situation."

Hundreds of girls. Violet Runyon. Courtney Mack. My God. Courtney Mack. Did Christine have something to do with Courtney Mack's fate as well? Had she also been one of Aunt Ginger's girls?

My mind raced through a thousand possibilities. Christine had developed a relationship with Violet. She knew Bart Runyon had made threats. Had she kidnapped Violet, knowing how easy it would be to pin it on Bart?

And Courtney Mack. Christine had been assigned to her case when she was a minor as well. Another at-risk girl being put into the foster care system. My God. Christine knew who the vulnerable girls were. The unwanted ones. The ones who wouldn't have people looking for them if they disappeared.

But Violet had people who cared. Why risk it?

"Are you sure you have never met with Leesha before?" I asked.

"Good," Gus said. "That's good."

"Who are you talking to?" Christine asked. "Do you need to finish your phone call?"

"I'm sorry," I said. "I'll have to call you back, okay?"

I pulled the phone away from my ear. I didn't hang up. I had no idea whether Gus could still hear what was going on.

"Leesha," I said to Christine. "Maybe you could check your files. Is it possible you worked with her before? When she was a minor?"

"I don't know what difference that makes now. Are you certain she's even using her real name?"

"I suppose we can find all of that out. I was just thinking you'd be in a unique position. If you had insight into Leesha and Vi—er ... Courtney's cases."

"Maybe," Christine said. "But the sooner I talk to Leesha in person, the sooner I can get started with getting her into a stable environment."

"I need to go with you," I said. "I really don't think Leesha can handle meeting someone new. I'll be happy to drive. Or you can follow me."

"I'm perfectly capable of getting myself to Waynetown Hospital, Mara. Are you all right? You've seemed a little ... off ... since you took that phone call."

"I'm fine," I said, gathering my briefcase. I'd left it on the floor beside the chair.

Christine paused. Then she raised a skeptical brow but shrugged it off.

"Suit yourself, I guess. What room did you say Leesha was in?"

"I didn't," I said. "At least, I don't think I did."

Christine grabbed a light black sweater off the coat rack in the corner. She twirled it and slipped her arms through it.

"Wait," I said. "We should wait. I've got a call in to Leesha's nurse. Before you go over there, I'd like to know how she's doing this morning. I don't want to upset her any more than she already is."

"I'm not going to upset her," Christine said, her tone growing more annoyed. She ignored me and started for the door.

Something had changed about her. She moved with purpose. She appeared ready to leave me in the dust whether I decided to come with her or not.

At that moment, I had absolutely no doubt that if Christine were ever in a room with Leesha Stevens alone, she would do her harm. It came over me like a black cloud.

All this time. She'd become Carla Gribaldi's friend. Kenya's friend. All this time.

Christine stormed out the front door. She didn't even bother to look back at me. I think had I given chase, she would have sprinted to her vehicle.

"Wait," I said. "Christine. We really should wait. You can't just barge in on Leesha."

She wasn't listening. She hit her key fob. Her red Honda chirped as she approached it.

"Christine!" I shouted.

She got as far as her driver's side door before two deputy sheriff cruisers drove up, squealed to a halt and boxed her in.

Christine looked back at me. There was no look of surprise. No shouted questions to me. But no resignation either. Instead, as one of the deputies emerged from her vehicle, Christine merely looked back at me, her eyes narrowing in anger.

"Ms. Schuler?" the deputy asked. "We have some questions for you. Detective Ritter has asked if you'd let us drive you down to the station. It shouldn't take long."

I froze.

"I told you," I said. "I'm sure it's to do with the investigation into Courtney Mack's murder. Ritter's been working alongside Tara Langley."

Christine's face changed. Relief. She smiled. "Of course. I'll do anything I can to help that poor girl. Even now."

As the deputy held open the door to the cruiser, Christine waved at me as she slipped inside.

33

I stayed far behind the cruisers as they drove Christine Schuler into the County Public Safety Building. I went through a side door. Gus and Sam were already waiting for me.

"Did she say anything?" Gus asked.

I shook my head. "She's sure? Leesha's absolutely sure?"

"She needs to get eyes on her," Sam said. "She needs to make a positive identification."

A moment later, Christine was led into one of the interview rooms. Sam led me into the adjoining room with the two-way mirror.

"Where's Leesha now?" I asked. "Sam, Christine wanted to go see her. She became adamant. If your deputies hadn't shown up, she was headed straight there. I wouldn't have let it happen. I would have stopped her."

"Mara," he turned to me, his voice cracking. "Of everyone involved in this thing ... you're the one who's done everything right."

"I don't understand. Bart Runyon said he gave Violet to a woman named Ginger Ivan. But he *knew* who Christine Schuler was. He would have recognized her. Why on earth wouldn't he have been the one to identify her all those years ago?"

"I don't know," Sam said. "He'll need to be questioned again. But he never told me he handed Violet physically to anyone. He only said the person who contacted him, who was going to take Violet to safety, was named Ginger Ivan. He was always fluid with the details. I could never pin him down on how this hand-off was supposed to have taken place. Maybe he never actually saw Ginger Ivan's face. One of his stories was that he was told to park at the gas station, go into the men's room, and wait there for twenty minutes. If that version was true, maybe he didn't see her. Or maybe he did and he's been lying about that too all this time."

Gus walked into the interview room. He was casual, apologetic.

"Sorry to keep you waiting," Gus said. "How've you been?"

"Good. How are you?"

"You look exactly the same though," he said. She gave him an odd look. "What's it been, ten years since you left the county?"

"About that. When are you going to retire? You've got to be eligible now."

"Not for years, if I have anything to say about it," Sam muttered.

"I can't retire," Gus said. "I've got too many ex-wives to take care of."

"Or you could just tell them all to get bent. That'd be more your style."

Gus laughed. He quickly put Christine at ease. They engaged in a few more minutes of banter. Then finally, Christine folded her hands in front of her.

"Will this Detective Langley be joining us?" she asked. "I'm not trying to rush you. I mean, anything I can do to help find out whoever killed that poor girl, you know I'm willing to do it. But as I told Mara, I don't really remember very much about Courtney Mack."

Gus nodded. "But she was on your service. That was what, ten years ago?"

"About that. I'd have to check my notes. What can you tell me about what happened to her?"

"Not much," Gus said. "As you know, it all happened outside of the county. I'm just doing Detective Langley a favor. And you as well. Rather than having you drive all the way out to Holden."

"I wouldn't mind."

"She was shot in the back," Gus said. "I can tell you that. We think she was trying to run away after possibly witnessing whatever happened to that chucklehead, Hoyt Marvin."

"I'd like to wring his neck," Christine said. "If someone hadn't already gotten to him. Giving poor Carla Gribaldi false hope again. She's been through enough."

"I won't argue that," Gus said.

There was a knock on the outer door. Sam put a light hand on my arm. When I looked at him, he held his index finger to his lips.

"Hey, Gus?" Detective Brody Lance poked his head in. "I'm sorry to bother you. Would you have a second to do me a favor?"

Gus apologized to Christine and stepped out into the hallway. He waited a few seconds, then came back inside.

"Christine, this is gonna sound crazy. It's been a crazy day. But would you mind if we borrowed you for a minute or two? Detective Lance is working a robbery. They've got a suspect in custody and they're bringing the victim in for a lineup. As it happens, the suspect was female, Caucasian, about your age and height."

"You think I committed a robbery?" Christine laughed.

"Yeah. Right. No. We just need to put together a lineup. It's standard. I've got two female deputies and one of our clerks in it. But we need a fifth."

"A decoy?"

"Something like that. It'll just take a few minutes. It'll be a good story for your friends maybe. I just got a text from Tara Langley. She's about ten minutes out. This'll maybe be better than us cooling our heels in here."

"I'm game," Christine said.

I held my breath. Christine left her seat. She followed Gus back out into the hallway. Sam and I waited a full minute before following them.

Sam led me through another door. This room had a large window on one wall. Two women sat in chairs in front of it. The blonde turned when I walked in. It was Leesha Stevens. She had color in her cheeks that hadn't been there the other day.

Her companion was Tonya McDevitt, the social worker assigned to her case.

"When they come in," Sam said. "I want you to take your time. They can't see you, okay, Leesha? And they can't hear you."

A moment later, a door opened to the adjoining room. Five women, including Christine Schuler, walked in. They stood on their marks and turned to face the window. I knew all Christine would see was a mirror on one wall.

Slowly, Leesha rose.

"Do you recognize any of these women?" Gus asked.

Leesha put a hand to her face. Then she pointed straight at Christine Schuler.

"That's her," she said. "That's Aunt Ginger."

"And where do you recognize her from?" Gus asked.

"She would bring girls to the group home in Bakersville. And then she'd come pick them up and I'd never see them again."

"You're sure?" Gus asked.

"I'm sure. That's her. I saw her every day for months. She told me I was lucky I was too old for her tastes. I tried to hit her. She spat on me. That was maybe five years ago. But I remember. Her freckles. I tried to hit her with a glass. It shattered. She bled a lot. Maybe she still has the scar. It would be on her left temple."

Gus leaned into the microphone so the women could hear him in the other room. "Will all you ladies turn to your right? And can you pull your hair back so we can see your left temple?"

Each woman complied. Christine looked amused. But as she pulled her hair back, even I could see it. A faint, crescent-shaped scar.

"That's her," Leesha said, trembling. "I swear to God. That's her!"

Sam nodded to Gus. Gus shut off the mic. He went out into the hallway. A moment later, everyone but Christine Schuler left the lineup room. I couldn't hear what was being said in that room. But a few seconds later, two deputies came in. Christine's smile faded as one of them produced handcuffs. Then she dropped to her knees, her face contorted with anguish.

34

A week later, Leesha asked me to come with her as she moved into her transitional housing. Not a group home. Not a shelter. Instead, she decided to take the kindness of someone who had reached out to help.

"It's pretty here," Leesha said. She sat in my front seat, clutching a grocery bag containing her meager possessions. A change of clothes, a new pair of shoes, and some essentials she'd picked out at the store. I offered to buy her an overnight bag, but she refused.

"All those red plants," she said. "What are they?"

"Hydrangeas. And those pink ones are Dinnerplate Hibiscus."

"It's secluded in back," I said. "The property butts up to the riverbank. There's a trail you can take. And if you like to fish ..."

The blue front door opened, and Kenya stepped out. She wore another of what was becoming her new staple, a blue and gold kaftan. She shielded her eyes from the sun with one hand and waved us in with the other.

Still clutching her paper bag to her chest like a shield, Leesha stepped out of the car.

"I'm so glad you came," Kenya said. She held the front door open. We walked inside. I smelled baked cinnamon. Kenya had a plate of muffins set out on the table.

"You baked?" I mouthed to her, then gave her an impressed thumbs up.

"Let me show you to your room," Kenya said. Leesha gave me a tentative look. I simply smiled, encouraging her to follow Kenya. This wasn't their first meeting. The morning after Leesha's admission to the hospital, Kenya had paid her a visit all on her own.

I waited in the kitchen while Kenya walked her down the hallway. A few minutes later, Kenya came back alone. She joined me in the kitchen.

"I'm giving her some privacy. Let her get acclimated to the room. She seems to like it. I gave her the one at the back of the house facing the river."

"Thank you for doing this."

"Carla wanted to. Did she tell you that?"

"No. Our conversation was brief. Sam did most of the talking."

"She's taking things pretty well, considering." Kenya went to her fridge and pulled out two small glasses. She poured milk in each and handed me one. Then she picked up a muffin off the plate on the table and set it in front of me.

"You bake now?" I asked.

"I'm trying lots of new things in my free time."

I peeled the paper off my muffin and took the first bite. It was delicious, buttery, with just the right touch of cinnamon.

"I'm impressed."

"Good. You should be."

"But baking. How long do you think that's going to sustain you?"

She didn't answer. She popped a bite of muffin into her mouth. After she swallowed it, she took a sip of milk. "So. How's Skip taking the news about Violet's case being reopened?"

"He says it doesn't have anything to do with him," I said. The truth was the tension in the office from what I heard had become intolerable. Caro was taking all her vacation days. I'd never known her to take even one in all the years we'd worked together. It meant she could stay away and get paid for close to two months.

"He has to reinstate you," she said. "The press is going to find out you're the one who pushed things. I heard Sam's giving a press conference about Christine's arrest later today."

"He wanted to avoid it. There are still too many moving parts. Missing pieces. And Bart Runyon refuses to talk."

"He's scared. There's a body count. He doesn't want his added to it. From everything I understand, the Shadow Brotherhood MC has a very long reach."

"But he was telling the truth," I said. "All these years. When he said he handed Violet over to Ginger Ivan, it was Christine Schuler. I still don't fully understand how he could claim he didn't know who she was."

"Did you talk to Sam about that? Because his original story about Ginger ... was that he'd been instructed to leave Violet in his truck while he went into that truck stop bathroom. He says he was told to stay in there at least twenty minutes before coming out. When he did, Violet was gone. He never claimed he saw the handoff. Just that Ginger Ivan would come get her and take Violet to safety."

"She would have gone with Christine," I said. "Violet knew her. She would have trusted her if she came to the truck door."

Kenya blinked back tears. "She was my friend. Me. Carla. Christine. My God, Mara, we had lunches together over the years. We supported Carla. Together."

"You can't beat yourself up over this."

"You sure about that? Skip Fletcher sure is. You've seen his statement to the press. That my incompetence during Bart's trial is what obscured the facts of this case."

"He's wrong. Sam's blaming himself too. It serves nothing."

"I hear she's talking," Kenya said.

"She is. Sam won't give me too many details. But Christine has confirmed her affiliation with the Shadow Brotherhood MC. She's been in a romantic relationship with a top-ranking member for twenty-five years. She's kept it a secret. When they searched her incident to her arrest, they found the same tattoos on her hip and tailbone that Courtney Mack had."

Kenya put a hand to her stomach. "She abused her position to feed young, vulnerable girls to those vultures."

"Yes."

Kenya picked up the remote control and clicked on the television mounted under her kitchen cabinets. "We'll see how good Sam is at this."

I checked my smartwatch. It was eleven o'clock. Kenya switched to a local channel. Any minute now, Sam would begin his press conference. After some herky-jerky camera work, the shot focused on a small lectern with the county shield affixed to it. A moment later, Sam walked into view. He wore his sheriff's uniform, including his campaign hat. He carried a single piece of paper. His terse, prepared statement that he'd had me look over just an hour ago. Skip had told me in no uncertain terms he didn't even want me in the building.

Sam cleared his throat. "Thank you for coming. I have just a few remarks. I'll open it to questions, but please understand this is an ongoing investigation so there will be many things I can't comment on. But I'd like to be as transparent as possible going forward. As you know, yesterday morning, Christine Schuler, a former county social worker, was arrested in connection with a national human trafficking ring. We believe Ms. Schuler abused her position and helped facilitate the kidnapping and trafficking of several young women."

Leesha came into the room. Kenya picked up the remote.

"No," Leesha said. "Leave it on. I'd like to watch it. In fact, turn it up."

Kenya's expression was unsure, but she did as Leesha asked. Leesha sank into a chair beside me as Sam gave the most general information about Christine's suspected role in the human trafficking ring. He said nothing about the Shadow Brotherhood MC. That, for now, would remain out of the press.

"I will not be making any detailed comment on the identity of our informants or the suspected victims involved. My office is cooperating with an already-established FBI task force on this matter. And please, I appreciate your understanding of the sensitive nature of this matter. Many of the victims involved are either still minors or were minors at the time. We believe they were put in harm's way. I'll have more to say in a few days. I'll go ahead and open it up to questions."

A dozen or more questions were shouted at Sam all at once. He pointed to someone off camera. Since the questioner wasn't mic'd, I couldn't make out what they were saying.

"Yes," Sam answered. "I hope and expect there will be further arrests made in conjunction with this investigation. I cannot comment on who or how many other individuals may be involved."

"Sheriff, is it true that you believe Violet Runyon might have been one of the young girls taken and trafficked?"

Sam took a breath. "Again, I can't specifically comment. But I have been asked to share something related to Violet Runyon's case."

Sam nodded to someone off screen. The camera panned wider. One of the deputies stood beside a covered easel. At Sam's direction, the covering was pulled away. There, right beside Sam, was a 16x20 photograph of Violet's latest age progression image. Beside that was the last school picture taken of a five-year-old Violet.

"Violet Runyon is one of dozens of young girls still missing in the state of Ohio. I'll be sharing photographs of some of the other missing children by the end of the day. But I would implore the public as we have been for twelve years. If you see anyone or know anyone who resembles this most current age progression rendering, please call the sheriff's crimestopper number. Violet would be close to eighteen years old today. If she survived."

"Sheriff, isn't it true you already located a young woman matching Violet Runyon's description?"

"No," he said. "That's not accurate."

"Can you at least explain how Christine Schuler's arrest relates to the Runyon investigation? Are you saying Bart Runyon, the child's father, is innocent of the charges brought against him?"

"I'm not saying that. Not any of that."

"But if Violet's alive. If you think she's alive, shouldn't Bart Runyon be set free? That's not some small mistake, Sheriff. You were the lead detective when Violet Runyon disappeared. How could you have missed this?"

There was a wave of murmuring in the crowd. Sam held up his hands. A moment later, he said he was done with questions. The camera panned back to the photographs of Violet Runyon.

"Leesha?" Kenya said. "Is something wrong?"

Leesha shook her head. "Violet. I never knew anyone named Violet. I told you. It's been years since I lived in Aunt Ginger's house. They didn't show me that picture. They showed me ones of a little girl. That one. She was just a little girl."

"Yes," I said. "Just like you, Leesha."

Leesha shook her head. "No. No. No. They didn't show me that one."

Leesha walked up to the television set. She put a palm against the most current age progression photograph. Then she turned back to us.

"I thought Violet was just a little girl. This picture? I know her. That's Carrie Ann."

"Carrie Ann?" Kenya and I said it together.

"Was she one of Ginger's girls?" I asked, heart pounding.

Leesha shook her head. "I don't know. I never saw her at Ginger's. I don't remember. But I know her."

"When did you know her?" I asked.

"When?" Leesha seemed confused by the question.

"Yes. Do you remember what year you met her? Where? Do you know where Christine ... er ... Aunt Ginger sent her?"

"Sent?"

Was something wrong? Was she having a breakdown?

"Carrie Ann isn't gone," Leesha said. "You don't understand. I said I know her. As in, now. I know her."

Kenya dropped her full glass of milk on the floor. It shattered and the milk made tiny rivers in the grout lines of her tile.

"Know," I repeated. "As in ..."

"Carrie Ann lives outside of Ann Arbor. Or at least that's where she was staying the last time I saw her."

"Leesha," I said. "When was that? When was the last time you saw Carrie Ann?"

"Two months ago," she answered. "If you give me a piece of paper, I can give you the address where she lives. I've stayed there with her a few times. Hoyt would send me there for parties her old man throws."

Two months ago. Lives. Not lived. It couldn't be possible. Not after twelve years. But Leesha insisted that Violet Runyon was still very much alive and that she knew where to find her.

35

A normal house. Two stories. A white-washed brick facade. This had been farmland twenty years ago. Now, there was a subdivision. Cut grass. Flowers growing. A normal house. A normal neighborhood. The house next door had a welcome sign hanging from it.

"Welcome," I said, my eyes focused on that sign.

"You're sure she gave you the right address?" Sam asked. He was agitated. Had been for the entire two-hour drive to a little suburb just outside of Ann Arbor. For two months, he'd thought I was on a hopeless, wild goose chase. But now Detective Gus Ritter sat in an interrogation room with Bart Runyon. And in another room just like it, Christine Schuler sat with special agent Palmer. Since early yesterday, she decided to fully cooperate with the FBI's human trafficking task force. She'd given names, dates, the locations of three houses, not unlike this one, all owned by high-ranking members of the Shadow Brotherhood MC. Fourteen young women and girls had been taken to safety, rescued from a life too unspeakable. They ranged in age from eight to nineteen.

Eight years old, I thought. And Violet had only been five.

Rescued.

I knew the statistics. It would still be too late for some of them.

"Mara," Sam said. "Did you hear me?"

One of the agents parked the surveillance in front of the house. The mailbox across the street had its red flag up. I could see the mail truck rounding the corner.

"Wait here," Sam said. "You can watch everything on the monitor." He handed me a headset. I slid into a seat next to one of the female agents named Lucas and put on my headphones. Sam got out, jogged over to the mailbox, and looked inside. He pulled out two pieces of mail, then put them back in the box, closing it.

I watched on the monitor as Sam gestured to two gray sedans parked further down the street. Inside each were two FBI agents. Now that we were across state lines, they technically had jurisdiction over what we were about to do. But one of them owed Sam a favor. This had been his case. He should be the one to do this.

He came back to the van and climbed in.

"Dusty Morrison," he asked me. "That's the name Leesha gave you? Morrison."

"Yes," I said. "Carrie Ann Morrison."

"There's someone in the backyard," Sam said. We could hear the whir of a lawn mower. A moment later, a teenage boy came into view from the backyard, cutting a straight path with a red push mower. He had over-the-ear headphones on and walked with a slouch. He wore a neon yellow shirt that read Wilbur

Lawn and Landscaping across the back of it. We'd seen a truck with the same logo at the entrance to the subdivision.

"Just wait here," Sam said. "I have a feeling this will be quick."

I looked back at the monitor. I could see the front door and one of the side windows clearly.

"Someone's inside," I said.

He turned to me. "Mara, wait here."

I didn't want to. I wanted to march up to that front door. But Sam had broken protocol and pulled a dozen strings to bring me this far. I did what he asked and hung back, waiting behind the van with my headset on.

He was casual as he walked up to the door. He rang the bell and waited. Two joggers rounded the corner on the sidewalk. I knew each of them had earpieces in, waiting for instructions from the agents in the nearby cars. Ready to move in if there was trouble.

I wanted to float through the monitor. I wanted to be at Sam's side. I had to be satisfied with the next best thing. Sam wore a tiny camera clipped to his tie. The image was grainy and jerked at first. But as Sam stood still, the front door and welcome sign came into focus.

The door opened. A middle-aged white man opened it. He wore a gray muscle shirt with faded lettering. He held a slice of pizza in one hand. He was fit. Trim. Maybe forty-five. I could make out ink on his forearms. I had no doubt if he took that shirt off, he would have the scythe tattoo of the Shadow Brotherhood MC across his back.

"Hello," Sam said. "Are you Dusty Morrison?"

"Who's asking?" the man said. His tone was curious but polite. He smiled at Sam.

"Mr. Morrison, would you mind stepping outside for a moment?"

I watched as Dusty peered around Sam. His eyes tracked the joggers as they went past his house. Dusty looked over his shoulder. He didn't protest. Didn't even ask another question. He simply stepped outside and off the porch, then took another bite of his pizza.

"Mr. Morrison," Sam said. "Do you have a young lady living with you? I'm looking to speak with Carrie Ann."

Dusty stopped chewing. He dropped his pizza to the ground. The two unmarked sedans pulled up and parked in front of Morrison's house.

"Mr. Morrison?" Sam said.

"He knows," I whispered.

"Sit tight," Agent Lucas said. "Just wait."

"What did she say to you?" Morrison said. "What did she say? What did she tell you?"

"Mr. Morrison, is Carrie Ann at home?"

Morrison took a step back. He faked to the right then started to run.

"Go!" Agent Palmer shouted through his headset.

Sam started chasing Morrison. The agents in the nearest sedan ran out, ready to cut Morrison off. The two joggers turned and gave chase.

But it ended quickly. Sam got to Morrison first. The man dropped to his knees and put his hands behind his head. This wasn't his first arrest.

"Move in!" Agent Palmer shouted from his earpiece.

I kept my eyes on the front door. A girl walked out. Thin. Blonde. Wearing cutoff jean shorts and a plain red tee shirt.

I don't remember making a conscious decision to step out of the van. But when Agent Lucas slid the door open, I followed.

I felt like a ghost. Floating. Existing beside myself as I made my way up the sidewalk.

The girl caught my eye. She looked at Dusty Morrison, lying face down on the ground as Sam fitted cuffs around him.

She walked toward me. Floating in a way, like I felt. Agent Lucas got to her.

"Honey?" she said. "Can you tell me your name? Are you Carrie Ann?"

I stood right in front of her. Her eyes, those pale blue, piercing eyes. The age progression photo was uncanny if she was who I thought she was.

Impossible. A dream. Alive.

"Honey?" Agent Lucas said again. "You're okay. We're not here to hurt you. But can you tell me your name?"

I felt lightheaded. The other agents had taken Dusty Morrison. He was screaming something. Sam ran to my side. He stared at the girl, thunderstruck, just like I was.

"Can you tell me your name?"

The girl stood straighter. She swallowed.

"My name is Sam Cruz," Sam said. "I'm the sheriff down in Waynetown. Maumee County. Do you know where that is?"

She nodded. Her eyes glistened.

"My name," she said. "Is ... I think ... is Violet."

36

I cannot imagine what she felt. I thought of Will as I always did. What would I do if he were taken from me? What would I do if I ever lost him? Would I survive it at all?

It could have happened. I'd worried about it in the days I found out my ex had committed federal crimes. Would he do it? Would he take our son and disappear?

It had been twelve hours since we found Violet Runyon. Twelve hours and twelve years. I sat in a hospital waiting room. They had brought Violet here. She was with a social worker. A psychologist. She was remarkably composed. Serene, almost.

They had told Carla what to expect. Funny that, I thought. What to expect. How could anyone prepare for a shock like this?

But Carla was calm. Stoic as she walked into that hospital room. For twelve years, I knew she'd prayed for this very day. Even knowing the miracle it would take.

Sam stood beside me, holding my hand.

"She hasn't wavered," Sam said. "They'll do a DNA test to confirm it. But she remembers, Mara. She said it was Dr. Christine who took her from her father's truck. She said she told her her mother wanted her to come home."

"She trusted her," I said. "Christine knew she would. Has she admitted it? Since we picked up Violet? Has Christine changed her story?"

"She claims she was forced into it. That the Shadow Brotherhood threatened to kill her and the rest of her family. At this point, there's no way to confirm whether that's true. But she's admitted to orchestrating the abduction of Courtney Mack and five other girls who were on her service. At risk. Reported as runaways. Violet was the only one of them with a family."

"Then why?" I asked. "Why risk taking her?"

"Money," Sam said. "Violet was blonde. Five years old. Her memory is remarkable. She knows she was taken to a house with a bunch of other older girls. Her description matches a lot of what Leesha said. From there, she went to stay with a family. She remembers them taking a lot of pictures of her but that's all. She moved around a lot after that."

"Pictures," I said.

"They told her it was for medical reasons," Sam said through gritted teeth. "Mara ... it's going to take weeks to debrief this girl. We don't know what horrors she faced and maybe we never will. But a year ago, she was sent to live with Dusty Morrison. He's a sergeant-at-arms for the Detroit chapter of the Shadow Brotherhood MC. He's talking now. A lot."

Agent Palmer rounded the corner. He extended a hand to shake Sam's.

"It's the big one, Cruz," he said. "I can't go into a lot of details, but with what the Schuler woman has told us, that girl in there, and now that scum Dusty Morrison, we've got corroboration on a lot of the operation. This may be one of the biggest trafficking rings we've ever busted. It extends to every chapter of the Shadow Brotherhood around the country. I'm ready to hand out roughly thirty arrest warrants. We've got intel on two more houses. We're gonna save a lot of women, Sam. Thanks to you."

"No," Sam said, squeezing my hand. "Thanks to her."

Carla Gribaldi walked out of Violet's hospital room. She had her back straight, but when she saw me, she ran toward me and collapsed in my arms.

"It's her," she whispered. "It's Violet. My God. It's Violet. The shape of her fingernails. Her toes. The little scar she has on her shin from the first time she tried to ride a bike without training wheels. She got that one only a week before they took her from me. And she has a little pink birthmark behind her left ear. My mother called it a stork bite."

"Oh Carla. Oh ..."

Then I cried with her. For all the years lost. And for all the years they would have together. It would be hard. Sometimes impossible. As Sam said, it would take time before Carla uncovered all the horrors her daughter had endured. But it was time they now had together.

The elevator doors opened. Tony Gribaldi stepped out. The color drained from his face when he saw his wife with me.

She let me go and ran to him. She leapt into his arms with the force of a battering ram. He absorbed it and held his wife close. She gushed, telling him all the things she'd just told me.

"We can't be sure yet," Sam said. "Like I said, we need to run DNA."

"You can," I said. "But she knows her daughter. The things she described. Only Carla would know them. I'm sure of that."

Sam nodded.

Carla took Tony by the hand and walked him over to us. His eyes glistened with tears, but he didn't appear able to speak.

Carla wiped her eyes. "She wants to see you two," she said. "You and Sam."

"Wait," Tony said. "I'm ... I have to ... I know what you think of me. I know what everyone thought of me."

"Stop," I said. "You've been trying to protect your wife. No one could have predicted what was going to happen."

"You did," Tony said. "You knew all along. Thank you. Thank you for bringing my wife's baby back to her."

"Go," Carla said. "Violet's waiting."

Sam hadn't let go of my hand. My heart pounding, we walked into Violet Runyon's hospital room. She was sitting on the edge of the bed.

She looked so much like Carla. Now that they were in the same room together the resemblance was even more marked. The same shape to their jaw. The same smile. The same nose.

"You found me," Violet said. "My mom says it was you. I wanted to come home. I just didn't know how."

"You'll be home soon, baby," Carla said. She came in and sat on the edge of the bed next to her daughter. It was the smallest gesture, but Violet rested her head on Carla's shoulder. Carla went very still. I knew she was afraid to breathe. So was I.

"I'm glad you're okay," I said. "Your mother never stopped looking for you."

"I didn't know how to get home," Violet whispered.

She looked exhausted. As she rested her head against her mother's shoulder, her eyelids started to droop.

"I'm afraid to go to sleep," Violet said. "Afraid I'm going to wake up and it's all a dream."

"No," Carla said. "But I know what you mean. I'm not gonna leave your side, baby. Come on. Let's get you tucked in. I'll be right beside you all the time. I'll never leave again."

Carla tucked her daughter into that hospital bed and pulled up the chair next to her. Violet locked eyes with her mother. I think she was afraid that if she closed them, Carla might disappear.

They had a long road to recovery, the two of them. But I knew a mother's love could bring a miracle.

Tears filled my eyes. Sam gathered me against him. We were intruders now. Carla looked at me and mouthed "thank you."

"You're welcome," I whispered. Though it felt more like Violet herself had given us all a gift.

Sam and I quietly left and closed the door behind us, leaving this new, fragile family the privacy they'd earned. There would be time for questions. The story would inevitably go national. But for now, I knew Carla Gribaldi's world was perfect.

For now ...

37

"You should be up there," Kenya said to me through gritted teeth. She and I sat against the back wall of the Maumee County Sheriff's Department press room. We disappeared into a sea of spectators and reporters. As Sam and Special Agent Palmer stood behind the lectern, several dozen cameras whirred to life. As I knew it would, the story had garnered national media attention. All the major cable news outlets had sent crews.

Violet wasn't here today. Two weeks ago, she and Carla had sat for an interview with *People* magazine. It was the only one she would give. Carla had allowed a single photograph to be taken of her and Violet walking hand in hand along the riverbank with their backs turned to the camera. She had hoped it would quell some of the curiosity, but so far it had only served to stoke it.

Carla was here though. She'd asked if she could read a prepared statement. She stood in the corner. She'd brought reinforcements. Two representatives from the Silver Angels victim's advocacy group had come with her for moral support and to field any hurtful questions.

Violet was safe. But she had years of recovery ahead of her. She'd spent twelve years in the custody of some of the worst people on the planet. She had survived. So far, she seemed resilient. But I prayed after this, both Carla and Violet would be able to recede into obscurity again.

"You're the one who should be up there," I said. Skip Fletcher walked out and took a spot beside Sam. I could see Sam go tense. He looked for me in the crowd but there was no way he'd be able to find me through the throng and the lights shining directly in his eyes.

"All right," Sam said, holding a hand up. "I appreciate you all coming today. I have a brief statement to make, then I'll turn the mic over to my colleague at the FBI."

"As of this morning, fourteen arrests have been made in conjunction with a nationwide human trafficking ring. My office has been working in conjunction with an FBI task force for weeks. In addition to the arrests, we've been able to bring nineteen victims to safety. While I cannot comment on the details of the investigation, I can tell you that the individuals involved will face both state and federal charges. This was a team effort. I'm happy to report all suspects were apprehended without injury to any law enforcement officers or to the victims themselves. I know you're already aware one of the victims was from this county, Violet Runyon. Her father, Bart Runyon, is facing new charges in conjunction with her abduction. As you know, a county social worker was involved in that abduction. My colleagues can speak in more detail perhaps, but I can tell you we're dealing with one of the largest trafficking rings in the country with tentacles that reached a double murder in Holden County as well as the death of an informant, an inmate here in Maumee County, as well as an attempt on assistant prosecutor Mara Brent's life. I can't divulge more on that yet."

The cameras continued to snap. Sam finished his remarks and handed the mic over to Special Agent Palmer. He basically repeated everything Sam had said. That should have been the end of it, but Skip Fletcher pushed his way to the lectern and took over.

"Thank you again for coming," he said. "As you may know, my office was integrally involved in this investigation. I want to thank my staff for their cooperation with Sheriff Cruz. Know that we will be prosecuting Bart Runyon and his associates to the fullest extent of the law."

"Mr. Fletcher!" one of the reporters shouted. "Will you speak to the involvement of former prosecutor Mara Brent in this investigation?"

"Is that ..." Kenya whispered. I sank lower into my chair. "Uh. Mara. That was David Reese, Channel 8."

"I didn't put him up to it, I swear," I said. I wanted to get out of here before anyone noticed I was sitting there. Kenya clamped her hand on my leg.

"Watch this," she said.

"Wait a minute. Did you put him up to that?"

Kenya shot me a wink.

"You suspended her," Reese said. "Isn't it true that your office, if anything, impeded the investigation into Violet Runyon's disappearance?"

"That is patently false," Skip said, though his face was turning red. "Ms. Brent has been reinstated to her position. It was an administrative issue that has since been rectified." I figured right about now, he regretted his choice to grab the spotlight.

"I can speak to that!" Carla Gribaldi stepped forward, flanked by the Silver Angels. "May I be allowed?"

Sam and Special Agent Palmer exchanged a look. Then Sam grinned. He cleared the way for Carla and practically shoved Skip from the microphone.

"Hello," Carla said. Her hand trembled as she flattened a piece of paper over the lectern. "I'd like to read from a statement I've written. You'll forgive me if I'm a little nervous. My family has been through a lot. First ... from the bottom of my heart I want to thank Sheriff Cruz and the FBI agents for bringing my daughter home to me. It's been twelve long years, but I never gave up hope that we'd see Violet again. I know you want me to say some things about Violet's father, but I won't be doing that. I'd like to let the justice system work in that regard. But I do want to make the public aware of something. There is one person I credit above everyone else for the break in this case. Assistant prosecutor Mara Brent. It was through her dogged determination that the true perpetrators involved in my daughter's kidnapping were brought to light. At the same time, there is one person who I feel impeded this investigation. That is Skip Fletcher. Rather than listening to Ms. Brent, he tried to silence her. So, for him to stand here and try to take credit for anything ... well ... I'm sorry. I wasn't going to say anything. I really wasn't. But I can't stand by and let him do that. It is my opinion that Mr. Fletcher has violated his oath of office and let down the citizens of this county. He is unfit for the office in which he holds, and I understand a petition is beginning to circulate asking he be recalled. I for one will endorse that effort. Wholeheartedly. That's all I want to say right now. I would just ask that you please respect my family's privacy while we all readjust to our new life together. Thank you."

Skip Fletcher appeared to have turned into a wax figure. His face had no color. His smile stayed frozen in place.

"Did you know she was gonna do that?" I said to Kenya.

Kenya had gone a bit waxen herself. "I ... did ... not."

Sam retook the lectern. He looked just as shocked as I felt. He and Agent Palmer fielded a few more mundane questions before ending the conference and retreating to the inner offices.

"Let's make a break for it before they see you sitting here," Kenya whispered. She grabbed me by the arm, and we made our escape. We practically sprinted down the hall. Kenya pushed open a side door that led back to Sam's office. When we got there, he and Carla were waiting for us.

"Well done," Kenya said. She pulled Carla into a hug.

"I was so nervous," she said.

"A recall petition?" I asked.

"We already have four hundred signatures," Carla said. "We need five hundred, but the Silver Angels have also mobilized. We're hoping to have the recall issue on the ballot by November."

"It'll pass," Sam said. "I just got a call from one of my deputies. There are protestors camped outside Skip's house."

"Oh my," I said. "I don't want the guy run out on a rail."

"I do," Carla said. "If he had his way, Violet would still be missing."

"Come on," Kenya said to her. "Let's get you back home to her. We can sneak out the side before anyone knows where to find you."

Carla hugged me. There were tears in her eyes as we pulled away. "I mean it. I'll do whatever I can. People need to know what really happened."

I thanked her again as Kenya led her out into the hall. Sam poked his head out and ordered two deputies to make sure they got to their vehicles unaccosted.

I plopped into a chair in front of his desk. "That was something," he said. "You okay?"

"Am I okay? Oy. You have no idea what kind of hellfire Skip's gonna try to bring."

"Let him. He's toast, Mara. I wouldn't be surprised if the county commissioners ask him to quietly resign. If he has any future political aspirations, he'd be smart to tuck tail and run. Wait a couple of years for people to forget his name, then start over somewhere else. If he lets this recall go forward, it's going to keep his name in the press for all the wrong reasons."

"I hope you're right."

"Kenya should run again. She'd win in a landslide."

"I don't know what she's thinking," I said. "She might like her retired life way too much."

Sam went to his desk drawer and pulled out a bottle of Scotch he kept there. He poured me a shot and one for himself.

He looked at the clock. "I'm officially off duty. So are you. You look like you could use it."

I took the glass and clinked it against his. "Thank you," he said. "But also, I'm sorry."

"For what?" I said, sipping my drink. It was smooth going down and warmed me.

"I should have listened to you earlier on this one. I've learned my lesson. I promise. From now on, I'll trust your instincts no matter what."

I wanted to say something self-effacing. To deflect. Instead, I took another sip and merely said, "Thank you."

"So you got him?" I asked. "The man who shot into my window that night?"

"We got him," Sam said, taking another sip of his Scotch. "Both Dusty Morrison and Christine Schuler have turned against the club in an attempt to save their own necks. Morrison fingered a hitman on the payroll of the Shadow Brotherhood. Palmer told me right before the presser that they picked him up just outside of Cleveland yesterday. He had the murder weapon used to kill Hoyt and Courtney Mack on him. I'm waiting for a report back from the lab, but I'm certain it'll match what we found out at your place. He's never gonna see the light of day again, Mara."

A chill went through me. It had gotten way too close to me. To Will. Sensing my unease, Sam moved in closer and kissed me on the cheek.

"You're safe," he said. "I swear."

"I believe you. But Morrison and Christine. They can't get immunity on this."

"They won't. Palmer's communicating with the US Attorney's office. Those two will spend the rest of their lives in federal prison. Christine will face state charges as well. They won't see the light of day again, either of them."

"Good," I said.

"We make a pretty good team, I think."

"I think so too."

"That is ... when I get out of your way."

I smiled. "At least you're coachable, Sheriff Cruz."

This got a deep laugh out of him. He set his glass down and came around the desk. He got down on one knee in front of me and for an instant, my heart seemed to short circuit and I couldn't breathe.

He gathered my hands and kissed them. "This is going to get harder, isn't it? You and me?"

"Not if we don't let it," I said. "And I like that phrase, by the way. You and me. We were a team on this one."

"Eventually," he said. "When I stopped being so pigheaded."

"Sometimes I'm the one who's going to be pigheaded, Sam."

"I suppose you will."

"Will ..." I said, my voice trailing off. "I said I liked the sound of that. You and me. But ..."

He leaned in close and kissed me. It wasn't chaste. It was slow and deep and warmed me far more than the Scotch.

When Sam finally pulled away, it took a moment for me to catch my breath. I hadn't been kissed like that for a very long time. Maybe never.

"You're a package deal," Sam said. "I get that."

"He likes you. No. He loves you."

"I love him too."

I searched Sam's face. There were so many unspoken promises in his eyes. In mine too, I knew.

"I want this," he whispered. "You. Will. Us."

I wanted it too. It wasn't a proposal he was making. But a promise. I'd been afraid to let him in. Will had been hurt so badly by his father. So had I. Was I brave enough to try again?

"Come on," Sam said. "Time for both of us to punch out. I think it's safe to go outside again. The vultures have moved on for now. I'll take you home. We can make dinner."

I took Sam's hand. As he stared back at me, I knew in my heart I could trust him. Will could trust him.

Not a proposal. But a step forward. I would bring him home with me. And I would ask him to spend the night.

NEWSLETTER SIGN UP

Sign up to get notified of Robin's new releases, plus get *Crown of Thorne*, a FREE exclusive legal thriller ebook novella.

SCAN TO JOIN
ROBIN JAMES'S
NEWSLETTER

ABOUT THE AUTHOR

Robin James is an attorney and former law professor. She's worked on a wide range of civil, criminal and family law cases in her twenty-five year legal career. She also spent over a decade as supervising attorney for a Michigan legal clinic assisting thousands of people who could not otherwise afford access to justice.

Robin now lives on a lake in southern Michigan with her husband, two children, and one lazy dog. Her favorite, pure Michigan writing spot is stretched out on the back of a pontoon watching the faster boats go by.

Sign up for Robin James's Legal Thriller Newsletter to get all the latest updates on her new releases and get a free bonus scene from Burden of Truth featuring Cass Leary's last day in Chicago. http://www.robinjamesbooks.com/newsletter/

ALSO BY ROBIN JAMES

Mara Brent Legal Thriller Series

Time of Justice

Price of Justice

Hand of Justice

Mark of Justice

Path of Justice

Vow of Justice

Web of Justice

Shadow of Justice

With more to come...

Cass Leary Legal Thriller Series

Burden of Truth

Silent Witness

Devil's Bargain

Stolen Justice

Blood Evidence

Imminent Harm

First Degree

Mercy Kill

Guilty Acts

Cold Evidence

Dead Law

The Client List

With more to come...

MARA BRENT SERIES IN AUDIO

SCAN FOR INFO ON
MARA BRENT IN
AUDIOBOOK FORMAT

Made in the USA
Monee, IL
10 February 2024

53263030R00215